MAKE THEM SORRY

SAM HAWKEN

MULHOLLAND
BOOKS

HODDER

First published in Great Britain in 2018 by Mulholland Books
An imprint of Hodder & Stoughton
An Hachette UK company

This paperback edition first published in 2019

1

A CIP catalogue record for this title is available from the British Library

Paperback ISBN 978 1 473 66225 4
eBook ISBN 978 1 473 66224 7

Printed and bound in Great Britain by Clays Ltd, Elcograf S.p.A.

Hodder & Stoughton policy is to use papers that are natural, renewable
and recyclable products and made from wood grown in sustainable forests.
The logging and manufacturing processes are expected to conform to
the environmental regulations of the country of origin.

Hodder & Stoughton Ltd
Carmelite House
50 Victoria Embankment
London EC4Y 0DZ

www.hodder.co.uk

Praise for the Camaro Espinoza series

'Hard-boiled action...Camaro Espinoza, who did tours in the Middle East, is tougher than an army boot...it's deeply satisfying to watch her take out an animal like Lukas.'

New York Times Book Review on *Walk Away*

'A trifecta of triumph...A complex and compelling protagonist (coupled with richly defined secondary characters), authenticity of voice and vista, and resonant timeliness...Camaro Espinoza is a name to remember, and readers will find themselves rooting for her despite the many liberties she takes with conventional law and order. Justice is in the eye of the beholder, after all.' *Strand Magazine* on *Walk Away*

'Sam Hawken has created a deep and dangerous female lead in *The Night Charter*. If you're ever in trouble and need a kickass heroine to get you out of it, look no further than army veteran Camaro Espinoza.'

Mari Hannah, author of the Kate Daniels series, on *The Night Charter*

'Camaro Espinoza, the intense and capable heroine of a series of novellas from Hawken, makes her full-length debut in this hard-boiled thriller...Camaro has an ironclad sense of justice...Hawken delivers a potent climax that winds its way through an unremitting firefight to a satisfying conclusion.' *Publishers Weekly* on *The Night Charter*

BOOKS BY SAM HAWKEN

THE CAMARO ESPINOZA SERIES
The Night Charter

Walk Away

THE BORDERLANDS TRILOGY
The Dead Women of Juarez

Tequila Sunset

Missing

For Mariann, who's had Camaro's
back from the start

MAKE
THEM
SORRY

CHAPTER ONE

CAMARO ESPINOZA WAS on her tenth shot when the man across the table started to list. His eyes were wet and he leaned heavily in his chair, but he didn't fall. Camaro lifted her glass. Whiskey burned all the way down.

They had two bottles of Jack Daniel's between them, both half empty. The man was named Waid, and he tipped the scales a hundred pounds heavier than Camaro. His round face was hazed with a bristly, semigrown beard, and he flushed pinker and pinker as they drank.

She'd been at the place for an hour and did her drinking at the bar. The sign out front said THE ALL-NITER, and it was stacked from front to back with denim and leather, men and women, and assaultive rock guitar played at heavy volume on battered speakers. The parking lot was jammed with motorcycles and more than a few pickups with Harley-Davidson stickers. A Harley logo was like a club seal, worn on hats and vests and do-rags. Camaro's T-shirt was emblazoned with the same, pulled tightly to her body over jeans and old motorcycle boots she'd worn since time out of mind.

There were eyes on her. Waid had been the first one to come calling. He put his hand on her rear, and she locked up his wrist and twisted until he backed off. He laughed, and they had a couple of beers before he made another move. Camaro deflected him toward two bottles of Jack.

One of the waitresses cleared a table for them and set up the shot glasses. Camaro took the first drink, an ounce and a half of Tennessee whiskey catching fire in her stomach. She put the glass upside down on the table between them. Waid did the same thing.

3

As they emptied the bottles, drinkers and partiers closed around their table. Camaro didn't know any of them, though some knew Waid. They cheered whenever he downed a shot, and cheered again when Camaro put away one of hers. They didn't seem to care who was ahead, or who might remain upright in the end. Only the competition mattered, raw and unfiltered like everything else in this place.

Waid leaned forward, arresting his slide from the chair. "Did I tell you how hot you are?" he slurred.

"Drink," Camaro told him.

He sought out his bottle, and managed to pour a shot though his hands were as unsteady as the rest of him. He studied the glass, brought it to his lips. He swallowed and belched, and for a moment he looked as though he might vomit on the spot. He laughed instead. "Another one bites the dust," he said.

Camaro pointed at the table. Waid had issues turning his glass over. He brought it down sharply on the tabletop. His arm slewed and he upset the collection of upended glasses by his right hand. They hit the floor, the silvery tinkle of them on the concrete scarcely audible.

"Damn it. I'm gonna lose count."

Her head was murky, and she felt heaviness in her limbs to go with the simmering heat below. She poured another shot, drank it, turned the glass over, and put it between them. She let herself sway backward in her chair. She didn't fall. Someone loosed a rebel yell.

"You're pouring 'em on the floor," Waid declared.

Camaro shook her head. "I'm drinking 'em."

"She's pouring 'em out!" Waid said to the assembled people. "You see it, right?"

A woman pushed forward. She spilled halfway out of a denim vest and wore no top underneath. The inky splash of a poorly drawn angel lay across one breast. "What's the matter, Waid? You got a problem with her?"

The man next to her cackled. The two of them teetered with beer bottles in hand. Camaro felt the ring of spectators close around the table.

Waid scowled. "I'm only saying she don't got the body for it. She's cheatin'!"

Jeers broke out. Someone pushed Waid and he nearly fell from his chair. He was slow to straighten, hanging on to the table with one hand. "Come on and quit," said the woman with the angel tattoo. "Quit if you can't take it."

"I'm not quittin'!" He grabbed his bottle and poured another shot. Amber liquid sloshed over the rim. Camaro didn't object. Waid did the shot, roared through bared teeth. "I'm a goddamned machine, baby!"

Attention shifted to Camaro. Everyone watched for the moment she could drink no more. Bass rolled from the speakers, pounding the barroom. The tempo merged with her heartbeat. She felt right.

She poured a shot. Waid regarded her with glazed eyes. She held up the glass between them, put it to her lips. Head up and back. Whiskey down. The glass rang when she slapped it onto the table. "Did that one go on the floor?" she asked.

Waid didn't answer. Pouring another measure took all his concentration. His tongue protruded from between his teeth as if he were a child doing a complicated math problem. He put his bottle too close to the edge of the table. It started to fall. The woman with the angel tattoo caught it. She and her boyfriend laughed at him. His pink face flushed a deep red. He drank.

Camaro waited. Waid extended his arm, hand gripping the glass. He turned it upside down, held, cracked the glass onto the table. He laughed, he hiccuped, and was violently ill.

Waid lurched out of his chair, heaving. He tripped over his own feet and into the arms of a trio of heavyset men nearly as drunk as he was. They went down, arms and legs tangled. Cheers turned to hysterical laughter before the ranks closed up and Camaro was alone at the table.

She rose from her seat. Someone drew her arm across his shoulders. Camaro let him whirl her, the room tilting, her senses askew. She fell into the hands of a couple of women who shouted congratulations into her face. She fell through to another table, pitched into the lap of a man drinking rum and Coke with a couple of others wearing leather cuts.

"What the hell?"

Camaro looked the man in the face. She was slow to focus, but she made out even features, a youthful look, and sandy hair. The man had only a patch of hair on the point of his chin, no beard, no mustache. Two silver loops of fine wire pierced one earlobe.

"You okay, lady?"

Camaro glanced around at the other men at the table. They were all the same: early thirties at most and not so rough. Weekend bikers who rode shiny bikes they probably never got their hands dirty fixing themselves. "I'm fine. I need my bottle," Camaro said.

"Looks like you need to lay off," the man said.

"What's your name?"

"It's—"

"No, I don't want to know. Let me up."

"I'm not holding you down."

Camaro made it back to her feet. The man held her wrist and kept her from falling. She looked more closely at him. "Help me find my bottle," she said.

The man looked toward his friends, but followed when Camaro pulled him. Together they pushed through to Camaro's table. A bar girl in a tube top collected the remains of the drinking game. Someone had their hand on Camaro's bottle. She snatched it away from them, and cradled it. She drank straight from the neck.

"Take it easy with that. You're drunk," the man told her.

Camaro kissed him on the cheek. "Not as drunk as I'm gonna be."

"You need me to call you a cab? How about you come sit at my table for a little while?"

"That's cute," Camaro said. She took his hand. "Follow me."

She led him through the assembled throng, underneath a nest of speakers, punishingly loud at close range, to a calmer outlet ending in a door lit with a red EXIT sign.

Camaro found the ladies' room and pushed through the door. The man behind her said something. She ignored him. In the small restroom there were three stalls and two sinks. A pair of women stood at the sinks, reapplying makeup in the cracked mirrors. Two of the stalls had visible feet below the closed doors.

"Hey, this is the *ladies'* room!" one of the women called out.

"I'm only...I'm sorry," said the man.

She dragged the man after her into the unoccupied stall and pushed the door shut when they were both inside. The mostly empty fifth of Jack Daniel's went on the toilet tank.

She grabbed him by the leather of his cut. They kissed in the close confines of the restroom stall, while outside the two women at the sinks complained. The air smelled of hairspray and sweat.

"Wait," the man said when they broke. "One second."

"Shut up and take my shirt off," Camaro told him.

7

CHAPTER TWO

THE POLICE CRUISER lit her up ten minutes after she left the All-Niter. Camaro wavered on the back of the Heritage Softail she rode but got to the side of the road. She killed the engine and removed her helmet. A sluggish breeze stirred the hair from her shoulders. In the dark, honey brown was the color of deep, old wood.

She stayed in the saddle as the cop approached. She was careful bringing out her wallet, careful again when extracting her license from its plastic holder. She felt steadier now than she had an hour ago, but only a little.

The cop was young and Latino, with perfect black hair and a spotless uniform. His name tag looked new. He shone his flashlight into Camaro's face. She winced, but didn't look away. "What's the problem, Officer?" she asked.

"Do you know how fast you were going, ma'am?"

"I don't know. Thirty-five?"

"Fifty. The *speed limit* is thirty. That's a school zone back there."

Camaro resisted looking over her shoulder. "It's the middle of the night."

"The school zone still counts. License and proof of insurance, please."

She thrust the cards at him. The cop played his flashlight over them. "Everything okay?" she said. "I didn't know it was a school zone back there. I would have slowed down."

"There are signs."

"I must have missed them."

He shone the light in her eyes again. "How much have you had to drink tonight?"

"I don't know. A couple shots. A beer."

"Uh-huh. You want to step off the bike while I check these out?"

Camaro swung off the bike and leaned against it. The cop went back to his unit. He turned on the inside lights. She saw him working on the computer terminal mounted to the dash.

It was a hot night and humid. Offshore winds kept it from being unbearable, but only barely. Sitting still, without the forward motion of the bike, Camaro sweated.

The cop came back after several minutes. He didn't return her cards. "Ma'am, I'm going to execute a field sobriety test. If you fail that, I'm going to have to place you under arrest."

"Okay," Camaro said.

He told her what to do and she tried to do it. She passed the eye exam, but stumbled on the walk-and-turn. The cop gave her three tries, but they weren't enough. Camaro put her hands behind her back without being told, and he cuffed her. He took the karambit from her boot, and confiscated the multi-tool on her belt.

She listened to him report the incident on the radio while they drove. It was around three o'clock in the morning, she ventured, and the streets in this part of Miami were almost completely still. In some places there was never a time when traffic didn't flow at least a little, but there was a sleepy side to the city tourists never saw. Camaro saw it now as the cop cruised empty streets lit with sodium-vapor streetlamps, past storefronts shuttered against the night.

At booking they relieved her of the contents of her pockets. The karambit and the multi-tool went into a bag with her keys, wallet, and cash. They asked if she was suicidal. If she said yes, they'd strip her and put her in a tear-proof gown before shutting her in a holding cell alone to wait for a psychiatric evaluation. She did not say yes.

They brought her into a room consisting of nothing but long benches made of molded plastic. The benches were bolted to the floor.

All around the periphery of the room were cells with glass windows and heavy doors. The benches were nearly full. The cells all had four or five people in them. Camaro saw a man sleeping on the floor inside one with his shirt wrapped around his head.

"Wait until your name is called," Camaro was told. "Watch some TV."

Three televisions faced the benches, each on a different channel. Men and women sat apart, but united in their attention to the TVs. Signs admonished them to refrain from talking, though some still muttered to one another and hoped the squall from the television sets would be enough to cover the sound. Camaro spoke to no one.

She judged time by the length of the shows parading across the screens. She broke the waiting time into thirty-minute chunks as late-night programming and infomercials ate up the hours. Camaro sat on the bench for a little over four hours before someone called her name. A policeman carrying a can of pepper spray and a baton, but no gun, beckoned her to the end of the row. She got up and shuffled past the others. Some watched her go, but most didn't care. No one seemed to care about anything.

"Espinoza?" the cop confirmed.

"Yeah."

"You're being released. Follow me."

He took her to a counter not far from where she'd been booked, photographed, and fingerprinted. They gave her the bag of her belongings, but told her not to open it until she was out. After that they escorted her down a side hallway to a locked door opening directly to the outside. She emerged alone into the rising heat of the morning.

"Hey there, Camaro Espinoza."

Camaro saw him standing on the sidewalk near a sedan parked in a red zone. He was rumpled, as if he'd been up all night or had been roused too early, but his beard was orderly and it looked as though he'd shaved his neck no more than a day or two before. "Detective Montellano," Camaro said.

Ignacio Montellano stepped toward her and smiled. "Hey, I thought I told you to call me Nacho. All my friends do."

Camaro didn't respond. She gripped the bag from the jail in one hand.

Ignacio's smile faltered. "You *do* remember me, don't you? Otherwise my feelings are gonna be hurt."

"I remember you. It's been a while."

"It has. So let's take a ride and we can get all caught up."

"I can walk."

"It's a long way back to your place, if you're still living in Allapattah. And I know you are, so don't argue."

Camaro looked past Ignacio. There was a large parking lot, mostly empty, and a dusty street with auto and tool shops squatting under the rising sun. An airplane's engine noise carried over high chain-link fences topped with curling barbed wire. They were somewhere west of where she needed to be, and she wasn't sure of the way.

"How about it, Camaro?"

"Okay, fine."

He opened the passenger door for her, and closed it, too. Once he was behind the wheel, he stoked the engine and turned the AC to max. Dawn lit the sky like a burning brand, and there were no clouds. It had been close to a hundred every day for the past week. July in Miami.

Ignacio fastened his seat belt, watched until Camaro fastened hers. Only then did he put the car in gear. "I guess you're wondering what I'm doing here," he said.

"I'm wondering where my bike is."

"Impound. I can keep you from going in front of a judge, but you still have to pay to get your ride back. Sorry."

Camaro tore open the plastic bag from the jail. She checked her wallet, stuffed it into her back pocket. A small roll of bills was intact. She hiked up the cuff of her pant leg, clipped the karambit to the inside of her boot. "I guess I owe you," she said.

"I don't keep track of things like that."

She looked at the detective. He was heavyset and fiftyish, but not old. His hair was still dark, though it had receded a healthy distance. Even his beard had no stray white hairs. As she watched, he fished a pair of sunglasses out of his breast pocket and put them on. They drove directly into the sun.

"I suppose it's been about a year," Ignacio continued.

"About that."

"Been keeping busy?"

"Yeah."

"Good, good. How's the charter-boat business? Still paying the bills?"

"Listen, I don't know what you want, but I don't have anything to say except thank you."

"Thank you is good. I can live with that. I didn't expect much better. It's not like we're buddies or anything. I only kept you out of prison when you killed all those guys." His expression remained neutral, eyes on the road, hands at ten and two.

"What *do* you want?" Camaro asked.

"Me? Nothing. I've been keeping Camaro Espinoza on my radar since then, that's all. If your name comes up, people know to give me a call. This morning I got a call. DUI? I had to have a look."

"Nothing to see."

Ignacio shrugged. "I suppose not. Though we're sitting here now and I gotta say, you smell like you fell in a bathtub full of booze."

She didn't answer. She sat back in her seat. Ignacio took the main street away from the jail, six lanes with a concrete island in the middle. The neighborhood shuddered with every arrival and departure from Miami International. Palm trees were a stab at making the cement desert into something resembling the better Miami, the sexy Miami, but there was nothing but business here.

"So you were drinking," Ignacio said. There was no question.

"I was."

"And then you got on that Harley of yours, figuring you'd make it all the way home to sleep it off?"

Camaro was silent.

"Seems dangerous," Ignacio said. "And you're such a careful girl."

"What's that supposed to mean?"

"Only that I figured you'd want to steer clear of any kind of trouble until everybody in Miami forgot who Camaro Espinoza is. That's the safest way to go. You make yourself noticeable, somebody might come poking around. They might wonder where you came from, or where you're going. They might wonder if you ever killed anybody. And why."

"You know why," Camaro said.

"I do. Now I keep an eye out."

Camaro let the miles slip by. She had a better idea of where they were. Soon they'd be in her neighborhood, where people kept small homes and families and worked hard for basic needs and simple pleasures. She thought she'd disappeared there, and there was no one left to know her name.

"If you're wondering what I want for helping you, the answer is nothing," Ignacio said. "I'm not that kind of cop. And I won't ask if we can be pals, because I don't think you really want one. Won't stop me from trying. I only wanted to tell you to keep on the straight and narrow from here on out. There comes a day I don't catch trouble before it finds you..."

"I don't see why you'd care."

"Maybe I don't like to see good people make bad choices."

They rode together in silence after that, the only sounds the rushing of the air conditioner's compressor over the car's engine. Ignacio never looked her way. He was careful to check his blind spots and use his indicators. He never broke the limit.

When they rolled down Camaro's street, she was ready to get out. The atmosphere inside the car was too chilly, and she could think of nothing to say she wouldn't rather keep to herself. He stopped in front of her one-bedroom rental, blocking the driveway and the red crew-cab pickup truck in the carport. He put on his hazard lights and shifted into park. "Home again," he said.

"Thanks for the ride."

"My pleasure. Let me give you my card. If you need someone to be your designated driver, I can help."

Camaro watched him produce the card like a magic trick. One moment his hand was empty, and the next the card was there. She didn't take it. "I'll do all right on my own."

"I only give one pass for DUI. After that, I'm inclined to let things play out."

She sighed and took the card. "Happy?"

Ignacio smiled. "Very."

Warm air rushed in when she opened her door. Camaro got out. She heard him call her name. She leaned back inside. "Yeah?"

"If you ever feel like you're gonna hurt somebody, maybe give me a call then, too, all right? I hear one of your neighbors got a pretty nasty beatdown after putting hands on his kid."

"I heard that, too."

"Remember me."

Camaro put the card in her pocket. "I'll remember."

"Okay. See you around."

She slammed the door and stood on the curb until Ignacio pulled away. She saw him wave over his shoulder. She didn't wave back.

"Yeah, see you."

He turned the corner and was gone.

CHAPTER THREE

THE GYM SMELLED of sweat and heat and straining muscles. It was loud inside, but not because of music. No music played in Miguel Anuria's place. It was a camp for toil and work and pain, and while fighting might have seemed like a dance, there was no dancing to be had.

Camaro went down hard on her back inside the five-faced cage in the center of the space. The woman sparring with her came rushing in. She scrambled to get inside Camaro's guard. Camaro caught one of her legs between her own and spoiled the attack. They rolled together, each trying to advance position. The woman put her hand on Camaro's chin to lever her away. Camaro clubbed two blows into the woman's head-gear to still her.

The woman's name was Laura Ogarrio. She was ten years younger than Camaro and slighter. As they tangled on the mat, the coiled muscles of Laura's arms and legs belied her size. They rolled again, this time with Laura on top and Camaro underneath.

Miguel shouted from outside the cage, "Laura, get your leg free! Use your knee and slip her guard. ¡Escúchame!"

Camaro felt the younger woman moving against her. Laura barred her chin with an elbow, dug in with a knee, and struggled to pull her leg from Camaro's trap. Camaro bore down, then released abruptly. Laura fell over her, both knees going to the ground. Immediately Camaro hooked the back of a leg, rolled up with an arm behind the woman's neck. Her hands locked together. Laura had nowhere to go.

"Damn it, *sobrina*," Miguel called. "She's going to put you in the choke! You got to find some leverage, girl."

15

Laura panted against Camaro's chest. Camaro's breath came in short, choppy bursts. They'd grappled for most of two minutes, an interval timer outside the cage silently counting off the seconds until the horn. They'd done two rounds of three minutes previously, standing and on the ground, and both were slick with sweat.

In this position, Camaro couldn't close the choke to end it. She felt Laura tense for a breakaway move. Camaro allowed her hook to loosen. Instantly they rolled, Laura surging on the canvas. Camaro held on until she felt the younger woman slip into position. She locked in again, the guillotine choke tighter than before. At this angle she was able to leverage the pressure with Laura's body weight, her grip the fulcrum.

"You gotta slip it, Laura. Slip it! Slip it!"

Laura struggled. Her movements fell apart, no longer considered or disciplined. She jerked against Camaro's grip, but found no way out. Camaro cranked the younger woman's neck until she felt it pop. Laura tapped Camaro on the side.

Camaro let go. Laura collapsed onto the cage floor. The interval timer sounded. The round was over but the match was done. Laura plucked out her mouth guard and lay on her back, lungs sobbing for air. Camaro was no different. She felt sore all over, and there was fresh pain in her right arm, still bothering her months after getting free of a cast.

Miguel unlocked the cage. He stood over the both of them with his hands on his hips. "I've seen better from both of you," he said.

Camaro spoke around her mouth guard. She was too tired to take it out. "She's quick. Strong."

"You're quick and strong. She's young and doesn't know all the tricks yet. What's your excuse?"

Camaro put a sweaty arm over her eyes. "Send me to the old folks' home," she said.

"Thirty-three ain't old!"

"It feels like it."

"Then you need to change how you feel. Get up and get showered. Somebody else needs the cage."

It was a minute before Camaro felt ready to rise. She rolled onto her knees. Around the perimeter of the cage, men and women watched her. Miguel had Laura on a stool and bent close to talk with her. Laura looked as though she was crying. She was the daughter of Miguel's brother-in-law.

A few heads nodded as Camaro left the cage. She stripped off her head protection and dropped it on a chair. She took a towel from a stack by the wall, mopped her face and neck.

"Excuse me?"

The woman had unruly black curly hair barely held in place by a strip of elastic cloth. She was skinny but had the widening hips of someone who spent a lot of time sitting down. Camaro thought she couldn't yet be thirty. The woman smiled, but the smile instantly faded.

"Yes?" Camaro asked.

"Are you... Camaro?"

"Uh-huh."

The woman put out a hand. She had unpainted nails, but they were carefully manicured. "I'm Faith. They told me to talk to you."

Camaro didn't shake her hand. She glanced around the room. No one looked their way. She examined Faith more closely. Faith wore no makeup and didn't spend much time in the sun. Everything about her said "office," and everything about her placed her outside the confines of Miguel Anuria's gym.

"Who's 'they'?" Camaro asked.

Faith dropped her hand. "Oh! I talked to Miguel and to, uh, Rey? I think that's his name. He does the beginner classes."

"Rey told you to talk to me?"

Another smile struggled to form. "I asked who the toughest broad in the joint was, and he said it was you."

"That's great," Camaro said. "I have to go."

Faith moved to intercept her. "I watched you spar with that other girl. She's good, but you're better. I've only been taking classes for, like, two weeks, but I think I can tell who's the best at this."

17

Camaro stopped. "Is this your first fight gym?" she asked Faith.

"Yeah."

"Okay, well, rule one is you don't come to the gym to make small talk. You come here to roll. So I'm glad you like it and I'm glad you think I'm good, but I don't really need this right now. I'm tired and I'm sweaty and I want to shower and go home."

"Wait," Faith said.

"Listen—"

"No, wait. I'm sorry. I don't know the protocol or anything. Can I…talk to you for a little bit?"

"I'm going to the showers."

"I can stay here for you."

"Then I'm gonna leave."

"We could talk next time."

Camaro shook her head. "I don't think so."

She turned her back on Faith and walked away. Faith didn't call after her.

CHAPTER FOUR

SHE WAITED IN her car in front of the gym for Camaro to come out, but Camaro never appeared. Faith Glazer realized too late that there must have been a second exit somewhere, and Camaro was long gone. Faith had to drive from Miami Beach to her apartment north of the Crossings, thirty miles away. Traffic was heavy. It took her over an hour to make it home.

Once parked, she snared her gym bag from the backseat and put it on her lap. She found her purse inside, and inside the purse a canister of pepper spray. She slung the bag over her right shoulder and got out of the car with her keys in her left hand, the canister in her right. She looked in a full circle around the parking lot before locking the car doors and stepping out into the middle of the street, well away from the other parked cars, ready for the walk to her apartment.

Faith knew the approaches to her apartment from every direction, and the exposure from the adjoining street. A six-foot iron fence enclosed the complex, but it ran parallel to a road with open curbs for parking, so there were always different cars directly outside the barricade. Pedestrians could look through. The bars of the fence were close enough together even a child couldn't pass between them, but visibility was still perfect from as far as a hundred feet away.

A large bush grew by her front door. She came in at an angle and found no one hiding behind it. Taking a last look behind her, she committed to the door, unlocked it, hustled inside, and secured it behind her. She had a dead bolt and a chain lock. Both of these were set before she looked through the peephole to see the empty doorstep and sidewalk beyond.

She didn't turn on her lights, and moved from room to room in the dark. The windows in her living room provided a clear view of the street, but the blinds were shut. Faith lifted a slat to peer outside. Only a few of the cars beyond the fence were familiar to her. Some belonged to boyfriends and girlfriends of people in her building. Others could have belonged to anyone.

She passed from the front room down a short hall to the bedroom. Vertical blinds concealed a sliding glass door barred with a heavy length of pipe. Faith hadn't trusted the simple, lightweight bar the door had come with. She looked out here, too. Her patio was enclosed by a square of privacy fencing, the space only four by three. No one was there. A single, rusting lawn chair sat alone.

When there had been no movement, and no sound in the apartment save the whisper of the air conditioner starting on a timer, Faith turned on the lights. She put her keys in a bowl by the front door, peered out through the peephole one more time, and went to the bathroom with the pepper spray still in her hand.

The pepper spray was never far from her. She slept with it beside the bed, and when she took her meals in the small dining area she stood it near the plate as though it were a salt shaker. While she showered, she kept the door to the bathroom locked and the clothes hamper propped against it.

Faith was sore all over, and it had been the same every time she came back from the fighting gym. Miguel's was not the kind of place where people learned cardio boxing, but a real gym where real fighters came to do their hardest work. It was what she had looked for before asking about lessons. She had absorbed everything she could from the place in the two weeks she'd gone there.

She wrapped a towel around her head and a robe around her body and went into the cool bedroom. Her bed was always made. She sat with her back against the headboard, clicking through channels on the television.

Someone rapped on the front door and rang the bell. Faith froze in place, the remote control in her hand.

She grabbed the pepper spray from the nightstand. When the doorbell rang again, she clutched the remote control so tightly the plastic squeaked. A single tremor became a cascade, and she shook all over.

"Faith?"

"Andrea," Faith said out loud. Where there had been ice before, liquid heat flowed. She breathed deeply.

Faith went to the door and checked the peephole. Andrea Marcus stood outside. She had something in her hands. Faith willed her heartbeat to slow as she undid the locks and opened the door.

Andrea brightened when she saw Faith. They were unalike in appearance, Andrea blonde and long-limbed, with the tight muscles of a runner. She would have no trouble in a place like Miguel's. She held a small cardboard box. "Oh, hi, you *are* home. I saw your car, so I figured... Were you in the shower?"

"The—?" Faith touched the towel on her head and blushed. "Oh, no, I... Is everything all right?"

"This got delivered to my door by mistake. I wanted to make sure you got it."

Andrea handed over the package. Faith weighed the box in her hands. It was solid, heavier than its size suggested. "Thanks. I don't remember ordering anything."

"Maybe it's a present."

"Maybe. Hey, I'd ask you to come in, but I'm kind of not dressed, you know?"

Andrea waved her off. "No problem. We'll get together some other time. Don't work too hard, okay?"

"Okay. See you!"

Faith was quick to secure the door. She brought the package into the dining area and set it on the table. The label was handwritten, her name and address perfectly printed with a black Sharpie. The lettering made her skin crawl.

Her fingerprints were all over it now. And Andrea's would be, too. And the postman's, and those of each one of a hundred other people who had handled her package from the sender to her doorstep. None of the prints would belong to him. She knew this without even having to ask, because he would never allow a single print to be left behind.

She found a knife in a drawer in the kitchen. She cut the tape on the package. There was balled brown paper inside for padding. Once she cleared it away, she saw the glass globe.

It was a snow globe the size of a softball, and it was not cheap. The wooden base was polished, with a brass plaque reading MIAMI, FLORIDA. Inside the globe, a thick layer of fake snow stirred around the foundations of a string of pastel-colored beach hotels.

On the walls of the dining area she had framed photographs of the same buildings. She had a print in her living room that she had bought at the Art Deco Historic District in South Beach. Looking at the little buildings now, she felt colder than she had before, as if the snow were all around her.

She took the snow globe to the kitchen trash and threw it away. Afterward she threw away all the packaging. She stood over the trash can and wrapped her arms around herself and held on until the tears came. She cried for a long time alone in the kitchen with no one to hear.

CHAPTER FIVE

CAMARO WAS AWAY on a charter all day. When the customers paid the balance on their bill, they left Camaro alone to hose down the decks and polish the wood and fixtures on the fifty-nine-foot custom Carolina she called the *Annabel*. It was a meditative activity, requiring no more conscious thought than breathing. Seagulls swirled around the pier, knowing she would cast off unused bait, and when she did they dove into the water to catch their prizes before they were lost.

She went into the galley and found a bottle of beer in the refrigerator. She opened it and drank her first alcohol of the day. Sitting in the fighting chair outside, she listened to the lazy activity of the marina: skippers shouting at dock boys and mates and the lick of water against hulls all around. Camaro pulled the brim of a sun-bleached Seahawks cap low over her eyes and looked out toward the marina office and the parking lot in time to see Ignacio Montellano lumbering her way.

"Oh, what the hell?" Camaro said under her breath.

He saw her watching, raised his hat and waved. He was in short sleeves, but still wore a tie. His service weapon was prominent on his hip, a compact Smith & Wesson automatic with a stainless steel frame. The holster was well worn. "Hey, nice to see you," Ignacio said when he came near.

"How did you know I'd be here?"

"Oh, educated guess. May I come aboard?"

Camaro gestured vaguely with her bottle.

Ignacio clambered onto the boat. He put his hands on his hips, his right resting against the automatic, and surveyed the vessel. His eyes were hidden by sunglasses with old-fashioned frames. "Have I ever told you what a nice boat you have?"

"You may have mentioned it."

"How much does a boat like this run?"

Camaro shrugged. "Depends."

"Ballpark," Ignacio said.

"I paid a little shy of five hundred."

Ignacio swept off his sunglasses. "Five hundred. Five hundred *thousand?*"

"Around that."

The detective whistled. "No wonder it's so nice. Say, you wouldn't happen to have something to drink, would you? Water is fine."

"Check the galley. Should be some bottles in the fridge."

Camaro didn't watch Ignacio go. She heard him inside the cabin, the slide and thunk of the door opening to let him out. The sun's rays slanted across the desk, partly blocked by the flybridge, painting shadows on the wood.

"That hits the spot," Ignacio said. He moved into her peripheral vision within the shade of the flybridge but still far enough to one side that Camaro was forced to turn her head to look at him. He leaned against the railing, a bottle of spring water sweating in his hand. Camaro's beer was almost empty. She drank the last.

"I don't remember calling the cops."

"No need. We're always around. Besides, I wanted to see how you're doing."

"Fine."

"Hit the bars lately?"

"There some law against that?"

"No, but I recall you getting into a little trouble a few weeks back."

"Everybody gets into trouble sometimes."

"Not your kind of trouble. Besides, it's a good thing to have a cop watching over you. Helps when things come up."

"So you said."

"Sure, sure. And I hear things."

"Like what?"

"Like I heard you took a trip to California around the New Year. How'd that work out for you?"

Camaro kept her face neutral. "It was fine. You keeping tabs on California, too?"

"Only on special occasions. You never know what you're going to find out. Such as you have a sister."

"I would have told you if you asked."

"Would you, though?"

"Maybe not."

"You named your boat after her."

"Yeah. So what?" Camaro returned. "Don't you have anything better to do? You have a wife? A girlfriend? Go spend time with her."

Ignacio looked thoughtful. He pulled from his bottle. "Yesterday was my birthday."

"Congratulations."

"My girlfriend, she broke up with me the day before because she didn't want to ruin things for me. I mean, I'm fifty-four, so it's not like a special birthday the way fifty-five is special. But I thought it was awfully nice of her. I had to cancel our dinner reservations, but it gave me time to catch up on paperwork."

"And now you're here."

"Now I'm here. So I *don't* have anything better to do with my time. I work and I read reports and I hear things which remind me, you know, Camaro Espinoza is still out there. I figure I'm doing myself a favor by staying aware before the next body comes across my desk."

Camaro shook her head. A seagull grazed the mast of a sailboat two slips over, hovering on the coursing breeze before setting down as lightly as a breath. "I'm not killing anybody today, so you can relax."

"You know, I thought maybe you weren't coming back to Miami after what went down in California. I did some asking around and they said you were spending your time in Virginia. Nice up there?"

"Depends on the place."

"Whereabouts were you staying?"

"Norfolk."

"Norfolk. Got a lot of ships there, right?"

"That's right."

"I never did much take to the water. Which is funny, because I was born on an island, but I don't like water I can't stand up in. Makes me nervous. Though that's one thing that's good when you're fat: you float like a bar of soap."

He laughed and Camaro smiled a little though she didn't want to. She let the silence grow between them until she said, "I guess you're going to keep coming around no matter what."

"That's the plan."

"Then you might as well take me to dinner."

CHAPTER SIX

IGNACIO LED HER away from the water, into the city to Hialeah. Camaro tailed his Ford on the back of her bike, signaling with her hand when they made turns, keeping a steady two car lengths back. Ignacio crawled, obeying whatever the speed limit signs said, though traffic careened around them as fast as it wanted to go. She found herself cursing him silently by the time they reached a sandy-colored strip mall on Palm Avenue and pulled into the small parking lot.

The restaurant was called Casa Berganza, and it looked like nothing from the outside. It was early evening, and the tables were occupied by a scattering of old-timers, dark-skinned Cubans burned leathery by long years in the sun. A domino game went on at one table, the ancient participants each looking a hundred years old. A round woman with streaks of gray in her hair found Camaro and Ignacio a booth near the front window where they could watch cars go by.

"I know it's a hole in the wall, but they have a *medianoche* here that's out of this world," Ignacio told Camaro.

A waiter who spoke no English came to them. Ignacio ordered waters and salads in Spanish. Camaro sat watching them. When the waiter left, she kept her eye on him all the way to the kitchen.

"I don't think he's a problem," Ignacio said.

"That's what everybody says before there's a problem."

Ignacio set aside his straw trilby and scratched the back of his neck. "That's the thing I wondered the most about you the first time we crossed paths. You don't trust people. How'd that happen?"

Camaro looked him in the face. "You're a cop. People lie to you all day long. You see murderers and rapists and every other kind of scumbag in the city. You telling me you believe everything you hear? Everything you see?"

"I try to keep some perspective."

"Okay."

The waiter brought their waters. Camaro squeezed a lemon into hers, pushed the crushed slice down to the bottom of the glass with her straw. Ignacio watched her and did the same. "In my line of work you see a lot of bad guys," he said, "but all that bad helps you see good a little bit better. It sticks out. Kind of like finding a diamond in the dirt, you know?"

"I don't know."

"So you don't get tired of being suspicious all the time?"

"Sure," Camaro said. "That's why I drink."

Ignacio smiled and wagged a finger at her. "Okay, I'll give you a point there. Sometimes you have to unwind. Me, I get a nice Cuban sandwich in front of me and it's like all my troubles disappear. The first thing I did when my girlfriend told me she was leaving, I went out and had the biggest *mixto* I could find. Extra everything. All that flavor..."

"All that salt," Camaro said.

"You aren't exactly doing your body any favors with the booze you're drinking."

"I work it off."

Ignacio touched his belly. "I don't."

The salads came. Camaro ate hers without dressing. Ignacio smothered his. The tomatoes were sweet and crisp, the lettuce fresh. Camaro picked out the onions. "You ever think about getting in shape?" she asked him after a while.

"Used to. But I figure at my age this is about as good as it's gonna get. So I live with it. My blood pressure's okay, and I don't have diabetes, so I'm set. You never heard the expression 'fat and happy'?"

"I've heard it."

"You've probably never been fat a day in your life."

"No," Camaro said.

28

"Not even when you were little?"

"Not even then."

"How about your sister? Your mother? Hey, maybe you have a nice, round *abuela* out there somewhere."

"No, nothing like that."

"Lucky genes, then," Ignacio said, and he wiped his lips with his napkin. "My family, we're all a healthy weight."

"This is healthy?" Camaro asked.

"Sure. I'm light on my feet for a big man."

Something tugged at the corner of Camaro's mouth. She shook her head. "Whatever gets you through the day."

They didn't talk for a few minutes. The quiet was only interrupted by happy exclamations from the domino game. The waiter returned to take their orders. Ignacio asked for the *medianoche,* and also for the churrasco. "It's Cuban-style," he told Camaro. The waiter went away.

"You're not Cuban, are you?" Ignacio asked her.

"Nope. My father was a Chicano from East LA, and my mother was from Canada."

"Latina?"

"White lady."

"That explains a little bit."

"Why I'm not as brown as girls down on the farm?"

"What farm? I'm talking more like Jenny from the block. My folks are Puerto Rican. I was born in Ponce, where my mom's from, but we moved to the Bronx pretty early on. You ever been?"

"To Puerto Rico, or the Bronx?"

"Either."

"Neither."

Ignacio made a vague gesture with his hands. "They're nice if you're from there. Long way from Miami, anyway. I wouldn't even be here if a good spot hadn't opened up, but I'm glad I came. Been here twenty-five years. I can't imagine living anywhere else. It's a great city."

Camaro nodded but said nothing. She looked out the window at the deepening shadows. In a couple of hours the sun would be down, and the city would glitter, spread out on a flat plain of wetlands like a fisherman's net set with stars.

The food came. The pressed sandwich Ignacio had ordered was perfectly browned, with diagonal stripes of darker bread where the flavor lurked. He tucked his napkin into his collar and parted the sandwich where it had been cut, an unconscious sound of delight escaping him. Camaro's plate was set before her: spiced beef served with plantain chips and rice. A floret of red pepper sat atop the meat, a splash of brilliant color.

She watched Ignacio eat with the reverence of a man at worship. She carved into her own meal, and the flavors balanced on her taste buds. The warmth of the meat soaked up spice and released it in an aromatic cloud. She ate more quickly than she intended.

"Places like this are where the real food of Miami is," Ignacio said after he'd demolished half the sandwich. "The tourists? They'll never know. Though I gotta be fair: there are some places in Little Havana that deliver the goods."

Camaro didn't reply. She ate in silence, aware of Ignacio watching her. The sense that she should leave the table, and then the restaurant, grew.

When the churrasco was all gone, Camaro gave Ignacio her full attention. "Is this you trying to be my friend?" she asked.

Ignacio tucked away the last of his sandwich. He chewed thoughtfully, then sipped from his straw. "You got me."

"I try not to make it a habit. Being friends with cops."

"Who's making it a habit? This is just us."

"And I'm not going to sleep with you. I don't care if your girlfriend left you."

"Whoa, lady, I didn't even ask. I'm too old for you anyway."

Camaro let the frown slip from her mouth. "You're not *that* old."

"Thank you for saying so."

"If you think I'm going to tell you everything there is to know about me, it's not going to happen, either," Camaro said.

"Your secrets are your secrets. I don't pry."

"Sure you do."

"Okay, maybe a little. I ask questions for a living."

"And there's something else," Camaro said, and she fixed him with a pointed finger.

"What?"

"I don't want you pulling strings for me. If I get into trouble, that's my business. I don't want to owe you anything. What you did for me before...I don't want it."

Ignacio took a thoughtful drink. "Okay, then. The next time you get caught riding drunk, I'll let them throw the book at you. But do you still want me to let them get you when you cross the line?"

"Which line?"

"You know the one I mean."

Camaro thought. "We'll talk about it when the time comes."

"Let's."

The waiter returned with the check. Ignacio reached for it. Camaro snatched it away. She checked the bottom line, brought out her wallet to pay. She paid in wrinkled bills, and added 20 percent for a tip. She noticed Ignacio watching her again. "What?"

"I noticed you don't carry a purse."

"Wow, you *are* a detective."

"No, I mean...you know."

"I don't need a purse, so I don't carry one," Camaro replied. "Besides, what would I put in it? Lipstick and throwing knives?"

Ignacio laughed. "That would be pretty silly, wouldn't it?"

Camaro put her wallet away. "I do what I want. You don't have to know anything else about me. I do what I want. I don't let people tell me who I have to be."

"You are something, that's for sure," Ignacio said.

"I need to go home. Thanks for dinner."

"You paid."

"Oh, yeah. I did."

31

CHAPTER SEVEN

HE LIKED TO watch Faith come and go. At first he thought he'd grow tired of the game, but after he'd done it for a while he realized he couldn't wait for the new day to start so he could be there when she woke up. He followed her all day long, and while she worked in the tall building downtown he snoozed sitting up behind dark glasses and no one ever knew the difference.

It had been enough to stay clear of her and watch from a distance at first, but eventually he found he couldn't help but get closer. That was when he started to leave the car and trail her into stores where she shopped, or sometimes into the building where she worked these days. He was always careful to veer away from cameras, and when this was impossible he wore a cap and big sunglasses to obscure his face. He looked down at the floor as he passed under the lens. There was nothing anyone could use to identify him.

The first time he saw Faith, she was eating her lunch on a bench outside the Pacific National Building, a stone's throw from the Metromover station in Brickell. He remembered the moment clearly, because she had her legs crossed and the smooth skin was exposed to the knee under a professional skirt he still felt was a little too short. There was nothing particularly beautiful about her, but it was an instant of connection.

He liked the way she wasn't tight or tanned or brilliantly blonde. Miami was full of such women. But she wasn't dark with Caribbean promises either. She was different. Special. It wasn't something he discussed with anyone, but he heard the occasional comment and he knew other men considered her plain, or at the very least not the model-quality lovely the unrealistic demanded. She had a too-broad mouth and an oddly quirky smile, and her hair never seemed to want to behave in the Florida humidity. He spent a very long time appreciating the modest swell of her breasts and her imperfect hips. A woman with a body like this was unthreatening, almost motherly. A woman without the sleek good looks of a commercial goddess would never turn her back on a man.

She wasn't secretly dirty either. He knew this. Once he'd left her at her work and traveled back to her apartment. He knew the passcode to the electric gate, and he used a set of lockpicks to get inside her front door. For two long hours he examined everything in her place, from the messy drawer where she kept her flatware to her collection of underwear. There were no hidden pieces of lingerie, no handcuffs in the nightstand drawer, no sex toys, no flavored lubricants. It excited him to think he might find them, but it excited him more when he didn't. She was pure. Eventually he rescued a pair of her underpants from the clothes hamper and took them with him. He kept them in his pocket, and on those nights when she came home and passed without seeing him, he put them to his nose and mouth and inhaled her scent deeply. Soon he'd need a fresher pair.

Tonight he arrived at her apartment a scant few minutes before she did. He barely had time to set up on the street opposite her building before she cruised by in her little Mazda. He breathed through the underpants while he watched her take her delightful precaution.

He put the underpants away and took up his journal. It had a plain black cover. He marked his place with one of her business cards. A pencil was held fast against the spine by a rubber band. He freed the pencil and flipped open the book to find the log of her day. Everything was listed—where she'd gone and when, all of it arranged day by day—and the records went back for weeks and months. Sometimes he was surprised by how long it had been.

When he was done taking notes, he set aside the journal and

watched her apartment. She was cleverer than she had been at the beginning. She never opened the blinds anymore. She knew he was there, and it made things harder, but it also made them more thrilling.

He got out of the car and crossed the street. He plugged in the gate code and slipped through. The day was failing, but it was still hot. He wore a loud Hawaiian shirt and cargo shorts and sandals. Anything else in this neighborhood might have drawn attention as something other. When he was downtown, he wore shirtsleeves and ties, and sometimes even a jacket. When he followed her to the grocery store, he wore a polo shirt and a pair of neatly pressed khakis. He was invisible to everyone, though not always to her. He felt maybe she sensed the connection between them.

Short bushes ran underneath the windows of Faith's front room. He pushed between them now, aligned his eye with the gap between the blinds and the edge of the window. His range of visibility was limited, but he was still able to see the dining area and a sliver of the kitchen.

Faith was at the table eating a salad. She bought salads in bags and expensive vinaigrettes no better than ones she could have gotten for less with a different label. She had a copy of *People,* because she was addicted to *People,* and while she ate she read.

"Excuse me. What are you doing there?"

He started and stepped back from the window. He quashed any look of surprise on his face. He belonged.

It was Andrea, Faith's neighbor. She was thirty-four years old and had more than one boyfriend. She possessed cheap beauty and knew it. He detested her. He smiled. "Hi, Andrea," he said. "It's me."

Andrea brightened. "Oh, hi! I didn't recognize you there. Is everything okay?"

"Tigger got out again. I was poking around in the bushes hoping to flush him out."

"You need to keep that cat behind a fence or something."

He nodded amenably. "You're absolutely right. As soon as the door opens, he bolts. Some cats don't want to be inside."

"Well, I haven't seen him. Maybe on the other side of the building?"

"I'll look there next. Nice to see you, Andrea."

"Nice to see you, too. Hope you find him!"

She waved and walked away, sorting her mail. He watched her go. His expression soured. Faith might have heard them talking. He walked back to the gate. He'd watch from the car for the rest of the night, and he would simply imagine what went on behind Faith's blinds.

CHAPTER EIGHT

CAMARO DIDN'T SEE Faith Glazer for a while. She was on the speed bag. The beginner class broke up, and Camaro heard Miguel's son Rey shouting out the date and time for the next session. The showers would be jammed for some time, but at least the floor of the gym would be given over to the experienced crowd.

She felt someone behind her. "One minute," she said. Camaro punched with her left hand, a rolling measure sending the bag rebounding in a steady rhythm, and switched to her right without breaking the pattern. She went left again and right again, concluded with a sharp right cross, and jangled the bag's mount. Camaro saw Faith.

"Hi," Faith said.

"You're back."

"I'm back."

Camaro flexed her fingers. Wrapped in elastic material, the bones of her hands were tight, her wrists straight. The wraps forced a fighter to learn proper positioning, and they prevented training injuries. She noticed Faith watching the movement. "Is there something about me I don't know?" Camaro asked. "Am I putting out a vibe?"

"A vibe?" Faith looked confused.

"You know...a vibe."

Faith's eyes widened. "Oh. Oh! You mean a *vibe*. No, it's nothing like that. I mean, if I were into that sort of thing I'd definitely be interested, but no. I'm only being friendly."

Camaro brushed past her. "Be friendly with someone else."

"Hey, wait! Maybe that's not everything. I told you I was asking around. And I watch you. I see what you can do. You're way stronger than me, and you know all the moves. I take the class, but I don't know how to do any of it."

Camaro regarded Faith. "How long have you been coming here?"

"A few weeks, I guess."

"You're not going to learn how to do anything in a few weeks. They'll give you the basics, but you're not going to be able to fight. There aren't any shortcuts. You learn, you roll."

Camaro waited.

"I wouldn't ask you if it wasn't important."

She saw Faith's expression swirl with panic, hope, and fear. Some people were easy to read. They had no secrets from anyone. "Is it boyfriend trouble?"

"Huh?"

"Your boyfriend. Is he smacking you around?"

"No, I don't . . . have a boyfriend."

"Then what is it? You're afraid of somebody, or somebody hurt you one time and you don't want to get hurt again? You live in a bad neighborhood?"

Camaro watched Faith's cheeks color. "I live in a pretty good neighborhood," she said.

"It doesn't matter, because I can't help you. It's none of my business. I come here to roll and that's it."

She left. Faith didn't follow. Camaro went into the locker room and stripped for the shower, wrapping herself in a thick white towel until she was safely ensconced under the spray. Hot water played over a network of white scars on tanned skin. Some she felt under her hands when she lathered up, but others had smoothed away like old rock faces against the sea, faded reminders of pain she had felt once upon a time.

Camaro was getting dressed when Faith reappeared. She still had color on her face.

"No," Camaro said.

"If I told you it was a matter of life and death, would it make any difference?"

Camaro reached for the tightly rolled fresh socks tucked away in her bag. She sat on a bench with her bare feet on the concrete and unrolled the socks. "I'd think maybe you were trying to get attention."

"No, I'm serious. I'm in danger. I need help."

"Call the police."

"I already did. They can't help me."

"Hire a bodyguard."

"Do you have any idea what that kind of thing costs?"

Camaro threw up her hands. "I don't know. I'm a fishing boat skipper, okay? I take tourists to catch swordfish. I don't hire out to people with problems. I don't know where you got that idea about me. I'm nobody. I like being nobody. So I'm sorry if you're having a hard time, but...no."

Faith's eyes were wet. Camaro busied herself with her socks. She thrust one foot into a waiting boot before doing the same with the other. She laced them up and pulled the knots tight. She heard Faith walk away.

Camaro exhaled. She held up a hand and found it out of tune with the rest of her. It was the faintest of tremors, and it came from the too-rapid beating of her heart.

She finished getting dressed and threw her sweaty gym clothes into the bag. She went out the rear exit to the back lot. The other day Faith had lingered out front. Camaro was certain she'd do the same today.

The evening sun was still brilliant, though colored with the peach and pink tones of encroaching evening. The small lot behind Miguel's gym was offset with concrete stanchions linked together with chains stained dark with age. A few cars bunched in the space, and a few motorcycles. Camaro turned to her bike and saw Faith Glazer there.

"I'll pay you a hundred dollars to listen to what I have to say. It'll take five minutes. If you still say no, I'll give you another hundred bucks."

Camaro kept walking. When the bike was between them, she dumped her gym bag on the saddle. "Who says I need two hundred bucks badly enough to listen to your story?" she asked Faith.

"If you want more, I can write you a check."

"And then you'll leave me alone?"

"I promise."

Camaro sighed. "Okay."

CHAPTER NINE

"I DIDN'T KNOW he was there until maybe three months ago," Faith told Camaro. "I don't know how long he'd been watching me by then. I mean, sometimes I'd get that creepy feeling you get when there's someone in the room with you, but they're not saying anything? I'd look, but there wouldn't be anyone. But one time I was in Publix and there he was. He was just *standing there* at the end of the aisle, looking at me."

They sat at a table in a small restaurant across Washington Avenue from the gym. It was a tiny place with a handful of colorful tables, all practically on top of one another. The walls were painted brilliant colors and the decorations were Colombian to go with the food. The patrons were mostly tourists, sun-blistered and loud, and their noise ensured no one heard anything spoken between Camaro and Faith. Faith ordered empanadas for the both of them, but neither took a bite once they were delivered.

"How do you know?" Camaro asked Faith. "How do you know he's the one?"

"Trust me, after a while you figure it out. The way he watched me. I knew it wasn't the first time. I started thinking about all the times I might have seen him before. I'm sure he's been by my work, too. I might have seen him by the pool at my apartment once. Or maybe it wasn't him."

Camaro leaned in. She had a bottle of Pony Malta by her elbow, but she hadn't touched it either. "What does he look like? Tall, short? Latino? White guy?"

"Definitely a white guy. He's not pale or anything, but you know the beach bums get as dark as they can. He's not like that."

"Hair color? Eye color?"

"I can't be sure about his eyes. His hair is dark. Maybe dark brown, but probably black."

"How old?"

Faith bit her lip as she thought. "Maybe forty? Could be younger. And he's not tall. I figure he's five ten or so. Not fat, either. He's got strong arms. He was wearing this polo shirt thing? I saw his muscles."

"How about a mustache or a beard?"

"None of that."

Camaro exhaled. "You need to take this to the police. You shouldn't be telling me."

"That's the thing: I *did* take it to the police. I told them everything I'm telling you. The guy's been watching me, peeking in my windows at night, sending me things in the mail. A couple of weeks ago he sent me a snow globe. I mean, I can recognize his handwriting on the stuff he sends me. But it's not enough for the cops. They want fingerprints, so they can identify him, and they want to know he's tried to break in or attack me."

"And he hasn't."

Faith kept her hands on the table to steady them, but Camaro saw her fingers twitch. "There's no way to prove it, but I think he's been inside my apartment. Nothing's missing, but sometimes I come home and I *know* he's been in there. Everything stays exactly the same, but he's been there."

Camaro felt her lip curl. "The cops don't care about that?"

"How can they when there's no evidence? I can't keep calling them every time I get scared. And what are they going to do? Dust my whole apartment for prints twice a week? So I take precautions. I don't go anywhere I might end up alone, and when I *am* alone I have my pepper spray. If he comes for me, and I get it in his eyes, I can run for it."

41

"Pepper spray doesn't work," Camaro said. "Anybody can learn how to fight through it."

"I don't know what else to do. That's why I started going to Miguel's—because I heard it was a good place to learn how to fight. But you know what it's like in these classes: everybody's the same and everything takes too long. I need to know how to take care of myself *right now*. I need someone to help me. One-on-one. A real teacher."

"Me," Camaro said.

"I don't know. Can you be?"

Camaro took up the Pony Malta and drank. She put an empanada on a small plate, but didn't do anything else to it. Her appetite wasn't there. She looked at Faith, at the way she sat and the way she looked back. She thought. "I have to know something first," she said.

"Anything."

"I have to know this is not some kind of boyfriend-girlfriend thing. I'm not saying I don't believe you, but I know this happens sometimes when people break up. They start making accusations and then it gets ugly. I don't want to be in the middle of something like that."

"There is *no way* this guy was ever my boyfriend. No way. I don't know him, I've never met him, and I don't know where he came from. All I know is he's a creep and he's not going away unless someone can *make* him go away. If it's not the police, then it has to be me."

"Do you think you have what it takes?" Camaro asked.

"I don't know what you mean."

"To hurt someone. Maybe kill them."

"If he was going to hurt me, then yes. I'd defend myself. I'm not going to be a victim."

"I don't think you should be."

"Will you help? Show me how to do what you do. Everything. I saw you tangle with that girl, and when you work out with the guys. I saw everything I needed to see. You know how to stop people like this."

Camaro picked up the empanada. She tore it in half. It was filled with spicy meat. "I need to make a call first. Depending on what I hear,

I'll do what I can. But I'm not promising anything. If someone wants to hurt you, they'll figure out a way to hurt you. Sometimes you can't stop it."

Faith sat up straight. "I'm *not* letting him hurt me."

"That's a start."

CHAPTER TEN

IGNACIO SAT IN front of the computer monitor with a pair of tiny reading glasses perched on the end of his nose. He typed with two fingers and his thumbs and managed a decent speed. The narrative of a case involving two junkies who had stabbed each other—one of whom died at the scene and one of whom managed to drag herself five blocks before expiring on the sidewalk—took form little by little. When Ignacio was done with his final report, he'd comb through it for the inevitable spelling errors and any details he had happened to forget. Only then would it be appended to the case's electronic file and dumped into a virtual outbox to join the others flowing out of Homicide Unit.

It was closing in on end of shift, when the daytime cops traded places with the nighttime cops. Fresh faces for new crimes. Already most of the cubicles around Ignacio were empty. The talk of other detectives was distant hallway chatter as the crews overlapped. He checked his watch, realized there was no reason to worry about it. No one was waiting for him at home.

His desk phone trilled, jarringly loud. Ignacio snatched up the receiver and tucked it into the crook of his shoulder. He kept typing. "Detective Montellano, Homicide Unit."

"It's Camaro Espinoza."

Ignacio stopped typing. "Camaro. You're calling me? Is somebody dead?"

"No."

"Is someone about to be dead?"

"Not that I know of."

He relaxed into his chair. "Then to what do I owe the pleasure? I don't think it's because you miss my handsome face."

"I need something from the police and I don't think I'll get a straight answer talking to anyone else."

"How so?"

"I met a woman. I don't want to get into how it happened. She told me she's being stalked, and she's been to the police about it. More than once. They told her there was nothing they could do."

Ignacio grabbed a pen and a yellow legal pad. "What's this woman's name?"

"Faith Glazer."

"And when did all this start? Did she give you dates?"

"She said three months, but it could have been longer. It's when she noticed."

"Got an address?"

Camaro gave it to him. He recorded all the information and scribbled a tail underneath it. "I'll look it up. Where can I reach you?"

"This number."

"We'll talk soon."

"Thanks."

"De nada."

Ignacio hung up and returned his attention to the computer. He swept the report away with a click and located another icon on the desktop in the shape of the police department logo. After two different log-ins, he drilled down to the search field he needed.

The database crunched for a little over thirty seconds. It returned a series of hits. Ignacio disregarded everything except the top result. He clicked it open. Notes and forms spilled onto his screen, internally searchable and with the handwritten originals scanned in.

Faith Glazer was twenty-nine years old, and she worked as a forensic accountant. Ignacio did not know what a forensic accountant was. She was for hire, skipping from temporary employer to temporary employer with regularity. The file listed four different work addresses over the previous year. All were banks or financial firms.

She recounted six instances of close encounters with her stalker. Twice she had seen him near her work, and three times in places of business or on the street near her apartment. Another time he'd been outside the fence around the lot where she parked. In none of the incidents had he spoken to her, or made any physical contact.

The reporting officer also made note of two times when Faith thought the stalker had been inside her apartment, though an examination of the premises showed no signs of forced entry. She said she was pretty sure he peeked through her windows at night, but had no times or dates to share.

There was more. Ignacio read it all. He picked up the phone and dialed internally. The line rang twice before a woman answered. "Detective Herrera. Special Victims. How can I help?"

"Detective, this is Ignacio Montellano over in Homicide. How are you doing tonight?"

"Clearing my desk before I head home."

"Yeah, same here. Listen, do you have a minute? I'm looking at a case forwarded to Special Victims not too long ago. It doesn't look like anyone was assigned to it, so I don't know who to talk to."

"What's the case number?"

Ignacio read the number off the screen. "The complainant's name is Faith Deena Glazer. I have an address if you need it."

"No, I have it. It looks like the case dropped in our laps about six weeks ago. It's on the board for someone to follow up on, but we haven't gotten around to it. Wait a minute: Is this a homicide case now?"

"Nothing like that, thank God. No, it came up because the MO of the reported stalker meshed with a potential suspect in another case, so I thought I'd chase down the details."

Herrera made a humming sound. "I'm not seeing anything unusual here. Though the behavior seems to be escalating, which is typical for this kind of thing. This suspect you're looking at, you're thinking he's good for a body?"

"Tough to say. I'll know more soon. But you're seeing what I'm seeing, right? This is a legitimate complaint."

"If it's not, then Ms. Glazer knows all the right buttons to push. I'd need to sit down with this file and really read it over, plus do interviews with the victim, but judging strictly from what I see here...yeah, it's legit. I'm going to move this up, because if he's doing some of the things she says he's doing, it's only a matter of time."

"He could hurt her," Ignacio said.

"At least. That's the thing with these stalkers: a little is never enough. He'll start with the harmless stuff—*creepy* stuff, but harmless—but he'll turn it up a few notches at a time until the next thing you know he's raped or killed the woman he's stalking."

Ignacio scowled at the file on his screen. "Tell you what: if you do look into this, keep me posted, okay? I don't want it turning into something one of ours has to handle. You know what I mean?"

"I do. Thanks for calling, Detective."

Ignacio hung up. He looked at the screen. He called up Faith Glazer's driver's license. She had a dejected expression in the photo, hair in disarray. "Sounds like you have a real problem on your hands, Ms. Glazer," he said aloud.

He called Camaro.

CHAPTER ELEVEN

CAMARO HEARD THE sound of Faith's car in the street. During the time she'd been living here, she'd learned the familiar noises, the voices and the cars and trucks. She knew when the Domino's Pizza driver was on her street because the engine on his dying car had a distinctive buzz that would only get worse if he didn't start maintaining his ride better. Camaro had the faces of everyone on the block tucked away, some with names and some without. She rarely spoke to her neighbors, but she knew them. For the better part of a year she'd avoided any contact with anyone on her street at all. Except for once, and a man ended up in the hospital. He belonged there.

She stopped in the living room to peek out through the blinds. Faith was out of her Mazda and struggling with an athletic bag. She wore yoga pants and sneakers and a T-shirt over an athletic bra, but none of it looked right on her. The band holding her hair barely kept the curls under control.

Camaro went to the front door, opened it, and pushed the screen door wide. "You're late," she said.

Faith hurried up the short walk, three cement squares sunk unevenly in the dirt and surrounded by listless grass. "I am so sorry. There was a power outage last night while I was sleeping and my alarm got switched off. I got here as fast as I could."

They moved inside, where it was cooler. Camaro let the screen door slap into place, closed the inner door against the day. It was dim with the blinds shut and the drapes mostly drawn. Camaro smelled the faint aroma of hair product in Faith's wake. "Next time you need to be here when I tell you," she told Faith. "I have a lot of business in the summer and not a whole lot of downtime. If you want to learn from me, get here. Set two alarms if you have to."

"I'm sorry. I won't even tell you that I got lost driving over here, too. I don't know this area at all. It's kind of...working-class. No offense."

"Bring your stuff out back."

They went outside. Camaro saw Faith looking around the patio at the equipment. A bench for weight lifting, a heavy bag the size of a man, a solid wooden crate, a battered wooden dummy called a *muk yan jong*, racks of kettlebells and iron plates and a mat patched with duct tape spread over one-quarter of the space. Overhead, tucked into the supports for the patio's roof, was a length of pipe wrapped in dirty cotton. A chin-up bar.

"Holy shit," Faith said. "You are hard-core."

"Put your bag down anywhere. Take your shoes and socks off."

Faith obeyed. Camaro stretched until her forehead touched her knees. Her legs were encased in black Lycra to midcalf, and she wore no shirt over a dark athletic bra with the lines of a tank top. When she straightened again, she gathered her hair and tied it back with a pink elastic band.

Camaro stepped onto the mat. Faith followed her. They stood face-to-face. "I'm going to tell you something right now," Camaro said. "And you need to *hear me,* all right?"

"Okay."

"I don't do this for fun. I don't do it to get a beach body. You understand? The things I do here, the things I'm going to teach you, are about saving your life. Over at Miguel's, they'll take it easy on you as long as you're paying the fee, and they know most of the people who come through the door are never going to throw a real punch in their lives. It's a game to those people. It's not a game to me."

Faith shook her head. "It is absolutely not a game to me. I'm sorry I was late. I won't be late again."

Camaro held her gaze. "This isn't about being late. This is about doing what you have to do to stay alive. I don't know how good a teacher I am. I've only done it once before and it went wrong. But I'm still going to try because whoever that guy is out there who's following you, he has to go down. All the way down. You have to put him there. I won't be able to help you, and no one else will, either. Not the cops, not your neighbors. It's going to be you...and him."

"I understand."

It was hot and the air lay thick against them. Camaro ran Faith through a series of warm-ups and stretches until Faith was drenched with perspiration and her face was flushed. They paused long enough for a drink of water before the rest: squats and lunges and kicks and push-ups, all done side by side. Camaro pushed herself until her body burned. When Faith fell behind, Camaro slowed only long enough to bring her back in tandem.

Faith screamed. Faith wept. Camaro wrapped Faith's hands in elastic cotton and turned her loose against the heavy bag. She saw the muscles in Faith's legs tremble. Hair plastered to her skin. Camaro urged her on until Faith staggered and collapsed onto the mat.

"Get up."

Faith held up a hand. Her lungs bellowed. "I'm dying. I can't get up."

"It doesn't get any easier than this. Get up."

"I need five minutes."

"You want five minutes, or do you want to hurt this asshole when he comes for you?"

"I can't."

"You can. Get. Up."

Camaro caught Faith by the wrist and hauled her to her feet. Faith swayed. Fresh tears streamed down her face. "This is too much. I'm out of shape."

"You are out of shape, but we're gonna fix that. You and me."

She grabbed a leather jump rope from where it lay coiled by the weights. She put it in Faith's hand. "A hundred skips. You can take thirty seconds after every twenty."

Faith looked as though she would say more, but she closed her mouth. She nodded. "All right."

CHAPTER TWELVE

HE HADN'T KNOWN where Faith was going. When he saw her in her workout clothes, he assumed she was headed to the fighting gym in South Beach where she'd begun taking classes. He'd gotten used to the commute, and the view on the gym's breezy street. But Faith made different turns and soon they were in a thicket of old housing and narrow throughways where the city's working poor struggled to hang on to the bottom rung of what used to be called the middle class. He did not like the neighborhood, nor did he care much for the people he saw. It reminded him of places he'd put behind him.

After a few strange detours he attributed to confusing GPS directions, they eventually found their way into the heart of Allapattah, and there Faith parked in front of a modest-looking house on a street thick with trees. He parked well back to stay out of Faith's sight, but not so far back that he couldn't see her all the way to the front door.

The woman in the house wasn't familiar to him. He looked at her through a small pair of binoculars. She was a bit taller than Faith and heavier with muscle. Toned arms and defined shoulders, body flat and tight where Faith's was soft. She didn't smile, not even when she greeted Faith at the door.

They went inside. He thought about moving closer, but he couldn't be sure if Faith would emerge suddenly and find him in the open. Instead he watched the dark, still windows and the red pickup truck in the driveway and imagined what he might see if he came near.

It occurred to him that this new woman was a lesbian. From the way she looked and the way she carried herself, it seemed obvious.

Faith was not a lesbian, but he sometimes thought it would be exciting if she was attracted to both men and women. Some nights he fantasized about two women, but both of them looked like Faith and he couldn't tell them apart. They made love to each other as well as to him and became one body.

An hour passed, then another, with no sign of Faith. It was too warm in the car, even when he rolled down the windows halfway. He busied himself writing down all the information he could ascertain, like the street number for the house and a few letters and numbers off the truck's license plate. The same idea kept coming back to prod him again and again, until at last the images unspooled inside his mind.

He had never seen Faith completely naked, but he had some idea of what was beneath her clothes. With the new woman he could conjure other details. Those details meshed with the daydream of Faith's body, and he saw the two of them together in bed as clearly as if he were watching them in the same room. A hot room, as overwhelmed with humidity and temperature as his car, and one that made their bodies wet.

In his mind he heard their sounds. Of course he'd seen the movies. Everyone had. He knew they were all fake, but sometimes he thought he heard the genuine passion hidden away inside them. He heard it now, echoing in the chamber of his skull as the sheets tangled around them and they moved together.

He pulled the pair of Faith's underpants from his pocket and covered his mouth and nose with the material. His body was abuzz with the vision. He breathed raggedly, drawing the last bit of scent from the underwear, concentration fragmenting into a million shards, each one reflecting the bedroom scene over and over until there was nothing else but Faith and the woman, Faith and the woman.

His chest hitched. His body spasmed. He felt heat and an insistent pulse. He snatched the underpants away from his mouth and gasped for unfiltered air. He clutched the steering wheel with both hands until he saw and heard and felt again.

Something moved in the corner of his vision. He saw a girl of eight or nine on a bicycle in the street in the shade of a full green tree. She stared at him, and her mouth hung open. He saw distress and confusion flicker behind her eyes. She turned her head and shouted, "Mama! Mama!"

He straightened up in his seat and twisted the key in the ignition. With the girl still watching him, he slammed the lever into drive and stomped the accelerator. His car leaped from its spot by the curb, wheels chirping. He accelerated down the street toward the woman's house. Despite himself he looked, but there was no sign of her or Faith. There was a bronze-and-black Harley-Davidson motorcycle in the carport.

Now he was beyond the house and moving toward the end of the block. In the rearview mirror he saw the girl joined by a woman in a blue housedress. The girl pointed down the street after his car, but he knew he was far enough away that they'd never be able to get the license plate. He reached the corner and hurtled around it, slowing only enough to keep the car from slewing completely out of control. He hyperventilated again, but it was different now. It was not the excitement he wanted, but the exhilaration of a moment passed successfully and no one the wiser.

He drove for fifteen minutes in no particular direction. The air conditioner chilled the air and the sweat wicked away from his skin. His spirits lifted still more. He turned on the radio to listen to snatches of music between commercials and DJ chatter. He almost sang along.

CHAPTER THIRTEEN

CAMARO HEARD THE shower running while she set the kitchen table for two. She had a pair of pork chops, absorbing the flavors of a dry rub, waiting by the stove on a sheet of waxed paper. Instead of glasses, she put out cold bottles of Gatorade straight from the refrigerator. She boiled water to steam vegetables.

After a while Faith emerged. She'd changed from sweat-soaked workout clothing into jeans and a loose blouse. Without speaking to Camaro, she took one of the bottles of Gatorade and cracked the seal. She drank until the bottle was half empty. "Oh, thank God," she said.

"There's more."

Faith collapsed into a chair. "I swear I thought I was going to die. I'm going to hurt so bad tomorrow. I hurt *now.*"

Camaro nodded. The water wasn't rolling yet. "Watch this pot."

She left Faith in the kitchen and took a turn underneath the shower spray. Her body ached, but Faith had it worse. Camaro dressed for home in a pair of pants with holes worn in them and a plain white T-shirt. By the time she returned to the kitchen, the water was ready for the vegetables.

Faith watched her while she worked. The pork chops had to go on at the right time. First a sear, and then a finish under the broiler. "Do I always get dinner after you torture me?"

"Today you do."

Faith drained the last of her bottle. "I'm out."

"Take mine."

Camaro stayed at the stove. A minute too long and the pork would dry out. "You didn't quit," she said without looking away.

"Haven't you heard of starting off slowly?"

"No time. From what I heard, a guy like the one who's been bothering you, he's going to keep stepping it up until he does something he can't take back. You want to be ready when it happens."

"You know a lot about this kind of thing?"

"No. But I know people who do."

Camaro put the pork in the oven. She set a timer. The vegetables were ready to come out of the steamer. She'd keep them in a bowl under a hot, moist towel. She knew Faith was watching.

"If we're going to do this, we'll need to meet three or four times a week," Camaro said. "The schedule's going to depend on my business. I keep odd hours sometimes."

"What is it you do again?"

Camaro soaked a towel under the hot tap. She shook the steamer out and transferred the vegetables to a bowl. She put the towel over the bowl. "I skipper a fishing boat."

"I would not have figured that out."

"What do you see me doing?"

"I don't know. Not a cop. A soldier, maybe?"

Camaro glanced at Faith.

"Were you a soldier?"

"Once."

"Do you have all kinds of medals and stuff?"

"Does it matter?"

"I'm an accountant. No medals."

Camaro came to the table with the bowl still covered. She set the bowl between their plates. "Everybody does something. I don't know anything about being an accountant. I use my computer to do my taxes."

Faith made a face. "You need a *person* to do your taxes. Especially if you're a small-business owner. The potential tax liabilities those software programs can miss are huge. Don't believe the hype."

"Okay," Camaro said.

"You're laughing at me."

"No. But I told you, I don't know anything about that kind of stuff."

"You know a hundred ways to kick somebody's ass, though, right?"

"Maybe."

"Maybe nothing. I saw the scars on your knuckles. You have them on your elbows, too. And then there's the one over your eye. It's pretty new. I think it is, anyway."

Camaro touched her brow without meaning to. She felt a stab of something dark. She went back to the oven. "You keep on learning to fight, you'll pick up some of your own. Stay at Miguel's, get serious. Sooner or later someone will break your nose."

"I don't even know what that would feel like."

Camaro peeked inside the oven. "It hurts. You get over it after a few times."

The timer went off. Camaro turned her attention to the food. She brought out the pork chops and served them hot from the oven. She fetched another bottle of Gatorade and sat down with it at the table. Faith pulled back the towel on the vegetables. Aromatic steam rose from them. They took turns portioning them out.

Faith was quiet while she tried the food. She nodded. "Good," she said.

"Eat it all. The protein will help your muscles, and the vegetables have the vitamins you need, plus carbs to get your energy level back up. Buy some apples and have two or three of them every day. Have salads, but make sure you put some chicken and cheese in them. Even better: eat the chicken and forget the salad. Nuts are good, too. Always keep some around."

"I feel like I'm going to start bodybuilding."

"Next time we're working with weights."

"I wish I hadn't said anything."

"It'll be worth it in the end."

Faith put down her fork. "You know, we haven't even talked about how I'm going to pay you."

"I don't want to get paid."

"I have to pay you something. You won't get rich, but this is worth money."

"I said I don't want to get paid."

"Then you're doing this just because?"

"Is there something wrong with that?"

"No. It's only...I guess nobody's ever done something for me just because."

"You need help. I can help. It's not about money."

Faith was quiet. "Thank you."

Camaro cleaned the last of her pork from the bone. "You have a gun?" she asked.

"No way."

"You don't like guns?"

"Not really. I mean, I've never had one. I've never shot one."

"There's a gun store with a range about twenty minutes from here," Camaro said. "I can give you directions. When you leave tonight, go there and buy a weapon. Get a recommendation from the guys, make sure it's something comfortable in your hand and something you can carry without a lot of trouble."

"I can't carry a *gun*."

"Do you want to make sure this creep who's coming around keeps his hands off you?"

"Yes, but that's why I'm learning all the other stuff. I don't need a gun."

Camaro reached across the table and touched Faith's wrist. "You need a gun. I can teach you everything about how to gouge somebody's eyes out or break their balls, but sometimes it's all or nothing. So get a gun. When you have something you like, we'll go out together and I'll show you how to use it. Even if you don't carry it with you, at least you can have it at home."

Faith put down her knife and fork. Half her pork chop was uneaten. "Do you really think it'll come to that?"

"I don't know. And you don't either."

Faith didn't reply.

Camaro stood and gathered her plate and flatware. "Remember what I said. Eat it all."

She went to the sink and rinsed the dishes. She heard Faith pick up her fork, and heard the scrape of a knife on the plate.

CHAPTER FOURTEEN

IGNACIO OFTEN WORE a jacket as part of the job, but in the depths of summer it became another thing to carry around. Short sleeves were better, but sometimes the higher-ups wanted a professional look. As he left the office and stepped into the heat of the afternoon, he slung his jacket over his shoulder and instantly felt trapped warmth that would turn into a sweaty burn if given the time.

He was halfway to his car when he saw Brady Pool crossing the scorched asphalt on his way inside. Ignacio caught Pool's eye and raised his hand. Pool changed directions. They met in the middle of the lane. "Back from vacation," Ignacio said. "Looking good."

Pool had dispensed with a jacket and wore a blue golf shirt with the police department's logo on the breast. It wasn't field wear, but likely he would work the phones tonight as other detectives caught the cases. Pool patted his belly. "I gained at least five pounds from eating all that food. They keep shoving it down your throat even when you beg for mercy."

"I've never been to one of those all-inclusive places."

"Well, you gotta go. Take Mara and head on down to Cozumel. Great atmosphere, friendly people...everything you want."

Ignacio frowned at Mara's name. "That sounds great, but Mara and I kind of split up."

"What? When?"

"Been a few weeks now. I didn't tell anybody about it, and you were on vacation and it's my problem anyway."

Pool gripped Ignacio's arm. "If you need something, you only have to ask, all right? Grace would love to have you by the house. We can watch some baseball, grill some steaks. Whatever you want."

"I appreciate it."

"Where you off to?"

Ignacio looked toward his car, and felt a shadow pass over him though the sun was brilliant. "Home, I guess."

"Take care of yourself, you hear me? I'll see you around."

"Yeah, see you."

They parted and Ignacio went to the car. He put his jacket over the passenger seat, and got behind the wheel. The interior of the car was nightmarish, even with reflective screens erected against the windshield. Ignacio put on the air conditioner full blast and didn't close the door until the vents started blowing cold air. By the time he was on the road, the temperature had plummeted. Soon it would be icy.

He didn't live far from work, and that was just as well. Miami traffic could be brutal, and he spent enough of his working day stranded in logjams full of cars. More people came every year. There were hardly any places to put them. Rents had been on the rise for years, and now there were complaints that a working family couldn't afford to live anywhere decent anymore. Ignacio sympathized.

The house he lived in had a decent amount of equity, but he was a long way from paying it off. It had been easier with Mara living with him, but now the bills fell to him alone. He didn't leave anything except the refrigerator running when he was out of the house to keep the electric bill down. The atmosphere grew thick during those hours, and it was sometimes hard to breathe when he returned.

Once he was inside, the ceiling fans and the air-conditioning units perched in the windows stirred things back to life. Ignacio took a shower and shaped up his beard and put on a tatty robe over boxer shorts and a T-shirt. He walked barefoot around the house. In the kitchen he opened the refrigerator and peered inside.

The shelves were almost entirely empty. Mara had been a light shopper, and didn't believe in buying more in a week than could be eaten in seven days. When she left it was up to Ignacio to stock the kitchen. He looked at a piece of cheddar cheese wrapped in plastic, a head of lettuce, and two bottles of Vitaminwater. In the door there were three eggs, some butter, and a squeeze bottle of mayonnaise.

"Okay," Ignacio said to himself. "We are going *out.*"

He re-dressed in knee-length shorts and a loose-fitting shirt. He wore sandals instead of shoes and no socks. On the streets he looked like every other Miami native, eyes hidden behind sunglasses, trilby perched on his head. The anonymity was appealing sometimes.

He decided to walk instead of driving, which was something people did in Miami less and less as the city continued to sprawl. He found himself on a street lined on both sides with small businesses, punctuated here and there with franchise restaurants. He browsed the window of a shop selling off-brand cell phones and other cheap electronics. He passed clusters of young men hanging out on corners with nowhere to go and nothing to do. They paid him no attention and he returned the favor.

In the end he pushed through the door of a little place with hand-printed paper signs in the window advertising sandwiches and other simple fare. The man behind the counter wore a plain white sleeveless undershirt and, around his waist, a stained apron. A boy in his teens worked in the kitchen. They looked enough alike that Ignacio assumed they were father and son.

A slight woman worked the half-dozen small tables in the dining area. The floor was scuffed and old, tiling too aged to be polished again. Ignacio sat with his back to the window and watched the family work, listening to the chatter from other tables and Latin jazz playing on a boom box on a high shelf behind the counter.

They brought him a pressed Cuban sandwich, and it was all right. He ate and washed it down with water. When he was finished, he sighed. A full stomach didn't chase away anything. He'd have to go back to an empty house, and sleep in an empty bed. And tomorrow it would start all over again.

CHAPTER FIFTEEN

FAITH WAS DEEPLY asleep, but then she wasn't. Her eyes snapped open in the darkness of her bedroom. She held her breath. She didn't know if she'd heard a sound, or if something else stirred her awake. She waited for it to happen again. She didn't breathe until she saw flecks of light in her vision. Nothing disturbed the silence.

She wanted to sit up in bed, but she was afraid to. She lay on her side facing the wall with her back to the window. The blinds were closed and it was almost entirely dark, even though there was a security lamp outside, which cast a brilliant cone of illumination on the end of the building.

Minutes passed. A metallic click came from the hallway and Faith flinched. She waited. It was the noise of the thermostat switching off the air-conditioning. It took time for her heartbeat to steady.

She had to get up.

When she rose, she did so abruptly, springing upright and throwing back the sheets in the same motion. Cool air played over her bare legs. She wore a long nightshirt with a MIAMI HEAT logo printed on the front. She was naked underneath.

The room was inky. A small amount of light bled in from the hallway. The bedroom door was half closed. She tried to remember if she had done that earlier, or if it had moved. Her heart quickened once more.

She slid out of bed, feet alighting on the carpet. She teetered on tiptoes, settled onto her heels. Nothing leaped out at her in the darkness.

She thought to turn on the light. She found she didn't want to give any sign that she was awake. She stole across the bedroom to the window and stopped there, a shadow in shadows, and put her hand against the thin plastic of the blinds. Her thumb found the edge of one slat and eased it upward. A crack of light pierced the room. She widened the gap.

Two bushes stood outside her window. They were frosted white by the security light. The fence was beyond them. No one moved in her vision. A glance at the bedside clock said it was a little past three in the morning. Even the last-call drunks were home by now.

The slat fell back into place. She was in the dark again. She went to the bedroom door. Her hallway lay ahead, the way dimly visible. She went down the hall, passing the empty kitchen, where no one could hide, and into the front room.

Everything was the way she had left it at bedtime. A stack of paperwork was on the dining area table, everything tucked away into folders. The photographs of the Art Deco District on the wall were smears of light and shadow in the dark. In the front room she saw the book she'd been reading, still splayed on its face. She saw the peanut shape of her remote control. The television was slate-gray and rectangular, like a slab of cut stone.

She stood motionless for what seemed like a long time. She made her way to the sliding glass door to her tiny patio. The blinds were like all the others, closed against the night. She felt breathless as she stood before them.

She looked. There was no one outside. The patio was undisturbed.

Faith turned in place. The atmosphere had changed. She felt exposed in the broader space. The thin material of the nightshirt seemed like no covering at all. She wished she'd put on a robe.

Light shone against the blinds in the front window. It was only the lamps that lit the sidewalk and parking lot. Half the blinds were dark, the other half bright, a slash of shadow from outside and nothing else.

She went to the window. She put her hand on the blinds and separated them. He was there.

The scream leaped out of her throat even before the sight of him registered. Faith jerked away as if electrocuted, tripped over her own feet. She tumbled to the floor and banged her shoulder on the coffee table. Her muscles protested, days of abuse by exercise coming to call. Faith kept screaming as she clawed her way onto her feet and ran to the dining table.

Her phone was there, plugged into a cord leading from the wall. The wire snapped as she jerked the phone from the table, one end still socketed into the bottom of the phone. She pressed her thumb to the phone's button to read her fingerprint, failed. Tried again and failed again. She tried a third time. The phone unlocked.

She dialed 911. The line rang. Faith stared at the front window. A shadow fell against the blinds, but she didn't know if it was the man or something else.

"This is 911 emergency," a male voice said. "Police, fire, or ambulance?"

"Police! Send me the police, please!"

"What is the nature of your emergency?"

"There's a man outside my window. He wants to attack me. He's going to break in. You have to send somebody *right now!*"

"Try to stay calm. I have an address on my screen, but I want to confirm it. Can you do that for me?"

"Yes."

The 911 operator recited the street address. Faith gave him her apartment number. In the background of the call, she heard the faint clicking of keys. "Ma'am, I want you to know a police officer has been dispatched to your location. It's only going to be a few minutes. Has the man outside tried to break in yet?"

Faith shook her head. She realized the operator couldn't see her. "No."

"Do you have somewhere in the apartment where you can lock yourself in?"

"The bathroom."

"Okay, go there. Don't come out until I tell you the officer is at your door. I'll stay on the line until they arrive. You're going to be okay."

Faith stumbled as she ran to the bathroom. She slammed the door and twisted the lock in the knob. It was completely dark. She put her back against the wall and slid to the floor. She felt sick to her stomach. She sobbed into the phone, "He's going to kill me."

"No one's going to kill you. Stay safe."

Faith held on to the phone with both hands. Her nose ran. The operator said more, but she heard none of it.

CHAPTER SIXTEEN

CAMARO SAW NO sign of the police when she drew near Faith's apartment. No lights flashed, no units parked on the street. Once she came to the gate and plugged in the security code, she saw a single patrol car parked with its headlights on and the driver's-side door open. The engine still ran. Soft lights glowed inside: the blue of the computer screen and the indicators on the dash.

She slotted her bike behind the police unit and killed the engine. The walk outside the apartment was clear of onlookers. In Camaro's neighborhood, people would be out on the street in numbers. It was different here.

A female cop emerged from the apartment at the same moment Camaro approached the front door. The cop stopped short and put her hand on her weapon. "Who are you?"

"I'm a friend of Faith's. Is she inside?"

The cop was white and older, and she scanned Camaro from head to boots. Her hand came away from her gun. "She said you'd be coming. Ms. Espinoza?"

"That's right. Is she okay?"

The cop shrugged. The name tag on her uniform read ADAMS. She consulted a small notepad she'd taken from her breast pocket. "About two hours ago she says she was awakened by something she wasn't sure of. She checked the whole apartment and didn't find anyone inside, but when she looked out the front window, there was a man. She says he's been following her for months. Is that true?"

"It's what she told me."

"She says she doesn't have any idea who he is. Do you?"

"No."

"So there's no secret boyfriend, or someone she's been getting close to at work? That kind of thing?"

Camaro looked past Adams. She didn't see Faith. "Look, I don't know her well. But she says she doesn't have a boyfriend and I believe her. This guy, he's a stranger. And nobody's doing anything to help with him."

Adams put away her notepad. "Did she say that?"

"Yes. Why?"

"We take this kind of thing seriously. A woman gets stalked, maybe the woman gets raped or beaten or killed. That's not something we want to have happen. So if she made a report about it, someone paid attention. But there's only so much we can do."

"She's not asking for a lot."

"We can drive by a little more often, and we can see if the detectives can shake something loose about stalkers in the area. Unless the guy decides to announce himself, he could be anybody. That's why we always look at ex-boyfriends and ex-husbands and people who might get the wrong idea from something she said or did."

"I'm going to go in," Camaro said.

"Sure. See if you can get her to take a pill or have a drink, because she really needs it."

"What are you going to do?"

"I'm going to drop by a few more times before my shift is up, in case I can catch the guy creeping around. Maybe he'll come back tonight, maybe he won't. But now you're here, so she won't be alone."

"Thanks."

"You're welcome. And when you get a chance? Move that motorcycle. You're blocking in the residents."

Adams went. Camaro passed through the open apartment door. She pressed it shut behind her and locked it. She looked around. The front room was empty, and the small dining area was too. It was possible to see the kitchen from where she stood. She saw a phone book on the dining table, still in its plastic door hanger. Pictures of Art Deco District hotels were on the wall. "Faith?" Camaro called.

"Back here."

Faith's voice sounded clotted. Camaro followed it.

Faith was in her bedroom on the bed, back against the headboard. Her hair was everywhere, and her face was blotched with red. Wads of tissue lay all around her.

"I'm here," Camaro said.

"Thank you for coming."

Camaro sat on the corner of the bed. "The cop says you need a drink."

Faith barked a laugh. "I could use ten drinks. But I don't have anything in the house."

"I'll pick something up for you later."

"I'm old enough to buy my own booze."

"Then what am I doing here? You want me to cook you breakfast?"

Faith trumpeted into a tissue. The skin above her upper lip was moist. Her eyes were swollen. She screwed her face into an ugly mask. She cried, and Camaro watched. Faith hugged herself. She was in a nightshirt and a pair of baggy sweatpants. She looked smaller than she was.

After a time she quieted. "I can't do this," she said.

"You are doing it."

"I don't know what I was thinking. You can teach me all you want, but I'm still scared. When I saw him tonight . . . I thought he was going to kill me, and I couldn't think of anything to do. Everything I learned was *gone*. He could have done anything he wanted to me. I couldn't have stopped him."

"You don't know that."

"I know exactly."

"So you keep at it. You train and train until you don't have to think. You don't have to remember anything. Your body does it all for you."

SAM HAWKEN

"Is that how it is for you?"

"Sometimes."

"I'm an *accountant*. Okay? I'm not some Amazon princess. I had an inhaler when I was growing up. I don't *do* stuff like this. I analyze records and I track transactions and I ensure proper bookkeeping. Nobody's ever going to look to me when they think, 'Oh, who's the toughest person I know?'"

Camaro stood. "I guess there's no point to going on with you," she said.

Faith's face blanched. "Wait! I'm not...I don't...Don't leave."

"Why not? You said it yourself: you're no good, and you're weak and you can't do it. I have better things to do with my time. I have a charter leaving in two hours. I should be on the boat getting ready. I don't need to hold your hand."

Faith's expression creased again. She dabbed her eyes with tissue. "Please. I don't want to cry anymore."

"Then cut it out!" Camaro said. "You want to feel sorry for yourself, it's your business, not mine. You came to me because you wanted *help*. So you could learn how to protect yourself. You didn't ask me to take care of your problem for you. You asked me to give you what you need to take care of the problem without me."

"I'm scared! Don't you get it?"

Camaro stepped forward. She lifted the hem of her shirt away from her jeans and exposed her side. Muscle lay flat under the skin. The skin itself was mottled with scar tissue. "You see that? I took three pieces of shrapnel in my side when a mortar shell went off fifty feet from me. I got shot in the leg dragging a man across a hundred yards of open ground while people tried to kill us both. You think I wasn't scared?"

Faith looked at her. Her mouth was shut, and the lips twisted. She said nothing.

Camaro grabbed the neck of her shirt and yanked it down to expose another latticework of scars, fresh pink and tender-looking. "I got this less than a year ago. The man who shot me put a gun in my face and told me I was gonna die. You think I wasn't scared then?"

"Camaro, I—"

Camaro cut her off. "I've got more. You want to see them? I've got broken bones and torn ligaments and stab wounds and anything else you want to name. And I was scared. I was scared every time."

Her voice faltered. She glared at Faith on the bed, and Faith shrank under her gaze, wringing a tissue in her hands.

"I'm sorry," Faith said.

"Don't be sorry. Make the *other guy* sorry."

"What do you want me to do?"

"Where's the gun?"

"What gun?"

"The gun I told you to buy. Where is it?"

Faith shook her head. "I didn't buy it."

"Why not?"

"I don't *like* guns! I know you told me to, but I don't like them."

Camaro sat on the edge of the bed. "You need to have a gun in the house. It's important."

"I'm afraid. I'm afraid of everything."

Camaro touched Faith on the leg. "We're going to work on it."

"Why?"

"Because I'm not going to let this happen to you."

CHAPTER SEVENTEEN

HE GREW AGITATED. It had been days and weeks since Faith had begun seeing the woman, Camaro Espinoza, and he did not understand what was going on. When he wasn't watching Faith, he felt worse, but he had to take time to find out about Faith's new friend. There was infuriatingly little to go on, but he did the best he could. All he knew was that Espinoza was a charter-boat captain and she had the interest of law enforcement in some quarters. She had been in the army and served with distinction. Why she was here, he didn't know, because she had no family he could find, or any ties to Miami at all.

This unto itself was not unusual. People came to Miami from everywhere to make a new start. Though the city was slowly sinking into the sea, they saw a future for themselves. It was a hopeful place, with much to aspire to. But it all took money, and sometimes money was hard to come by. He knew this.

One day he left Faith at work and returned to her apartment. He lay down on her bed, smelling her on the pillows and sheets. Afterward he straightened everything to leave no sign. She had recently washed all her underthings, so there was nothing in the laundry hamper, which upset him, but there would be other times. He spent a while looking at the pictures on the walls. She loved the Art Deco District and those brilliantly pastel old buildings. She had books on her shelves filled with photographs of them, and of the traces of the past still visible here and there around the city. He looked for the snow globe he had sent her, but she hadn't kept it. He was not surprised, but he was still disappointed.

He returned to her work in time to see her leave the bank building and walk to the parking garage a block away. Once she was on the road, he trailed her as he always did. Sometimes vehicles slipped between them and obscured his view, but he gave his car the gas and moved ahead so he could always see the outline of her hair around the head-rest of the driver's seat. He wanted to touch her hair, but he had never been that close for more than a few fleeting seconds. He also knew that the moment they made contact it would be over.

Sweet agony was watching her park her car in the lot outside her apartment building and walk carefully to her door. He'd lost count of the number of times he'd seen this exact same thing, and watched her vanish before the sun went down and the soft glow of her lights illuminated the blinds from within.

She'd seen him, of course. He'd suspected it for a while, but the night she came to the window there had been no mistake. He had to be particularly careful now. But she *had* come to the window, and this was the most important thing. She'd known he was there and she came to him, and this proved to him that they had a connection beyond watcher and subject. She wanted him, even if she didn't fully understand it yet. And he wanted her more than anything he'd ever wanted in his life.

Tonight he'd creep up to her window and try to catch her in bed asleep. He wouldn't try to break in. He wanted only to see her in the dim room. Not too much to ask.

He waited, and the sky stained with rose before drifting into a deep, angry red as the sun settled. Thin clouds lay like fingers bathed in the light. He looked up at them as the day faded. They vanished into a night colored with the lights of the city. It was impossible to see a star.

Time passed. Faith's lights went out one by one. He imagined her dressing for bed in the darkness. She did not wear much, he knew. The thin material of her nightshirts hung loosely against her imperfect body. In recent weeks she'd started to tan, a result of long runs around Camaro Espinoza's neighborhood. She was looking more like Miami.

The real Faith had begun to vanish. He wanted her for her flaws. He wanted her because she was the most unique woman in the world.

He had sat alone in the darkness for a long time, not moving, when his phone trilled. He checked the number and saw it was blocked. He frowned. It was probably a robocall from some scammer in a rented office somewhere trying to fish for credit card numbers. He did not need such nonsense ruining his night with Faith, but he knew he had to answer.

He pressed Accept and put the phone to his ear. "Yes," he said. His voice sounded strange to him. On his vigils he spoke to no one. It was the silence of worship.

"Are you watching her?"

The man on the other end of the line had a deep voice. He had seen the man only once, months ago, an envelope of money passed under the table of an expensive restaurant. Other envelopes followed, but they came by courier. They spoke once a week.

"Yes, I'm watching her. She's sleeping now."

"Is it safe?"

"Yes."

"Then do it."

A tingling sensation crawled between his shoulder blades. "Now?" he asked.

"Yes, now. Do it and get it over with. I'll be in touch."

The man on the other end severed the connection.

He sat very still, the phone remaining against his ear. He turned toward the apartments and Faith's darkened windows. His skin crept with adrenaline. He shuddered, and his teeth clicked together. He made himself be calm.

When he was ready, he put the phone away and got out of the car. He crossed the street. He felt his stride lengthening, lungs expanding. It was the moment. It was the moment.

It was now.

CHAPTER EIGHTEEN

WHEN SHE RETURNED to Miguel's gym, the beginner class was in session. Already the numbers had thinned from where they had been only weeks before. Still more would drop out and more and more until they were replaced by fresh faces in a new round of classes. Most of these people would quit, too. It was an endless cycle.

She changed and put her things away and went back onto the floor. It was late and only the most dedicated fighters spent time in the gym at this hour. Camaro was one of three besides Miguel and Rey. She saw the two men talking at the desk near the stairs. A pair of fighters were in their own worlds elsewhere, drilling with heavy bags and dummies, practicing controlled destruction.

Camaro decided to warm up with some stretches and a few basic calisthenics. She found herself distracted. An itch at the base of her skull wouldn't fade, even when her muscles began to burn in the workout itself. Her eyes strayed toward the stairs again and again, but no one appeared. Even the other two fighters in the gym had done enough, and they left for the locker room.

She was in her fifth set when Rey approached her. Camaro sweated heavily, closing out with ten sitting twists that set her core on fire. She had two more sets to complete and then she would step things up. To be at the edge of exhaustion was to be in the right place.

Rey watched her. She finished out the twists, collapsed onto her back on the mat, and breathed. Once she had her wind again, she asked, "What?"

"Your friend," Rey said.

"What friend?"

"Faith. In the beginner's class."

"What about her?"

"She quit."

Camaro sat up with effort. "What are you talking about?"

"I know, I was surprised, too. Whatever you were teaching her, it was working. She was the best girl in the class. I was going to suggest she take it to the next level and really see what she could do. But she didn't come in tonight. She never missed a session before."

The itch was there. It became a tiny coal. "Did she call to quit?"

"No. But I've seen it before. You get people who are real dedicated, and you think they're gonna be something special, and they just stop. They miss one class, then they're gone for good. Guess she got tired of it."

Camaro rose to a knee. She was hot and sore. It had been easier once. "Can I use your phone?"

"Yeah, sure."

She went to the desk by the stairs. Miguel nodded at her. "You're going to shut me down again tonight. Last one out."

"I like it when it's quiet," Camaro replied.

"Hey, it's not like I have a life or anything."

The man smiled. Camaro didn't. She grabbed the phone on the wall and dialed Faith's number. It rang a half-dozen times before switching to voice mail. She hung up and tried again, then a third time. She left a message. The perspiration on her skin was almost gone. She stared at the phone. "I don't think I'm staying," she said finally.

"You haven't even worked the bag. And we have to go over your ground game. We got some new battle ropes I thought you might want to break in, too."

Camaro barely heard him. "I have to go."

"Don't cut corners! You have to stay sharp."

"Next time."

In the locker room she hurried through her cleanup, washing her face and arms in the sink, skipping a shower. She got into her jeans and boots and hooked a .45 in its holster against her hip. Having the weight there was good.

Half the lights were out when she emerged. Miguel and Rey lingered by the stairs until she came. They descended together. The neon on the street-level windows went out. The gym plunged into semidarkness. As the banks of lights extinguished, Camaro felt drawn along, out of the gym and into the lot behind the building. The night air was heavy enough to feel. Camaro heard Rey talking, but the words themselves were lost in the roar of her bike's engine.

Nighttime in South Beach was a busy time. Camaro was aware of minutes passing with every clutch of cars blocking the way and every stoplight. The sidewalks were busy with tourists seeking pleasure. None of them knew where Camaro was going, or cared who she was. Camaro breathed in through her nose and out through her mouth, but even that was not enough.

She saw the apartment complex in her mind's eye, and Faith's apartment. The door was open and it was quiet and dark inside. No one else was around, not a neighbor or a cop. In her imagination she did not go inside, but she knew she had to. She was not afraid to fight, but she was afraid to see.

She picked up speed on the bike, hurtled from lane to lane. The exit was just up ahead.

CHAPTER NINETEEN

SHE DIDN'T KNOW how he'd gotten inside, but it didn't matter. She hadn't heard him enter, and she hadn't known he was there until he was on top of her. His body pressed her to the bed, and when she screamed it was into his covering hand.

Faith heard him now in the front room, wrecking everything. There was the sound of falling books, and the shredding noise of cloth coming apart. She thought maybe he was cutting her furniture to pieces. He'd already dissected part of her mattress with an ugly knife. Scattered bits of fluff were all around Faith on the floor. The drawers were out of her dresser, dumped and searched top and bottom. He'd pulled the furniture away from the wall.

It was hard to see. One of her eyes was swollen shut. She found him and she did everything she learned. She went for the balls, and for the throat and the eyes. She hurt him, but then he hurt her. Her body throbbed where he'd punched her, where he'd kicked her when he threw her to the ground. The collar of her nightshirt was torn. She lay on her side with one hand holding it up to cover herself. She thought it would happen then, when he started to strip her, but instead he descended into a sudden and vicious fury. He beat her with a closed fist and an open hand. The kicking had been the worst, and when she took a blow to the stomach she vomited on the carpet. He talked the whole time, but she understood none of it. The language was meaningless to her.

She heard her phone ringing again and again, but it was in the other room. There was no landline in her apartment, no bedroom phone. It didn't matter anyway, because he never would have let her call the police. He might have strangled her with the cord.

He was in the kitchen, clattering through her pans. Something fell to the floor and shattered. Moments after that, something else broke. He was rampaging through her cabinets, one after the other. He had asked her for nothing in any way she could comprehend.

She turned her head where she lay and looked under the bed. A few scattered socks and a single shoe lost in the space. The vision in her good eye was cloudy. She focused on each object in turn. Her nose was broken and it was hard to breathe. Camaro had been right: it hurt, but it was not the worst thing.

It took a few moments for her to fix her eye on the gun. She kept it under the pillow beside her as she slept, and when they struggled on the bed it fell between the mattress and the wall. After he moved the bed, it fell still further and it rested out of the light with the butt toward Faith. Faith's heart tripped when she looked at it.

There was pain in her skull and neck when she rolled her head to look toward the bedroom door. She still heard him in the kitchen. He was searching something else, maybe her refrigerator, though there was nothing to find among the frozen Lean Cuisine meals and salad fixings she'd bought for her new diet.

Faith knew he would return. It was inevitable that he would, and it would be more terrible than it had been before. He was stronger than her, and she was hurt.

She looked at the gun. It was five feet away from where her hand rested on the carpet. Her body was a webwork of agony. She didn't want to move. She had to move.

Rolling onto her side was torture. Making it onto her belly caused her stomach to churn again. She swallowed hard to keep down what was left. She pushed with her bare feet and clawed with her hands, and wormed her way under the edge of the bed. It was crawling through a field of broken glass. It was an impossible task. The gun seemed no closer, though she knew it must be. She stretched out for it.

When she was halfway underneath the bed, she extended her arm as far as it could reach. Her fingertips settled on the polymer frame of the weapon. It was chilly to the touch. Faith panted as if she had been running for a long time. Her open eye bleared with tears.

She forced herself farther. Her hand closed around the weapon's grip. She had it. Breath exploded from her lungs. She tasted dust and carpet fibers.

He seized her by the ankle. Faith croaked as he dragged her from underneath the bed by both feet. The carpet burned her flesh, and her nightshirt bundled up around her armpits. The room opened up as she came clear of the bed. He spat. He grabbed her by the material of her shirt.

Faith rolled onto her back and brought the pistol with her. The man's face blanked. Faith pulled the trigger and hit him in the throat.

Blood burst from the wound. The man recoiled, grabbing at his neck. Hot red jets painted Faith and the space around them. Faith pulled the trigger again and again. Bullets carved wet holes in the man's chest. He collapsed, gagging on his own fluids. Faith managed to sit upright. Her finger worked against the pistol's trigger, but there were no more rounds to fire. The slide was locked back.

The man's legs twitched. The flow of blood between his fingers slowed. His face was smeared with crimson. He gurgled once, and then he was still.

CHAPTER TWENTY

Ignacio was not sure of the time when the phone rang. He'd been dreaming of something, but the dream was gone in the instant he awoke. He thrashed in the bed, disoriented in the dark. His hand landed on the phone. He accepted the call. "Montellano," he said.

"It's—"

"A little after midnight."

He checked the red numbers of the bedside clock. It was 12:04. "Brady?"

"I have a body here. I think maybe you ought to come out and see it."

Ignacio rubbed his eyes. "I'm not working nights."

"You're going to want to see it."

"What's happening?"

Pool clucked his tongue. In the background, the sound of low discussion. Ignacio saw the busy scene as if he were there. "I have a single white female, aged twenty-nine, who shot an unknown white male, approximately forty years old, six times in the neck and chest. He broke in, beat the hell out of her, wrecked her place, and when he came back to finish the job, she got him with a .380 she took possession of a day ago."

Ignacio pushed back the covers and sat on the edge of the bed. It was dark in his bedroom, but light slanted through the window from his neighbor's security lamp. "What's this girl's name?"

"It's Faith Glazer. She's an accountant. Works downtown."

"Wait a minute. I know about her."

81

"I know you do. I have Detective Herrera from Special Victims here, and she says you called her a while back about a stalking case. But that's not why I'm calling."

"So why are you calling?"

"Camaro Espinoza is here."

Ignacio straightened up. "You sure she's not the shooter?"

"No, it's Glazer. The deed was done before Espinoza arrived on the scene. We have witnesses to that effect. But I know you have your ear out for this woman and she's here, right now, talking to Glazer. I can't keep them apart."

"I'll be there as soon as I can. Send me the address."

"Don't take too long."

Ignacio was half dressed before his text alert pinged and Faith Glazer's address appeared. By the time he got to his car, the route was programmed in, and the phone talked him all the way there. He saw flashing lights two blocks out. He turned onto the street and saw two men with crime lab windbreakers examining a car parked against the curb. The car's doors were open wide, and its dome light gleamed.

The apartment complex had a secure lot, but the gate was open to admit emergency vehicles. There were two crime-scene vans, an ambulance, a fire truck, and three police units in addition to Pool's unmarked Crown Victoria. Ignacio saw Camaro Espinoza's motorcycle. Her helmet was on the ground. Ignacio slipped into the knot and killed the engine. He found Pool outside. The idling fire truck was loud. The uniformed officers had tape up. The neighbors were kept well back.

"You look rested," Pool told Ignacio.

"That's funny. Can I look at the crime scene?"

"Be my guest."

Pool led him through the open door of the apartment. The front room was demolished, the couch slashed to ribbons and stuffing everywhere. The same had been done to the room's only chair. Everything had been turned over, from the television to the cable box. In the dining area the table was upside down. Pictures had been torn from the walls and smashed before being ripped from their frames. "What the hell?" Ignacio said.

"This guy was very angry. He worked Glazer over something awful."

"Sexual assault?"

"No, thank God. Looks like he wanted to tenderize her a little bit first."

"Where is she now?"

"Next door with a neighbor friend. Espinoza's there, too."

Ignacio walked the apartment. The kitchen was as wrecked as all the rest, and even the refrigerator had been moved, pulled away from the wall to expose the coils. Every cabinet was open. It seemed as though the intruder had smashed every dish Faith Glazer owned. Ignacio shook his head.

The body was covered with a plastic sheet while the crime-scene investigators did their work. A woman with flame-red hair gave Ignacio a sour look. "If you people keep trampling through here, it's going to make our job harder."

Blood had splattered the wall and ceiling and soaked into the carpet. The dead man was an awkward shape under the white plastic. "I'd like to look at the body."

"It's been processed. Go ahead."

Ignacio lifted the sheet to expose the corpse. The man's dark shirt was sodden with congealing blood. His face was pallid, smears of red from his ruined throat like brilliant, unreal paint. There were bruises on his face, and three perfect fingernail gashes on his cheek. "I have no idea who this guy is. ID?"

Pool looked on. "Nothing. He had an unlocked phone in his pocket we're going to check out, but at first glance it looks like he never made any calls with it. There's nothing in the history, anyway. Car keys in his other pocket go with a Buick out on the street. I'm having them turn it over."

"Got to be something good on the registration."

"Rental car."

83

"Of course," Ignacio said.

"Weird thing is, the trunk's full of phone books. Like, a ton of phone books. I have no idea what he'd want with all of them. And they're new."

"Has to mean something."

"Maybe. The important thing is he's dead. And I have to say this for Faith Glazer: she may have only owned that gun for one day, but she's a good shot. Any one of those bullets would have killed this guy, and she put six into him."

"Hard to miss at close range."

"I've seen people miss from a foot away."

Ignacio nodded. He put the plastic sheet back in place. "I want to talk to her."

"Glazer?"

"And Espinoza."

"You want to take this one off my hands?"

Ignacio looked at the room in disarray. "Yeah, I think so."

CHAPTER TWENTY-ONE

THE NEIGHBOR'S NAME was Andrea. Camaro didn't think anything of her. She seemed pleasant and ordinary and pretty, and she wasn't afraid to open her door when Faith needed somewhere to hide.

The police brought Faith fresh clothes and took her nightshirt away as evidence. Now she huddled on Andrea's couch in sweatpants and a Florida State University sweatshirt. She wore socks but no shoes. Even with a blanket around her, she shook. Camaro didn't sit next to her. She watched from a chair close at hand. She told Andrea to make some soup. Anything hot would do.

Faith's face was a mass of bruises from chin to hairline. The swelling around her eye was pronounced. She pressed a plastic bag of ice against the injury. The cold made her shiver more, but there was no helping it.

Camaro had examined Faith when she found her. There was nothing broken except her nose, though it was possible the blow to her eye might have caused a fracture. Only an X-ray would tell for sure. The paramedics arrived. Camaro told them what they had to know. Faith needed a hospital, but the police had to sign off on it first. Camaro ground her teeth and waited.

A detective named Pool interviewed Faith before a woman detective arrived to get a second interview. This detective stayed in the room with them, making calls and writing notes. Camaro did not want to talk around her.

She heard Ignacio's voice before she saw him. When he appeared in the front room of Andrea's apartment and caught sight of Faith for the first time, Camaro saw a stricken expression on his face that lasted only until he hid it behind another, more studious look. He nodded at Camaro. "Ms. Espinoza."

"Detective."

The woman detective stood up. "Detective Montellano, I'm Detective Herrera, Special Victims. We talked on the phone."

They shook hands. "Yeah, that's right," he said. "You were following up on this."

"Not fast enough. Look, I'd like to release Ms. Glazer to the hospital. Are you taking the lead on this one?"

"Seems like it. And she *should* go to the hospital. She's already been here too long. But I'm going to want to talk to her."

"I have notes, if you want to go over them."

"In a minute."

Ignacio approached Faith. She didn't look at him. Her bad eye was toward him, and she had done nothing for a while except stare into the middle distance with the eye that still worked. He didn't try to touch her. "Faith, my name is Ignacio Montellano. I'm a detective with Homicide Unit. I'd like you to go to the hospital for a full examination. I'll be by after you've rested. Okay?"

Faith blinked. She glanced toward Camaro. Camaro inclined her head. Faith turned to Ignacio. "Okay."

Ignacio straightened. His voice sharpened. "Okay, let's get her out of here. Grab the paramedics and tell them I want the works once she gets to the hospital. We'll share information as it comes in. Detective Pool will oversee the rest of the crime-scene examination, and I'm going to follow up with Ms. Espinoza. Faith, take care of yourself. You're in good hands."

Herrera summoned the paramedics. They brought a stretcher even though Faith didn't need one, and they secured her before carrying her away. Herrera disappeared with them. There was only Camaro and Ignacio. "So now what?" Camaro asked.

Andrea appeared. Ignacio put up a hand. "I'll be out of your hair in a minute, ma'am. I need to talk to this witness alone."

The woman swallowed hard. She disappeared. Camaro looked at Ignacio and he looked at her.

"Did you know this was going to happen?"

"Not tonight. But I knew it would eventually."

"Whose idea was it for her to buy a gun? Yours?"

"Yes. And it's good she had it—otherwise she'd be dead now."

Ignacio lowered himself onto the couch. He touched the abandoned plastic bag, half full of melted water. "It's not like I don't believe you, but I need to know: Do you have any idea who this guy was?"

"No. I've never seen him before."

"That situation in Glazer's apartment is not normal. I don't work stalker cases or rape cases, but I've done plenty of homicides. I've seen what people do."

"The guy was crazy."

"Oh, sure. No doubt. But crazy people are generally crazy about *something*, you know? They have a thing. Like this guy, he has a trunk full of phone books. I'm sure the shrinks will talk about how it's some kind of OCD, or whatever, but it's a thing."

Camaro remembered. She leaned forward. "Phone books?"

"Yeah. You know something?"

"I'm not sure."

"Whatever it is, I have to figure it out. That's the problem with these kinds of cases: the guy's dead, but we have to have all the answers."

"Are they going to charge Faith?"

"I don't think so. It's self-defense. Anybody can see that. Stalker decides he's tired of watching and she has to do what she has to do. Can't argue with that. Public-service homicide."

"I should probably go to the hospital and watch over her."

"Why? The wacko's dead."

"It's something I have to do."

Ignacio regarded her. "I think I get it. But listen, I'm going to have to get a full statement from you. You have to repeat everything you told me about this case *for the record*. You ready to do that?"

SAM HAWKEN

"You can't keep my name out of it?"

"You came to the crime scene. I can't cover up something like that."

Camaro looked toward the door. The emergency lights flashed blue and red ceaselessly. "All right."

Ignacio rose from the couch. "One more thing: You have a permit to carry that piece?"

She touched the weapon under her shirt. "I do."

"So you figured out Florida doesn't submit to NICS, huh? Nice way to skirt around any legal troubles you might have out of state."

"You want to see my papers, Detective?"

"No, I don't. And it's Nacho. *Nacho.*"

"I'll see you soon."

"Yeah. You will."

CHAPTER TWENTY-TWO

LAWRENCE KAUR WAS forty-seven years old but looked thirty-nine. He had perfect hair and an even tan from long hours on the water. He kept his body fit with daily sessions in a private gym with a personal trainer. He ate a fully organic diet made up of purely vegetarian nutrients. His breakfast this morning was toast with black beans and avocado, a Samoan coconut, and tapioca porridge, served with fair-trade coffee and a large glass of Florida orange juice squeezed right in the kitchen. The in-season oranges were always the best, and Kaur's chef chose only the finest and freshest ingredients.

Kaur still read a newspaper, though newspapers were passé. He liked to go through the stock reports and single out key accounts in the long rows of tiny letters and numbers. All this could be gotten through his iPad, but he preferred the tactile sensation of paper and ink, even when the latter left dark smudges on his fingers.

He sat in the breakfast room of his house, a glassed-in box, which allowed in sunlight from every direction. Spread beyond the teak deck outside was the full expanse of blue water off Key Biscayne. The previous day's lingering clouds had vanished overnight, and the sky was a perfect shade of robin's egg. Sometimes, like this morning, Kaur had to eat breakfast with his sunglasses on. Life was simply too brilliant.

The sound of voices drifted over to him. He didn't look up from his paper. A minute later he heard his assistant clear his throat. "Mr. Kaur? Mr. Roche is here to see you."

"All right, John, tell him he can come in. And tell Enrique to make something for Mr. Roche."

"Yes, sir. Right away, sir."

Kaur heard Roche's footsteps approaching. Only when the legs of a chair scraped the floor did Kaur set aside his paper.

Brandon Roche was in his early fifties, darker than tanned, with heavy eyebrows, which made him seem perpetually angry. It did not help that he rarely smiled. He wore a cream-colored linen suit with a white shirt underneath and no tie. He looked ready for a trip on a sailboat. It was Saturday. "Larry," Roche said. His voice was cold iron.

"Brandon. I didn't expect to see you today. I have Paul handling any weekend matters."

"We missed," Roche said.

Kaur froze. He ran his hand over his newspaper to make a crease. "Okay," he said.

"You do understand what that means."

"Yes, but maybe you'd like to explain it to me again. I don't think I grasped the urgency of the situation."

Roche shook his head. "Don't make light of this. We missed and now the police have her."

"What about our man?"

"He's dead," Roche said. "Which is good for us, because dead he can't talk. I heard from my people that there are three different detectives involved in the case, and any one of them might have gotten our man to say things he shouldn't."

"I didn't think you'd let someone sloppy do this."

"I wouldn't, but it doesn't mean it couldn't happen. I also didn't anticipate he'd obsess over his subject."

"What do you mean?"

"I mean sexually obsessed. They found a pair of her underpants in his car."

"That's sick."

"Yes, it is."

"But I don't understand. You told me he had every angle covered. It would be no problem if we decided to go all the way with this. That's what you *told me*, Brandon."

"I know what I told you. I didn't lie. It turns out she bought a gun. I suppose our man didn't secure the weapon before he did the rest. She managed to get ahold of it, and now he's dead. No one could have foreseen it."

"You should have."

"I'll accept that. But the more pressing matter is what to do to recover from the situation as it stands. Faith Glazer is still alive, and she has to know we're responsible. She might not have known before, but she's going to be certain now."

Enrique entered the breakfast room with a platter. He presented Roche with a mirror image of Kaur's meal, poured a cup of coffee for him. A wisp of steam danced around the brim. "There you are, Mr. Roche. The best breakfast you'll have all week," Enrique said.

Roche didn't look at him. "I'm not hungry."

"But, Mr. Roche—"

"Enrique!" Kaur interjected. "Mr. Roche says he's not hungry. I'm sorry, but you'll have to take it away."

The chef's shoulders sank. He collected the platter. He reached for the coffee, but Roche put his hand over the cup. "Leave it," he said.

"Of course, Mr. Roche. And if you change your mind, I—"

"That will be *all*," Kaur said.

Enrique fled. Kaur and Roche regarded each other across the table. Roche sipped from his cup, the coffee black. "We'll need to contain this," Roche said.

"That's not my job. It's yours."

"Then you don't object if I take things to the next level?"

"Beyond killing the woman? What next level is there? I'm not some kind of crime boss, Brandon, I'm a banker. I deal with clients and accounts and you handle the security. I agreed we needed to work together on this, but that's only because you promised me plausible deniability. Is there any way she can *prove* we ordered it?"

Roche rested his elbows on the table. He tapped steepled fingers against his chin. "Proof is a difficult proposition, but if she decides to talk there will be people who'll listen. And that's not something we can afford. Not now."

"Then take care of it. Just…take care of it. I can't have this on my plate."

"It'll be done."

CHAPTER TWENTY-THREE

CAMARO HAD TO wait a long while to see Faith at the hospital. These things took time. She was patient in the hallway, seated on a chair with a flattened cushion and slightly clammy vinyl upholstery. When a nurse signaled her, she went into the room.

Faith's face was bandaged so her injured eye was covered completely. Cuts and bruises had been treated. Faith looked as though she'd gone through a plate-glass window. Camaro saw that they had her on an IV drip of pain meds. Something to take the worst of it off, but not so potent as morphine.

It was dim in the room. Faith's good eye flickered open. She smiled faintly, and beckoned Camaro closer with a hand covered in tape, the IV tube leading from it. "Hey," she said. Her voice was cracked. "Long time no see."

"How are you?"

"How do I look?"

"You don't look good."

"Awesome."

"I've seen worse. You'll make it."

"They told me if I hadn't fought him, he would have done it to me anyway, and maybe he might have done more."

"That's true. You don't want to be someone's victim."

Faith made a weak fist and bumped it against Camaro's. "Girl power," she said.

Camaro looked around the room. It was small, but a large window dominated one wall. It was almost impossible to tell the sun was up

93

because a blackout shade covered nearly the entire square of glass. Only a little light seeped in around the edges. Outside it would be a beautiful day. In the hospital, it would be the same as always.

"You don't like hospitals?" Faith asked.

"What?"

"Hospitals. You don't like them."

"What makes you say that?"

"You have a look."

"I'm tired of visiting people in them. People I care about get hurt by people who shouldn't be allowed to breathe the same air as the rest of us."

Faith seemed to think about this. Her eye closed. Camaro thought she might be sleeping. The eye opened again. Faith's voice was stronger now, but laden with fatigue. Soon there would come a long, narcotic sleep. Camaro had been there, too. "I know what you want."

"What's that?"

"You want to know who he was. Why he followed me."

"Don't *you* want to know?"

"No," Faith said.

"It doesn't matter?"

"He was a crazy person. What does it matter why crazy people do what they do?"

Camaro heard something in Faith's voice. It wasn't fear, but it was difficult to identify. "I think you should know. It's better if you know."

"I said I don't *want* to!" Faith stirred on the bed. "I don't care."

"Maybe not now, but later you will. Believe me, you'll want a reason."

Faith fell silent. Camaro let her quietness go on. Finally, Faith said, "I'm not going to stay here long. I have things to do."

"You stay until you're ready," Camaro said. "You don't have to like it, but you need the help."

"No, I have to go."

Camaro put her hand on Faith's. She felt the rough surface of the tape, and the cool plastic of the IV tube. A moment of memory flashed, of another hospital in another place far away, but not so long ago. Camaro shook it off. "Look, I know you want to move past this, and the guy is dead, but that doesn't mean you have to start running. You don't have anything hanging over you anymore. So take the time you need and get well. Don't rush it."

"Would *you* lie in a bed somewhere and let people take care of you?"

"If I had to."

Faith looked away, toward the shaded window. "I want to be stronger than that."

"There's being strong, and there's being stupid. Don't be stupid."

Faith turned to Camaro again. Something kindled behind it. "Who do you see when you look at me?"

"I don't know what you mean."

"All of this . . . it's not only for me. I'm just somebody you met one day."

Camaro felt her cheeks warm. "You needed help. That's all."

"Who was it? A friend? A sister?"

"That's enough," Camaro said. "You don't need to worry about it. You're my friend. I'll watch out for you."

"Are we friends?"

"Yes."

The slightest of nods. "Okay."

"I'm going to go," Camaro said. "You have my number. Call me whenever you need to. Doesn't matter day or night."

She turned to go. Faith called her name. "You did a good job, Camaro. Don't think you didn't."

"Rest now."

She left the room and eased the door closed behind her. Her chest was tight. She breathed until the pressure lessened. Up and down the hallway it was quiet, the only bustle coming from the nurses' station at one end. There were no visitors except Camaro.

On the first floor, her phone rang. It was Ignacio Montellano's number. She answered. "Detective," she said. "What is it?"

"Where are you?"

"I'm leaving the hospital. Where are you?"

"Right now? I'm watching them cut open our guy. You should be here. *So* much fun."

Camaro stepped out into the sun and was dazzled. She took Wayfarers from her back pocket. "I've seen what people look like on the inside."

"I'll bet. Listen, I'd like to sit down with you and have a talk. Remember the restaurant where we ate? You can meet me there?"

"I think I can find it."

"Good. Come by in two or three hours. We'll have some lunch."

Camaro looked around the parking lot. She realized there was no one to watch out for anymore. "What do we have to talk about?"

"I have questions. They're easy questions. So how about it?"

"I'll see you."

CHAPTER TWENTY-FOUR

THEY SAT IN the same booth as before. It was busier than it had been, the midday crowd at their tables eating rich food. The air was full with overlapping, even overpowering aromas. Every time the kitchen door opened, another gust of cooking scent billowed into the dining room. Camaro dug into a plate of *pernil asado,* pork shoulder braised with onions in its own juices and spices. Ignacio seemed to eat nothing but sandwiches every day.

He inquired about Faith and he commented on the food. He was slow to come around to the rest. Camaro found herself wanting to speak before he asked his questions. She knew this was his game.

"I know what you're thinking," Ignacio said after a while. "You're thinking I'm making an excuse to sit down and eat with a pretty lady again."

Camaro snorted. "That's *not* what I was thinking."

"Yeah, we covered that, didn't we? Still, I know when people see us together, they're going to wonder."

"I don't care."

Ignacio smiled. "I think that's what I like the most about you. You really *don't* care. You're you. I know a lot of people act like they're something they're not, but you don't make any excuses for yourself. Not even when you're making big-time mistakes."

Camaro pulled away a piece of pork with the tines of her fork. The meat came apart easily. She put the bite in her mouth, chewed slowly, and watched Ignacio until she swallowed. She followed the bite with beer. The spice and the cooling drink balanced exactly. "What mistake am I making now? You said yourself this was an open-and-shut. Self-defense. The guy Faith shot was some wacko. That's all."

"Let me tell you something about police work, okay? It's not always about the person who does the crime. It's about the people *around* that person. So Faith Glazer, she gets a pass, but then people start asking me, 'Who is this Camaro Espinoza? Where does she come in?' That's when things get complicated for you and me, because we have history. I have to have my story straight."

Camaro frowned. "There's no story to keep straight. Faith needed help. I helped her. And if I *hadn't,* that asshole would have raped and killed her last night."

"She bought the gun because of you?"

"I suggested it, yeah. So what?"

"Did you have any reason to suspect the stalker would attack? Is that why you told her to buy a gun?"

"She didn't even buy the gun until it was almost too late," Camaro said. "What do you people want? For her to have nothing?"

Ignacio made a gesture of surrender. "Hey, I'm not the one asking, okay? I'm going to put it in the report that Ms. Glazer was in fear for her life, and she asked for help from a friend and from the police. The friend said she should learn to fight and buy a gun. So she did."

"You think someone will want more than that?"

"Who knows? I want to make sure it's airtight, that's all. Because if it turns out you and she *did* know he was coming, or if you precipitated the attack, it opens up a whole can of worms."

Camaro took up her beer. She drank. When she put the bottle down, it banged on the table. "Would anybody even ask that if it was a man who got attacked?"

"They might."

"No, they wouldn't. Because nobody cares what a man does. But when it comes to a woman, it's all, 'Did she ask for it? Was she leading him on?' And that's bullshit, Detective. It's bullshit! And you have to know it. How can you not know it?"

Ignacio's expression turned somber. He nudged his plate away. His sandwich was unfinished. "Yeah, I do. I'm not defending it. People get weird ideas when it comes to this kind of thing."

"Yeah, well, fuck them."

"Can I put that in my report?"

"In capital letters."

Ignacio laughed. Camaro's scowl melted. They laughed together.

"That's a new one," Ignacio said when they finished. "You laughing."

Camaro let her face settle. "Yeah, whatever. Is there anything else?"

"I'd really love to know more about this guy."

"So would I."

"Here's the weird part: no ID, no fingerprints in the system, but I'm pretty sure he's not an American. He had a notebook in his car with times and dates, but the rest is all in some kind of foreign language. Now, this doesn't mean anything by itself, but I'm thinking again: not American. They've been fingerprinting people entering the U.S. since 9/11, so he ought to be somewhere, right? Nothing. But he has some tattoos, including one in the same language from the notebook. At first I thought it was Hebrew or something, but it's Armenian."

"What does it say?"

"Armenia's kind of far away from Miami. I'm going to talk to someone who can help me out, maybe get someone on the notebook. And who knows? Somebody might recognize his picture. Not that I think every Armenian in Miami knows every other Armenian. You know what I'm saying?"

"Sure."

The check came. Ignacio snatched it away before Camaro could touch it. "Not this time. I'm putting it on the department's dime. Meeting with a witness. Enjoy the free food."

"I told you I don't want to owe you anything."

"You don't. It's like it never happened."

Camaro shook her head. "I can take care of myself, you know."

"Absolutely. But it never hurts to have friends. Faith Glazer figured that out. She found you just in time. It's lucky."

Something sparked in the back of Camaro's mind. "Yeah," she said. "That is lucky."

Ignacio paid the server in cash. "I need a receipt," he told the man. "And that's it, Ms. Espinoza. We are officially out of police business. Thank you for your cooperation, ma'am. You've been very helpful."

They got up from the booth and left the restaurant. Ignacio held the door for Camaro. She didn't object. Her thoughts were elsewhere.

CHAPTER TWENTY-FIVE

THE DOOR TO Faith's apartment was festooned with police tape, but it was possible to duck under the yellow strips and gain access to the inside. The door was broken. Camaro assumed it was because the police needed to force entry when they arrived. The stalker, the man without a name, hadn't needed such blunt methods. He was quieter, quicker, and he knew how to get in and out without being seen. He'd been on Faith before she even realized he was in the room.

Camaro looked around. Her jaw worked, muscle flexing under the skin. She surveyed the overturned couch, the shredded cushions, and where the man had cut open the bottom of the furniture to look inside the frames. Camaro knelt beside a chair turned upside down and peered in through the gaping hole in the black fabric usually hidden underneath. She saw nothing.

Everything that could be broken had been broken. In the front room Camaro walked over the torn remains of a print that used to hang on the wall. In the dining area she saw where the man had methodically punched out the pictures of the Art Deco hotels and searched the frames.

It began to coalesce around her, the sensation of order in the chaos. The man had gone from room to room, and from likeliest place to unlikeliest place, tearing the apartment down to the carpeting. At first it seemed like rage, and the image of destruction was complete, as though a terrible storm had ripped through Faith's home. Camaro saw him, all in black, hands protected by gloves, searching and searching until his search brought him back to Faith and the barrel of her gun.

In the bedroom, blood was all that remained of the man. It was possible to make out the shape of his fallen body from the pattern on the floor, and there was also a void where Faith had been. A smell lingered in the room, partly gunpowder and partly fear, underpinned by the fresher scent of whatever Faith used to perfume the air.

Camaro looked in the closet and in the bathroom. All the contents of the medicine cabinet and the cabinet underneath the sink were spilled onto the floor. After a while Camaro returned to the front of the apartment. She cast a closer eye over the destruction. She went into the kitchen.

Faith's garbage can was kicked over, but the contents did not appear to have been searched. Camaro righted the plastic bin and opened it. A dirty coffee filter had spilled grounds all over everything inside, and there were more than a few apple cores and discarded empty trays of packaged fresh vegetables. Camaro put her hand in the soft, wet mess and felt around until she found what she was looking for.

She extracted the phone book, still in its plastic bag, from the bottom of the garbage can. She dropped it on the counter by the sink. She washed her hands before taking a wad of paper towel and wiping the detritus from the phone book's bag.

The phone book was like any one of a half-dozen different kinds dropped on people's doorsteps all over the city. This didn't matter to her. The book itself would tell her nothing. She wiped coffee grounds off a white square on the lower edge to reveal a printed name and address. The company's name was Gold Coast Direct Marketing. The address was in Liberty City. Liberty City was not on the coast.

Camaro took her phone from her pocket and snapped a picture of the address label. She dropped the bag and the book into the trash. She wiped the mess off the counter before throwing away the wad of paper towel. She left the apartment.

"Hello?"

Andrea was there. She looked drawn and tired. No makeup concealed the darkness under her eyes. "Hey," Camaro said.

102

"Is Faith back already?"

Camaro stepped away from the door. "No, she's still at the hospital. It'll be a day or two."

"Is she...okay?"

"It's better now she's in the hospital."

Andrea looked past her. "Why were you in there?"

"She asked me to bring her something."

The woman saw Camaro's empty hands. "But..."

"I couldn't find it."

"If you see her, tell her I'm thinking about her, will you? I feel so guilty because I had no idea someone was creeping around. And I'm pretty sure I saw him a few times. I mean, I thought he lived here. He told me his name and everything."

"What was it?"

Camaro moved closer to Andrea. The woman retreated the same distance. "Eduard. I think."

"Did you tell the cops?"

"No, because I didn't even think of it until later on. I remember the first time I saw him, though: he was bringing phone books around to all the units. Later on he was by the pool or in the laundry room. He was just *here*, you know? But he couldn't live here, right? I mean, this is a nice complex and the people aren't weirdos."

Camaro didn't come any closer. She watched Andrea cling to one elbow, arm tight across her belly. "There are creeps all over," Camaro said.

"He could have picked me," Andrea said. "He was crazy, so he could have picked me. It could be me in the hospital right now."

Camaro had nothing to add. "I'll tell Faith you said hello," she said. "I'm sure she'll like that."

She started to walk away. Andrea called after her, "He is dead, isn't he? Really dead?"

Camaro looked back. "They don't get any more dead."

Andrea's lip curled. "Good."

CHAPTER TWENTY-SIX

IGNACIO RETURNED TO his desk to find several messages waiting. He sorted through them before calling the number on the top slip. "Hey, Willy, how are you?" he asked when the line picked up.

Willy Marshall drove a patrol car in Boca Raton. He was an old-school cop, and he knew the names of people on his beat and stopped to help kids with their bikes. When he spoke, Ignacio heard the squelch of a radio in the background. "Ignacio! I thought I missed you."

"Only by a little bit. What's up? You have something for me?"

"Yeah. Let me pull over."

Ignacio waited. He thumbed through the message slips. He liked them better than voice mail.

Willy spoke up again. "I took a picture of your DB's tattoo to the priest over at Saint David's. That's the Armenian church around here. Father Hayrapetyan."

"That's a mouthful."

"Yeah, it's all like that with the Armenians. He's a nice guy, though. Real helpful around here. And he was able to translate the tattoo for me."

"So what does it say?"

"It says—let me check my notes—'The armed struggle and right political line are the way to Armenia.'"

"What the hell does that mean?"

"Father Hayrapetyan says it was the motto of some Armenian militant organization that disbanded back in the '90s. A lot of those guys were military or former military, and they were about breaking up Russian control over Armenia before it all fell apart. He told me a lot of other stuff, too, but I'll be honest and say most of it went right over my head. I didn't become a cop to major in Armenian history."

Ignacio chuckled. "Me neither. Listen, Willy, thanks for checking it out for me. I need somebody to go through this notebook, because it's all in Armenian. Tell Father Whatsisname I owe him a beer. Do Armenian priests drink beer?"

"Hell if I know. But I'll tell him. And maybe he can look through the notebook for you."

"We'll see how it goes. Take care, Willy."

"Nice talking to you. Don't be a stranger."

Ignacio ended the call. He pondered the phone. He reached for the receiver again. Someone called his name.

The woman was very short and very dark, her hair cut almost to the scalp. She wore a black suit with a skirt and low heels. A visitor pass dangled from a clip on her lapel. "Are you Detective Montellano?" she asked again.

Ignacio stood and nearly upset his chair. "Yes, ma'am, I'm Detective Montellano. Ignacio Montellano."

He extended his hand and she shook it. Her grip was firm, the handshake brief. She had a serious face and distinct frown lines. Ignacio thought she might be fifty. "My name is Trina Pope. I'm a special agent with the Drug Enforcement Administration. I was wondering if we might have a word in private."

Ignacio glanced around the bullpen. Most of the cubicles were empty. A few detectives worked at their computers. "More private than this?" he asked.

"Much more private."

"The captain's out. Why don't we talk in his office?"

Pope allowed him to lead her. They stepped into Captain Palmer's corner office. The blinds were already partly drawn. Pope closed the door behind them. She shut the blinds entirely. She said, "I understand you caught a case overnight involving a woman named Faith Glazer. What can you tell me about it?"

"Looks like a stalking case. Ms. Glazer told Special Victims she'd been followed for several months by an individual she feared might attack her physically. Turns out she was right. Last night the man broke into her apartment and assaulted her. Luckily she had a gun."

"I see. Do you have an identity for the stalker?"

"Not yet, but I'm working on it. He might be Armenian. Maybe an Armenian-American, maybe from outside the country. I won't know until we've looked everywhere we can look."

"What makes you think he's Armenian?"

"It's a tattoo he's got. I did some checking and it's from some group in the old country. Also, Ms. Glazer said he spoke to her in another language besides English. She said it wasn't Spanish, and when we saw the tattoo and the notebook in his car, full of the stuff…"

"Faith Glazer is in the hospital right now," Pope said. It was not a question.

"Yeah, she was banged up pretty badly."

"Is she under police protection?"

"Uh, no. The guy stalking her is dead. Should she be?"

Pope took a step toward him. "How much do you know about Faith Glazer?"

"She's some kind of accountant. I don't know a whole lot more than that."

"So she didn't tell you anything which might make you suspect there was more to this matter than a simple stalking case?"

"No. Look, what is this all about? I was going to do my due diligence and try to identify this guy, but the case is open-and-shut. He was a freak and she killed him when he came after her. It's happened before."

Pope nodded. She lifted one of the slats in the blinds and peered outside. "It's a little more complicated than that. I'm going to need everything you put together for this case, and we're going to combine it with the case file we got from Detective Herrera in Special Victims.

Then we're going to ask you to ease off a little bit while we put things in order."

" 'We'? Last I heard, the DEA doesn't handle homicides. And this doesn't have anything to do with drugs."

Pope dropped the slat. "You don't know what this has to do with, Detective Montellano. And as far as who's going to handle it from here on out, let me introduce you to someone you already know."

She opened the office door. Ignacio saw a man standing there. "Hello, Nacho," Special Agent Mansfield of the FBI said. "It seems like we just talked."

CHAPTER TWENTY-SEVEN

SHE FOUND THE office in Liberty City on the second floor of a building with mostly empty offices. The ground floor used to be a showroom of some kind, but the tall, broad windows were completely boarded up and painted an aquamarine bleached halfway to white over the years. Trash settled into the cracks and hollows of the storefronts on the street.

Camaro parked her motorcycle by the curb. The bike was unsteady, the surface of the road eaten away by time and neglect. The sidewalk was worse: concrete squares pitched and angled against one another like a child's imitation of the real thing.

The building looked abandoned at first, but Camaro heard voices when she stepped into the stairwell off the street. A radio played, and someone talked loudly in Spanish on a speakerphone. The stairs were narrow. The paint on the walls bubbled from water infiltration.

Gold Coast Direct Marketing had a printed paper sign tacked by the open door to the office. Camaro went inside. An oscillating fan on a stand stirred the sodden air. The windows toward the street were open and no air conditioner ran. The front office was larger than it needed to be because there was no furniture in the waiting area and only a desk. Instead of a coffee table and a couch, there was a two-foot-high mound of telephone books in plastic bags identical to the one in Faith's trash.

Two rear offices had their doors open. Camaro saw that one office was empty. In the other, a man worked with his back to her, shuffling through a pile of flyers on a battered desk. Camaro stepped into the doorway and cleared her throat.

The man turned around. His shirt was open to expose the undershirt underneath, and both materials were soaked with patches of sweat. He was Latino, his mustache and half-grown beard flecked with white. "What the hell?" he exclaimed. "What do you want? ¡Sal de aquí!"

"Who are you?" Camaro asked.

"Who am I? Who are *you?* What do you want? No work today."

Camaro pointed to the phone books. "You distribute these?"

"You need a phone book? Take all the phone books you want."

"I don't want a phone book. I want to know about someone who took them around."

The man squinted at her. "You police?"

"Do I look like police?"

"No police, no warrant. No warrant and I don't have to say nothing. Get out."

Camaro's right hand made a fist by her side. "Hey, asshole, I want to know about phone books someone took north of the Crossings. He's a black-haired guy, about this tall. Foreign. Maybe forty? Something like that. Do you remember him?"

The man opened his hands. "Look, lady, I don't know names. People come in, we pay them cash to take the stuff. You see these? Flyers for a strip club. Whatever people want spread around, we spread around. This man—who is he?"

"I don't know. That's why I'm asking!"

"You don't know, I don't know. So go away. I have too much to do."

He turned away. Camaro caught him by the arm. The man made a squawking sound when she dragged him around, and again when she grabbed the front of his shirt. "I am not done talking to you. You have to keep records. How do you pay taxes? Give me a name. Do you know the guy? A name."

The man gripped her wrist, but she did not let go. This close to him Camaro smelled sweat and the perfume of bodywash intermingling. "I'm telling you, I don't know. I really don't know."

Camaro lifted one foot and swept the karambit from her boot. The man made a yipping sound when she put it against his neck. The edge curved flush against his skin but didn't cut. "I don't believe you," Camaro said.

"He's not from here, I don't think!"

"Then you do remember him."

"Sure, sure. He talked funny. With an accent, like he don't know English. Maybe Russian or something. His name was Eduard. Yeah, Eduard!"

"Eduard what?"

She pressed the karambit harder against the man's flesh. The tip dug into soft tissue below the ear, the skin drawn tight. A vein pulsed visibly.

"I can look for the name. In the book. We keep a book."

"A record book?"

"Yes. Records. But it will take a minute. It's a big book. Everybody goes in."

"I don't give a rat's ass how big the book is. Find it."

Camaro let him go. The man sagged against the desk. Flyers tumbled to the floor around their feet. When Camaro pushed him, he moved, slipping on the papers. He rounded the desk and searched a lower drawer and found a ledger as thick as one of the phone books. He fished in the breast pocket of his shirt and produced a pair of reading glasses. He sorted through the pages, his lips moving silently as he read.

"Hurry up," Camaro said.

"A moment. Yes, it's here. He took thirty phone books. His name is Eduard . . . Serafian."

"Eduard Serafian," Camaro repeated.

"Yes, that is him. He's a weirdo. I didn't think he would be a good employee. And he never came back for his money. He took the phone books and disappeared with them. I remember him now. I don't know why I didn't think of him before."

"I don't know, either," Camaro replied. "Now . . . did he leave an address?"

CHAPTER TWENTY-EIGHT

CAMARO FOUND THE home of Eduard Serafian in Wynwood, some fifteen minutes outside Liberty City. The transition between neighborhoods was typical Miami, from the rougher outlines of Liberty City to what was turning into an enclave for artists and their benefactors. Gentrification was the word here, and though much of the working-class history of Wynwood remained, it was being painted over, like an old fence gussied up for a new owner.

The place was a duplex, one unit on top of the other, kept behind a chest-high fence. The short driveway was locked in, and at this hour it seemed that the residents on the ground floor were at work. The entire lot was paved over, with only a couple of wispy trees on either side to allow for green. Compared to Camaro's neighborhood, where the trees had grown to encompass everything, it seemed desolate.

She parked opposite the house and watched it until she was absolutely certain no one was home. What she could see of the apartment through the open blinds was too dark and still otherwise. She knew Serafian was never coming back.

She dialed Ignacio's number. He was slow to pick up. "Oh, hey, honey," he answered.

Camaro sat up straight in the saddle. "'Honey'?"

"How you doing? Everything okay?"

"This is Camaro Espinoza."

"Right, right. No, I didn't forget."

She moved the phone from her ear and looked at the display. Ignacio Montellano's name was in block letters above the timer measuring

111

out the call. She talked to him again. "Is this some kind of weird thing you do?"

"Lunch? I don't think so. I've got a lot of stuff going on here."

"What the hell are you talking about?"

"Oh, you know, I have to talk to some sources."

She listened to the background of the call. She heard nothing, not the bustle of the street nor the sounds of an office staffed with cops. It was perfectly silent. "You're not alone."

"No. No, I'm not."

"Do they know who's calling you?"

"I haven't said anything to them about it, but I'll keep it in mind."

"Listen, I wanted you to know I got a name for the wacko who broke into Faith's apartment: Eduard Serafian. The phone books he had were his cover to get into the apartment complex. Once people got used to him, he pretended to live there. He's definitely foreign. He had an accent. I tried to find out more, but the man who gave him the phone books couldn't tell me anything."

Ignacio's voice brightened. "That's awesome! Good news for her. I'll have to send her something."

"I'm in front of the house right now. It's in Wynwood. I'll text you the address. I don't know if you can get permission to go in, but there might be something inside. It's bothering me. He wanted something. Faith didn't tell me, but I think she knows."

"Don't pick out anything yet," Ignacio said. "I want to help."

"How soon can you get here? I can't hang out on the street all day."

"Let me get back to you, okay? I'm in a meeting, so I might be a while."

"The address is coming. Text me when you're on your way."

"Will do. Love you!"

The call ended. A crawling sensation moved across her forearms. She rubbed them and it went away.

She looked up at the house again. Nothing had changed. She crossed the street.

Up close there was no sense of anything amiss. The place was small and painted bright yellow with white trim. A green awning made shade for the front door, but the windows upstairs were bare to the sun, the face of the house a northern exposure. She moved along the fence until she saw narrow stairs leading to the second floor. Serafian's door was the color of baked clay.

No one passed on the street, though she wasn't far from a busy thoroughfare. The sound of traffic carried to her, as did the distant, angry blare of a horn. A few moments later, there was a brief skirl of a siren. Camaro looked up and down the street before she went over the fence.

She surveyed the ground floor, peered into each of the windows in turn. Shadowed rooms and life on pause. The people who lived there weren't wealthy, but they had some nice things. They were clinging to the bottom rung of the middle class in a city that wanted to price them out of town.

When she was satisfied, she mounted the steps to the second floor one at a time, listening for a raised voice, a shout, or any indicator of someone who cared or even noticed that she was somewhere she shouldn't be. It didn't come.

Serafian had a cross hanging from a small hook on the door. It looked as though it was made of stone, but it was lighter than that. It had been inscribed with lettering Camaro didn't recognize. It wasn't Arabic, and despite what the man at Gold Coast Direct Marketing said, it didn't look Russian. Camaro didn't know what kind of name Serafian was, but the rest of it had to be Armenian.

She tried the door. It was locked. The only window on this side was by the door, but too far from the steps to see through.

Camaro kicked the door in.

CHAPTER TWENTY-NINE

IGNACIO ENDED THE call with Camaro and stuffed his phone into his pocket. He grinned at Pope and Mansfield. They looked back at him. "Trouble?" Pope asked.

"No, no trouble. That was my girlfriend. One of the ladies she works with is having a baby. She wants to get something nice. They've been working together a long time."

Pope raised an eyebrow but said nothing else.

Mansfield leaned against the captain's desk. "I know this is something of a shock to you, Detective. And God knows I never expected to talk to you again after that disaster with the Cubans last summer. It's just the way things worked out."

"Right. Is this about Cubans again? Or some kind of terrorist thing? That's what you do, isn't it?"

"Most of the time. And no, it's not about Cubans. It's about . . . well, I'm not sure I'm cleared to tell you everything you want to know, but I can tell you some. For example, Special Agent Pope and I are part of a small task force investigating offshore money laundering. The kind of money laundering that puts cash in the pockets of American enemies."

"Miami used to be the money laundering capital of the United States," Pope added. "In the '80s there were banks popping up on every corner, and every single one of them was flush with drug cash. All the major construction projects in Miami had a little dirt on them, whether they knew it or not. That's how the profits moved around."

Mansfield nodded in agreement. "Did you know you can bring a suitcase through the airport packed with twenties, and nobody would ever know? That's half a million dollars walking around. Multiply that by dozens. Hundreds. You couldn't turn around in this city without bumping into a stack of cash."

Ignacio looked at Pope, whose face was unreadable. He looked at Mansfield. "You're talking about ancient history. Miami's not Little Colombia anymore. It's not *Scarface* out there."

"No, it's not, but that doesn't mean the problem has gone away. The last time we worked together, things got a little messy. Lots of corpses and a lot of questions. I'm hoping that won't happen this time. I'd like to get on top of it before it has a chance to really get out of hand. As for this case, let's stick to the general outlines. Let's talk about money laundering happening right here, right now, in Miami."

"Is that an FBI thing?"

"Oh, sure. We have hundreds of accountants working for the Bureau. Financial crime is what we were born to do. For a while there, if you didn't have a degree in accounting, you wouldn't get very far in our line of work."

"Are you an accountant?"

"Me? Hell, no. I have trouble balancing my checkbook. No, that's not my area. I come at problems from a completely different angle, but it's money that got us into this. You see, about a year ago we received an anonymous tip. It was a fragmentary piece of data, basically part of an accounting record showing a substantial cash deposit into an account we have an interest in. Now, there's nothing particularly shady about the account at first glance, but it has a history, and when we see big money going into it..."

"Drug money," Ignacio said. "That's why Special Agent Pope is here."

"Special Agent Mansfield..." Pope said.

"Right, right. Detective, let's not get ahead of ourselves. Like I said, there are things I'm not sure I'm cleared to tell you. I have temporary permission to bring you in on this because of the situation with your dead man. Whether I can bring you in all the way, I don't know. But I *do* know you can be trusted to keep your mouth shut."

"Thank you?" Ignacio said.

"It's a compliment," Pope said.

"Okay, then. So some money goes somewhere it shouldn't. And you can't tell me where the money came from because it's classified. What does all of this have to do with my dead body? Is he a money launderer when he's not attacking women in their homes?"

"I understand you confiscated a notebook on the scene."

"Who told you that?"

"Is there a notebook?" Pope asked.

"Yeah. But it's all in Armenian. The guy's got Armenian tattoos on him, too. Seriously, how do you know what I have? How did you even know I was working this? Do you have access to our system?"

"It doesn't matter, Detective," Pope said. "The important thing is we're here."

"Exactly," Mansfield agreed. "It'll make more sense once I've told you the rest. You see, we've been watching that account because it's attached to a construction company that doesn't build anything. Sure, there are a lot of construction companies in Miami and only so much work to go around, but this company has never built anything. Anything *ever*. It exists solely to process cash from dirty sources."

"I follow you," Ignacio said.

"Good, because this is where it gets interesting. The ownership of this company is part of what I can't tell you right now, but it's an essential piece of the whole investigation. I can tell you it's a bank, and like Agent Pope said, there are a lot of banks in Miami with, uh, questionable pasts. Some are worse than others, but all of them have a little bit they don't talk about at board meetings."

"I'll bet."

"We thought the tipster would stay silent, but we got more information later on. Additional cash moving into this construction company's account, and some indication the money was moving out fully laundered. This is information we might have gotten through a subpoena, but there are ways to cover up this kind of transaction. So what we got was hot stuff, straight from the source."

"Someone inside the company?"

"The company has no employees. It's controlled entirely from the outside. You have to understand: this company is only a *thing*. It's a machine that makes clean money. That's literally all it does, and it does it by playing with numbers inside the system, making hard currency into ones and zeros in an electronic account somewhere."

"I need to sit down," Ignacio said.

He took one of the office's seats for visitors. He rubbed his forehead. "So you're telling me this person, your informant, he's in the bank, or he's working for some accounting firm, or what?"

"You're getting warmer," Pope said.

"We got information for about six months," Mansfield said. "And then the source shut down. So we started digging, because we hoped we could find out who the informant was based on the information we had. What we got was compelling, but it was only pieces. We couldn't act on it, not without stirring up the situation and maybe blowing the case altogether. It took about three months to isolate a half-dozen people who might have the information we received. It took another month to narrow it down from there. And finally we had one name."

"Faith," Ignacio said.

"Yes. Faith Glazer was the informant."

CHAPTER THIRTY

CAMARO STEPPED INSIDE the apartment. It smelled of old cooking, and the interior was stuffy and hot. She kicked aside pieces of the door frame and nudged the door itself shut with the toe of her boot. With the blinds down and the light from the open door cut off, the apartment was reduced to a dim cave.

In her back pocket, Camaro had a pair of light leather gloves. She put them on. She moved to the window air conditioner and pressed the power button. It started to blow on the highest setting. Camaro notched it down to soften the noise of the fan.

She did not know what she expected to find. The apartment was neat and kept clean, the area rug in the middle of the room vacuumed and the hardwood of the floors swept. A few framed pictures hung on the wall, including one of the Carlyle, a hotel in the Art Deco District that millions had seen in movies and on TV shows about Miami over the decades. Camaro remembered seeing it on TV as a kid, and when she came to Miami she saw it in person. It was less impressive in the daytime, but at night, as in the photograph, it glowed with light.

Camaro moved closer to the pictures. There was a thin film of dust on the glass of one, barely visible. On the picture of the Carlyle, there was none.

From the front room she wandered into the small dining alcove. A simple table topped with Formica sat with two old-fashioned chairs. In the kitchen she found a refrigerator with almost no food inside, but a full complement of pots and pans in the tight cabinets, all of which looked as though they'd been used frequently.

One half of the duplex was given over to these communal spaces, but the second half was private. Serafian's bedroom was surprisingly large. He had a bed with a cast-iron frame painted flat black. On the wall over the headboard was another cross, this one featuring a cruci- fied Jesus writhing in agony. On the opposite wall, a framed painting of the Virgin Mary, expression intense. Being trapped between both made Camaro feel cold despite the mugginess of the room.

The bed was made. Besides the religious items there were no other decorations. Camaro looked for photographs of Faith under the bed and in the drawer of the nightstand, but there was nothing. She moved to the closet and shoved aside the accordion door. Serafian's clothing was sorted into little wire baskets, or hung in an orderly fashion. He owned casual clothing and suits. He had six pairs of shoes of varying fanciness. He had expensive socks, but also socks that looked as though they'd been purchased at a dollar store. Some of his shirts included touristy logos. Some were very much of the yuppie variety.

Camaro pulled one of the basket racks away from the wall to look behind it. No hidden evidence of Faith. She didn't exist here at all.

Serafian's bathroom was the last stop. She found it in the same con- dition as the rest. Shaving kit with fresh blades and a brush for mixing and applying lather. The tub was thoroughly scrubbed, and the plastic shower curtain had no mildew or buildup on it at all. The tile under Camaro's boots looked as though it had been scoured with a tooth- brush.

She looked up. Overhead, a square screen was embedded in the ceil- ing, large enough for a person to fit through. Screws held it in place. At one corner was a semicircular scrape in the paint.

Camaro glanced around. In the corner was a tiny footstool made of wood and carved with a heart. It served no purpose. She put it di- rectly under the screen and stood on it. With her hands extended, she gripped the screen's mesh.

The multi-tool was still on her belt. Camaro studied the screws on the screen. She selected a flathead screwdriver. She went to work on one corner until the screw dropped into her cupped hand. She repeated this three times before gently tugging the screen out of its place.

A black space opened up beyond the hole. Camaro saw nothing. She stepped down from the footstool and went into the kitchen. A minute's rummaging turned up a flashlight. She brought it back to the bathroom, along with one of the chairs from the dining area. Standing on the chair, her head was even with the ceiling. She shone the flashlight around.

The equipment stowed in the space was wrapped in resealable plastic bags. Camaro removed them piece by piece. Eduard Serafian had a tripod, a high-resolution digital camera with a variety of lenses, a parabolic microphone, and a small case filled with things that looked like microchips with wires attached. Camaro didn't know what they were, but she could guess.

The last things to come out were a pair of gun cases. Serafian owned a rifle and a handgun. Both were well maintained and smelled strongly of oil. He preferred hollow points for his pistol and full metal jacket for his rifle. Both of the weapons were of Eastern European make.

She crouched on the bathroom floor with the things all around her. After a while she went into the space again and found another resealable plastic bag farther back from where everything else had been, barely reachable. This one contained a cell phone and three different passports. All the passports showed the face of Eduard Serafian, but his name and his style in the pictures were different in each one.

CHAPTER THIRTY-ONE

BRANDON ROCHE HAD just turned onto Eduard Serafian's street when he saw the woman, Camaro Espinoza. He did not know her by sight, but he knew her regardless. She moved away from a parked Harley-Davidson motorcycle and crossed to stand in front of Serafian's house. Roche applied the brakes and slipped up to the curb. He cracked the windows of his Audi and killed the engine. The air conditioner's blast whispered away to nothing. Instantly the heat of the sun soaked into the black body of the car. Roche felt it reaching through the windshield to cling to his suit jacket.

Espinoza stood for a long time watching the house before climbing the fence. When she disappeared from sight, Roche keyed the Audi back to life, but didn't start the engine. He voice-dialed his phone through the car's Bluetooth and waited for the other end to pick up. "It's Roche," he said when the call was answered.

A woman responded. She had the clipped, low tone of an emergency dispatcher. "Mr. Roche, what can I do for you?"

"I'd like to make arrangements for a passive surveillance."

"Yes, sir. What do we need?"

"I'm looking at a Harley-Davidson motorcycle. I'm not sure of the model. It's one of the bigger ones. Let me give you the license plate number. I want someone to put a marker on it. Nothing fancy. Something we can use to keep tabs when we need to."

"I'll have someone on it right away. Is there anything else I can do for you, Mr. Roche?"

"Yes. I want a complete workup on a woman named Camaro

121

Espinoza. I have a little information already, but I want the whole story. Deep background. Everywhere she's ever been and everything she's ever done. Also give me a list of known associates and anything else that might be useful."

"Absolutely, sir."

"And I need it on my desk by this time tomorrow."

"No problem, sir."

"That's all for now."

He hung up without letting the woman reply. He waited a few minutes for Espinoza to reappear, but she didn't. Roche tried not to grit his teeth. Instead he scratched at his knee with his thumbnail, the contact making tiny rasping sounds. It grew increasingly more unpleasant inside the car. Sweat gathered at the center of Roche's back and under his arms. He turned over the engine and let the air-conditioning run. Within a few minutes, the temperature plummeted to a chilly sixty degrees.

Espinoza came out. Roche watched her stand still on the curb, lean and tightly bound. She turned her head and Roche thought she was looking directly at him, but he knew he was invisible behind the tint of his windshield. The angle of the sun also helped, though in a few hours looking down the street from his direction would be impossible.

She unwound and crossed. Roche observed her movements. She was careful, balanced. He recognized her body language in himself, and in the men who trained him. "Who are you really, Ms. Espinoza?" he asked aloud.

She leaned against her motorcycle. She glanced his way, but now he was certain she had no idea he was there. Her eyes were hidden by black Wayfarers. He saw her gather the hair off her neck to cool the perspiration there. He felt no desire for her, but he knew not every man would feel the same way. She wasn't beautiful. Roche decided that "striking" was a better word.

His phone rang. He said, "Answer phone."

"Brandon?"

"Mr. Kaur."

"Don't 'Mr. Kaur' me, Brandon! Where are you?"

"I won't tell you, and you don't want to know. This conversation isn't happening and you have nothing to do with it. In fact, you ought to hang up right now."

"I'm looking over the accounts."

"You shouldn't do that."

"Why not?"

Roche sighed. "Every time you open a file, that file leaves a trace. That trace can be followed directly back to you, especially if you're using the computer in your office or in your home. Everything has to be anonymized. If you want to have a look at the accounts, it can be arranged."

"I don't *arrange* things with you. This is my bank. *Mine*. I decide what I look at and when."

"Then I suppose there's no argument to be made. If you want to go to prison, that's your concern."

"It's not like that. I only want to be informed."

"You *are* informed. Everything you need to know, I will tell you. Beyond that, your best course of action is to go on as if nothing has happened. Go play golf, or racquetball at the club. Take the boat out. But don't look at those accounts again."

Espinoza was on the phone. Roche wished he could hear her.

"I'm closing the files now," Kaur said.

"Good. I'll be in touch."

"When will you—"

Roche killed the connection and settled into his seat. He watched Camaro Espinoza. She didn't go anywhere. The cop came.

123

CHAPTER THIRTY-TWO

CAMARO CHECKED HER watch when Ignacio's car made the turn onto Serafian's street. Ignacio waved.

She waited until he parked, and met him in the middle of the street. He surveyed the house. "So this is the place," he said.

"Looks like it."

"It's a good thing you didn't go in there. I've got probable cause to search, and if you did anything you shouldn't, we might run into trouble down the line."

"Yeah, all right," Camaro said.

He glanced at her. "I don't like the sound of that."

Camaro was quiet.

"Okay, I *really* don't like the sound of that."

"I may have taken a look around."

Ignacio took his hat off and covered his face with his forearm. "Tell me you didn't leave your fingerprints all over the place."

"No, I was careful."

"She was careful," Ignacio said to himself. He put his hat on. "You think you can go without breaking the law for thirty minutes?"

"Gee, I'll *try*, Detective, but you know how it is."

Ignacio shook his head. "What did you find? Not that you told me, because I'd be an accessory after the fact."

"You should see for yourself, anyway."

They went up together. Camaro let him take the steps first. He entered through the broken door, tsking at the damage. He took a sealed package of latex gloves from his pocket, stripped it open, and put on

124

the gloves. He turned a full circle in the middle of the front room. "Looks normal," he said. "If I didn't know the guy was a pervert, I'd never guess. But that's the way it goes."

"The bathroom has what you want."

She led him in. Serafian's gear was laid out on the floor of the bathroom, the guns unloaded and set aside in the bathtub. Ignacio made a low whistle. "Now what does a guy need with all this stuff?" he asked.

"I don't think he was some peeping Tom."

"You got that right. Creeping on Faith Glazer was only his sideline. I'm thinking he was some kind of a spook, but we won't know until we can get a handle on him. It's like he doesn't exist in the United States, outside of a couple of driver's licenses and a lot of speculation."

Ignacio knelt and traced his hands in the air above Serafian's surveillance gear. Camaro went to the bedroom window. She opened the blinds and looked into the yard of the next house over. It was cramped, too, but the owners let some grass grow. There was a worn track outside a battered old doghouse. No sign of a dog.

"I'm not an expert at this kind of thing," Ignacio said. "But you don't have to be an expert to know what most of this is. These little wire things, I think they're probably bugs. I've seen something like it when the tech guys go to work. Little doodads. You can put 'em inside a phone. If anybody used landlines anymore. Nowadays we usually hide them in the electric sockets. Every room has one of those."

Camaro returned to him. "He was a watcher. But he had skills. Those guns are for real."

"Yeah. I don't recognize them. European?"

"The rifle's an APS-95. It's Croatian. The pistol comes from Turkey."

"Croatian, huh? Don't know if that fits what I got so far. Serafian has Armenian tattoos on him, and he has an Armenian name. He spoke another language during the attack."

"People who knew him say he had an accent," Camaro said.

Ignacio stood. He looked at her. "'People'? You've been talking to people?"

"There's a guy in Liberty City who day-hires to pass out flyers and phone books...things like that. It's how Serafian moved around without anybody noticing him. Once they got used to seeing him, he stopped even bothering."

"Oh, man, I really want to know about this guy. Maybe I would have let it go before, but there's something happening. I talked to the FBI and DEA today. They're both all over this."

"Why?"

Ignacio's face pinched. "I'm not sure how much I ought to tell you, what with you breaking and entering and God knows what else. This is the kind of thing that ends careers. You don't make friends with people on the other side."

"Hey," Camaro said. "I'm not on the other side. I'm on this side, with you. The same side Faith is on. This guy didn't drop out of the sky, not with all this gear. If you're talking to the feds, I *know* it's something I need to hear about. For her."

He searched her face. He sighed. "I think Faith Glazer is in some serious shit, pardon my language. Money laundering at least. Maybe more. And before you get up in my business about it, I don't know a lot. They told me some, but it's not enough for me to build a solid case, if that's the way I want to take it. The way these federal guys go, they'll pull rank and before you know it you're on something else because the old case is gone. I mean *gone*. It goes down a hole and never comes back up again."

"She's a crook?"

"I didn't say that. But she has information, and the feds are gonna want to get it out of her. I'd like to get my piece, because I don't like loose ends. Which means I can't have you playing cowgirl and busting down doors and interrogating witnesses. That's not how it's done. You understand me?"

Camaro bit back the first word that came to mind. "What do you want me to do?"

"For right now? Go home and get back to doing whatever you were doing before. Visit Faith. Cheer her up. If I need you, I'll ask for you."

"You'll tell me what's going on?"

"How much do you really need to know?"

"I put the gun in her hand," Camaro said. "I'm the one she came to when no one else would help. This guy is dead, but if there's another guy behind him, I want to know she's safe from him, too."

Ignacio considered. She saw the thoughts play on his face. "All right, all right. I'll keep you in the loop. But this is off the books. Way, way off the books. I don't want to be pulling slugs out of people, okay? If somebody's going to do any shooting, it's gonna be me. I'm the law around here. You're a civilian."

"Whatever you say, Detective."

127

CHAPTER THIRTY-THREE

FAITH KNEW THEY were outside the door before they made a sound. She woke in her bed at the hospital, alert. It took a moment to orient herself in the half-light of the room. They'd removed the bandage from her left eye. It was still swollen, but she could see enough to know this was not her home. She was away from what had happened. The man was dead.

A shadow passed over the slender window in the door. Bodies moving. She heard the murmur of voices. The door opened and an older man stepped through, followed by a black woman in a suit almost identical to her companion's. Both of them wore sober expressions. She didn't know them by sight, but she knew who they had to be.

"Ms. Glazer," said the man, "I'm Special Agent John Mansfield with the Miami field office of the Federal Bureau of Investigation. This is my colleague, Special Agent Pope of the Drug Enforcement Administration."

"Hello," Faith said. Her voice caught on the word.

"Do you know why we're here?"

"Yes."

Mansfield stepped closer. Pope was his shadow. Her face was stone. Mansfield continued, "I'm not the agent you contacted originally, but your information came into my possession and it's now my case. Everything you sent from the first piece of information onward, I and my people have been working on."

"Okay."

Mansfield smiled a warm smile, but the expression didn't reach his eyes. "The things you gave us are tantalizing. And I don't think I need to explain why we want more. The presence of Special Agent Pope should give you some idea of the scope of what we're talking about. This is not about dollars and cents. It's about serious crimes committed by serious people. You got a little taste of how serious they can be."

Faith shuddered. "The police say he was crazy."

"He was definitely crazy, but that's not why he was there. The coincidence is too strong. I've been to your apartment and I saw how he turned it over. He was looking for something, and the people who sent him know you took it and they want it back or destroyed. Right now the only option I see is for you to hand it over to us before things get any worse."

Faith took a deep breath, held it, let it out. Her eyes closed and she did it again. She opened them. "I can't help you," she said, and this time her voice was steady.

Mansfield's smile vanished. "Excuse me?"

"I said I can't help you. I don't know anything about what you're telling me and I don't have any information to give you."

"Wait a minute," Pope spoke up. "You know lying to a federal agent is a crime, don't you?"

Faith let her gaze drift to Pope. She felt light. She was calm. In the theater of her mind, she saw her wrapped hands pounding the heavy bag on the patio behind Camaro's house. The slap of the leather, followed by the thud of the bag absorbing the impact. The jolt in her arms and shoulders. *Breathe,* Camaro said in her ear. *Keep breathing.*

"Ms. Glazer, are you listening to me?" Pope asked.

"I hear you. I'm sorry, but there's nothing I can do. I don't know either of you, and I don't know how I can help you. I'm an accountant. That's all I do. I don't have anything to do with criminals or anything like that. So I'm sorry if you got me confused with someone else."

Mansfield stepped closer. "Ms. Glazer. Faith. We *know* it was you. And we know you know. It's the first thing you said when we came in the room. This was inevitable, from the first file you sent us. Narrowing it down was easy. We have hundreds of people whose only job is to track down information like this. It came from you. It couldn't have come from anyone else. You're not that good at covering your tracks."

Faith did not reply.

"Ms. Glazer, this is in the interest of the American people and their allies," Pope said. "Do you understand that? I gathered you did, based on what you passed to the FBI. Now, I don't know why you would suddenly deny you're involved, but if it has to do with security, I can assure you it's safe. We've already made arrangements for you to receive a twenty-four-hour guard."

Faith's gaze flicked toward the door. "There's someone out there?"

"Not yet," Mansfield replied, "but there will be. We'll be on you every minute of every day. Nothing like what happened to you is going to happen again. We won't allow it. So there's no reason not to tell us what we want to know."

"We need the complete files," Pope said. "Everything you have. We need to illuminate this situation from the inside. Where the money comes from, where it goes, and whose hands it touches along the way. We can take the whole thing down, but it starts with you. If it's not your safety that's the problem, is it something else? Do you want to be paid? Because that's not out of the question."

Faith's shoulders drooped. She rested her hands on her stomach and looked down at them. She felt their eyes on her. When she looked up again, they still stared. *Breathe, Faith,* Camaro said.

"Please," Mansfield said.

"I can't help you. I'm sorry."

The two federal agents stepped away from the bed. They conferred in whispers. Pope abruptly left the room. Mansfield remained. His face was neutral. "Faith, I'm going to go now. And I understand you're going to be discharged soon. So what we're going to do is give you two days. Over the next forty-eight hours, I want you to really think about where you're going next. Because I can guarantee if we have to put pressure on you to get what we need, there will be damage. The question then becomes whether you go on with your life, or whether you go to prison. Those are your options. Think about it."

He left. Faith was alone. She cried.

CHAPTER THIRTY-FOUR

THE PHONE RANG by Lawrence Kaur's bedside at ten past one in the morning. He started from sleep, and cast around wildly with one arm before he laid a hand on the receiver. He yanked it free of the cradle and pressed it to his ear. "It's the middle of the night."

"This business never sleeps," said the man on the other end of the line.

All fogginess left him. Kaur sat up in the bed, hand clutching the receiver. His heart thudded. He realized he couldn't speak. He forced himself to. "Señor Lorca."

"Don't use my name. Your NSA is able to pick a name out of all the calls being made all over the world. I don't want them monitoring this conversation."

"You don't have to worry about that. My home line is completely secure. Mr. Roche, my security director, sees to that personally."

Carlos Lorca said, "If only Mr. Roche was better at resolving other problems."

"I don't know what you've heard, but—"

"Please, don't do me the disservice of lying. I already know more than you think, and I am unhappy with everything I hear. First you allow this woman to have access to critical records. Then you allow her to leak these records to the authorities. And *then*, despite everything, you didn't eliminate the threat before it got worse."

Kaur got out of bed. He walked to the bedroom window. It was twice as tall as he was, and encompassed the entire wall. The ocean lay beyond, perfectly black under the moonlight, highlighted only by the occasional ripple turned faintly silver. "I don't know where you're getting your information, but it's not entirely accurate. The woman, Faith Glazer, was only a temp. We brought her on to do some auditing for another client entirely. How she got access to *these* accounts we can't say for sure, but I can say that it wasn't something we did deliberately or out of carelessness. You are a valued client, and your father was before you. We have always done what we had to do to maintain your anonymity and your security. We want your business."

"Your business and my business are not always the same."

"I understand that. But we respect everything you do."

Lorca grunted. "Where is the woman now?"

"My understanding is that she's in the hospital."

"Is she talking to anyone?"

"Not to my knowledge."

"That's not good enough! I want information on her, and I want it all the time. Everything you know, I want to know. Do you understand what I'm saying to you, Lawrence? Daily. And if your Mr. Roche doesn't like that arrangement, then he can take it up with my people in person."

Kaur took a step back from the window. "You have people here?"

"It can be arranged."

"That's not necessary. We have everything we need. You don't have to expose yourself."

"I am already exposed. The moment this woman gained access to my accounts, I was exposed. And you...you did nothing to prevent it. It's a disappointment it will be difficult for you to assuage, Lawrence. Very difficult."

"Give us time," Kaur said, and he hated the note of pleading in his voice.

"I've already given you too much time. You wasted months when you could have put a stop to it immediately."

133

"We had to know it was her. And we had to know who she was sharing information with. It's all part of containment."

"And now? How will it be contained?"

"She'll be eliminated, of course. But we still don't know if she has backups, or where those backups might be located. There are a lot of moving parts, Señor Lorca. You have to understand—"

"No excuses! Solve the problem."

"I swear to you, it's already in hand. Your accounts have been moved and all trace of them was erased. It's like nothing ever happened. Once we have the files she copied, there will be absolutely no evidence of any kind. Even if she were alive to tell the story, no one would believe her without proof. I believe in Mr. Roche. He can bring this to a firm conclusion."

"Don't try to sell me, Lawrence."

"It's not a sell. It will be done."

The line went dead. Kaur called for Lorca, but he was gone. Kaur's hand shook as he held the silent phone.

He didn't go back to sleep. He put on a robe and crossed the bedroom to the wet bar. He poured himself two fingers of sixty-year-old Macallan whiskey and downed it without sipping. He poured another but this time made himself take nips from the tumbler. The impact of the drink was astringent, almost too much to bear, while oaky tones followed in a cloud.

His bedroom had a desk and an Aeron chair. He sat and brought his computer to life. The monitor glowed painfully in the darkness. Kaur accessed his secure e-mail and addressed a message to Brandon Roche. Without specifics as to who called and from where, he laid out the urgent message of Carlos Lorca. He made no admonition in closing. The information in the e-mail stood for itself.

When he was done, he took up his whiskey and walked back to the window. He decided to go out onto the deck, and from there he felt the cooler breeze of early fall coming off the Atlantic. The weather in Miami never truly turned cold, but it was possible to feel the difference in the seasons carried on the wind.

Kaur nursed his whiskey for most of an hour. He thought of Faith Glazer only once, and his stomach soured when he did. He flung his empty tumbler over the rail. It caught moonlight, a tiny glint lost immediately in the greater darkness. The tumbler fell somewhere into the sand below. Kaur didn't hear it strike the ground.

CHAPTER THIRTY-FIVE

IGNACIO WAS BACK at his desk early. He logged in to the computer and saw all the evidence from Eduard Serafian's home had been checked in overnight. Each piece had its own digital photograph, sharp and flatly lit. Someone from the technical section had taken a look at the things Ignacio thought were bugs and confirmed that this was exactly what they were.

The pages of Serafian's notebook had also been scanned in, the notebook itself messengered to the FBI care of Special Agent John Mansfield. Ignacio scrolled through the scanned images, looking at the strange alphabet the Armenian language used. It was like hieroglyphs, though at least hieroglyphs looked like something and not squiggles on paper.

He picked two dozen pages at random and ran off copies. He collected them from the printer and left the bullpen. In fifteen minutes he was in his car, headed north toward Boca Raton. The drive was forty-five minutes, depending on the traffic, and Ignacio played Viva on the satellite radio. He missed the between-songs chatter of the local Miami stations, but not the commercials.

His phone led him directly to Saint David Armenian Church, set beside a busy roadway bustling with traffic. The parking lot outside the church was mostly empty. Ignacio parked and got out. The sun bore down on him like a hot rock wrapped in wet burlap.

Inside it was comfortable. He stood in the lobby, taking in the icons on the wall, framed in gold leaf, and smelling the strong odor of incense. A rack displayed church literature, almost all of it in

Armenian. By the door was a box for donations, the label in Armenian and English.

He stepped inside the sanctuary. The ceiling was high and the space suffused with a gold color from hanging chandeliers. At the far end an arch stood over what looked like a smaller replica of the church itself, a painting of Mary and Jesus inside. Fresh-cut flowers were everywhere.

He moved farther in until a voice called out from behind him, "May I help you, sir?"

Ignacio turned. He realized he was still wearing his hat. He took it off. A man in a dark suit with a clerical collar stood in the doorway to the lobby. His beard was salted with gray, but he was younger than Ignacio expected. "Father Hayrapetyan?"

"Are you Detective Montellano?"

"That's right," Ignacio said, and he showed his identification. "You are Father Hayrapetyan, right?"

"I am. But please, you can call me Stepan if you want."

"Okay, but only if you call me Nacho."

"Nacho?"

"It's what my friends call me."

Hayrapetyan nodded and smiled. He came closer. "Then Nacho it is. I see you're interested in the church."

"I've never been inside an Armenian church before."

"I think you'll find it's not too different from any other church."

"Yeah. Listen, is there somewhere we can sit down?"

"You said you have something for me to read?"

Ignacio produced the printed pages from inside his jacket. "These are scans of a notebook kept by a suspect who stalked and assaulted a woman. I don't have anyone who can read it."

The priest took the papers. "I understand this man is dead?"

"He was killed."

"That's a shame. He may have been a criminal, but the Lord says all men can be redeemed."

"Not this one, I don't think."

"Let's go to my office and have a look at these."

In the administrative area, the only sign of religiosity was the occasional piece of art depicting Christ or his mother. Away from the exotic scent of the sanctuary, the air had the clean blandness of a commercial park. Father Hayrapetyan looked over the pages as he walked, leading Ignacio deeper into the building until they came to an office filled with books. Books overflowed from the shelves behind the desk and took residence on the floor, on the corners of the desk, and even against the door, preventing it from being opened all the way. Father Hayrapetyan had two chairs for visitors, but one was completely given over to more books. "Please sit," the priest told Ignacio.

The priest sat behind the desk in a large leather chair. He spread the pages on his blotter. He read quietly, and occasionally made an astonished noise under his breath. "Is it something?" Ignacio asked.

Hayrapetyan shook his head. "This man was very disturbed."

"I kind of got that."

"No, I mean he was twisted. I assume there's more of this?"

"A whole book's worth."

"I imagine it's all the same."

"We figured it for some kind of logbook. Tracking his victim's movements."

"It is, but there's more. Obviously the narrative, if you can call it that, is fragmented because I don't have all the pieces, but what is here is genuinely upsetting. How badly hurt was the woman?"

"He beat her up pretty good."

Father Hayrapetyan's face creased with pain. "I don't know what to say. Armenians are people like anyone else, and there are good ones and bad ones, but when you live in a country where most people couldn't tell you what an Armenian is . . . well, you can't help but feel personally affronted when someone does a terrible thing. We're still living down the Kardashians."

Ignacio hesitated. "Uh."

The priest smiled. "It's a joke. And Lord knows we need one right now."

"What exactly did he put in this book?"

"Much of it has to do with the various sexual things he wanted to do with this woman Faith. I won't bother you with the specifics of it, but there was going to be a lot of pain and humiliation involved. There are references to keeping her like a pet, to killing her in ways I'm sickened to read, and more. In between all the ranting there are notations made of her every move. When she went to lunch, when she left her apartment, when she came home from work. All of it."

Ignacio digested this. "I think maybe it was a good thing he got shot dead, Father. Not that I want to say it in a church."

"No, you can say it. He absolutely should have been shot dead, because if he hadn't been, he would have committed unspeakable acts. The fact that he only beat her is, sad to say, something of a blessing."

"Does it say anything about who he might be working for? Where he came from? I didn't see any phone numbers anywhere except hers, but he was in contact with someone who kept their calls a secret. I was hoping there might be something in there I could use."

"I'm sorry, but no. Maybe if I had more. Are you sure he was employed by someone?"

"Watching somebody like this is a full-time job. And maybe he was wrong in the head, but somebody had to pay his rent. I'm sorry you had to read all that."

"Don't be sorry. Someone had to. It might as well be me. I can pray for him, but I think it's a little too late to save this man's soul."

"Way too late." Ignacio stood up. "I want to thank you for your time, Father."

"Not at all. But before you go, Nacho, I thought I'd share something with you. Officer Marshall—William—he showed me a picture of this man's tattoo and I translated it for him."

"It's some kind of motto," Ignacio said.

"It is. Of an Armenian group called Hayasdani Azadakrut'ean Hay Kaghtni Panag."

"I hope there's not a quiz after this."

"The Armenian isn't necessary. Essentially it means 'Armenian Secret Army for the Liberation of Armenia.' They were a militant group I barely remember from when I was a young teenager. They wanted to force the Turkish government to acknowledge the Armenian genocide and cede territory for an Armenian homeland. They disappeared twenty-five years ago and haven't been heard from since."

"So they were, like, terrorists in Turkey?"

"Unfortunately, yes. They killed a few dozen people over the years, and injured more. But it's passing away into history now. As Armenians we still want the same things, but we don't go about it in that way. The HAHKP never spoke for the majority of Armenians."

"Thank God for that."

"Yes, thank God."

"I should go."

"Let me walk you out."

Ignacio let the priest escort him. Before long they stood outside the front doors of the church, with traffic droning past. "One last question," Ignacio said. "Do you think any of these 'secret army' guys ever came to the United States?"

"I don't know. But it seems at least one of them did. God be with you, Nacho. I'll pray for your safety."

CHAPTER THIRTY-SIX

KAUR'S SECRETARY BUZZED the intercom. Kaur touched the speaker button. "Yes?"

"Mr. Roche to see you, sir."

"Send him in. And bump my next appointment by thirty minutes."

"Yes, Mr. Kaur."

The office was on a corner of a mirrored-glass tower in downtown Miami, with a spectacular view of Miami Beach. The building was constructed in 1984, and the funds to erect it had come from the booming business done by M&I Bank and Trust. The valuation of the real estate had risen astronomically since then. The office was itself one of the most expensive spaces in the city by square yard.

The double doors to the outer office opened. Kaur caught a glimpse of Ms. Caits, his assistant, before Roche swept into the room and shut himself in. Roche came no closer. He stood at the doors with his mouth turned downward. It was a full minute before he spoke. "You should have told me about Lorca's call right away."

"I needed time to think over what he said."

"Did he threaten you?"

"Not in so many words."

"I see."

Roche came closer. He had a folder in his hands. He flexed it between them. Kaur saw the tension in the tendons on the backs of his hands. Kaur said nothing until Roche sat down. Outside the window, a helicopter flew past, its racket silenced by thick glass. The sea was green.

"We expected this," Kaur said lightly. "Right? We expected it. This isn't ideal, but it's not a disaster."

"He understands we couldn't kill the woman outright?" Roche asked.

"I explained it thoroughly."

"I'm sure you did. In the meantime, he's probably wondering how to take this to the next level. I intend to act before he gets a chance to put his foot in it."

The folder now sat on Roche's knee. Kaur gestured toward it. "What's that?"

"This is our new problem."

Roche handed over the folder. Kaur opened it on his blotter. Inside was a stack of pages a quarter inch thick, and on top of it a black-and-white photograph of a woman staring directly into the camera. A driver's-license photo, or a passport. Kaur looked into her face and saw nothing but pure calm. She had obviously had her nose broken more than once, and a scar cut through her eyebrow. He lifted the picture out of the way. "Camaro Espinoza? That can't be a real name."

"It is a real name and she's a real person. She's also a real problem, because she's involved with both Faith Glazer and with the police."

"So she's a policewoman?"

"No, she's the captain of a fishing charter. There's information on her boat, the *Annabel,* in the file, but it's not interesting or important. What's troubling is she's a decorated military veteran, a licensed bail fugitive recovery agent, and a woman with a difficult past, which, quite frankly, I've never seen with someone who's not in prison."

Kaur continued to sort through the papers. Included were military records. Time served in Iraq and Afghanistan. She was a health-care specialist, which Kaur assumed was some sort of nurse. She'd been honorably discharged three years previously, her last station Fort Irwin in California. Her Miami license said she'd been in Florida for two years.

"This woman is the reason Faith Glazer had a gun. It's the only explanation I have for it. I heard the name in Serafian's reports, but he said she was some kind of personal trainer. Cardio kickboxing. That sort of thing. He didn't look any deeper—otherwise he would have found what I found: registrations for multiple firearms, and a concealed-carry license. She owns guns, she knows how to use them, and she was training Glazer to fight back. Our man is dead and Glazer is still alive because Camaro Espinoza helped that happen."

On the last page of the report, Kaur found a picture of the *Annabel*. "That's a nice boat," he said.

"Forget the boat," Roche said. "The point is this: she was talking to Glazer, and now she's talking to the police. I had my people do some deep digging, and she has some sort of connection to a homicide detective named Ignacio Montellano. Montellano is handling Serafian's death. And even though we were sure to insulate Serafian from anyone trying to dig up his identity, when I went to his house to clear out his equipment I found *her* there already. And later the cop came. Montellano."

Kaur closed the folder. "What do you think she's telling him?"

"The more pertinent question is, whose side is she on? Depending on whether Glazer told her everything, she knows about us. And she tracked down Serafian. The link between the bank and Serafian is dead. No one will ever be able to follow it, but she'll put together what she can. Whether she takes it to the police or tries to take advantage herself, we don't know."

"I don't see what the problem is," Kaur said. He got up from the desk. "We silence her. We silence her, we silence Glazer, and maybe we silence the cop. And then that's it."

Roche glared at him from his seat. "That's it? Are you listening to yourself? Days ago you were begging me to make this airtight. Now you have me killing two women and a *cop?*"

"Then why bring this to me at all? I don't have the answers! You're the one who's supposed to have the answers!"

"I'm bringing this to you because I think we might have to consider a deal. If we kill one woman, that's not a hardship, but we start killing too many people and there will be questions. The FBI and the DEA are already on the case. They've spoken to Glazer already. It's only a matter of time before something breaks for them."

Kaur put his fingertips to his temples and worked them in a circle. "This is not happening. This is not happening in my office."

"Larry, listen to me."

"No. Listen to me. Everything I told you before stands. If this means people have to die, then so be it. This is what we allowed for all along. This woman, this Camaro Espinoza, she's some opportunist looking for a payday. Maybe she thinks she'll get it from us. Who knows? She won't get rich going to the police. So deal with it. *Deal* with *it*."

"If you say so," Roche said.

"I say so. Do your thing. Get it done."

CHAPTER THIRTY-SEVEN

THE CLOCK BY Camaro's bed made a dull buzzing sound day and night. It was old. She had found it in a closet when she moved into the house. At first the buzzing drove her crazy, but eventually it became part of the background noise of the room, along with the fan of the window air conditioner. She settled into the sounds of the night and the neighborhood, and she slept well. Tonight she woke.

Without changing positions, she glanced at the clock. It was past last call. Outside the neighborhood was tranquil, with not even the wail of a siren to break the quiet. The air conditioner circulated cool air. The house was settled.

She closed her eyes and looked for sleep. The tinny sound of metal scraping on metal made her open them again.

She tensed on the bed under the thin blanket. She was stripped to a T-shirt and underpants, and the skin on her legs prickled. Without rustling the bedsheets, she put out a hand and rested her palm on the grip of a .45 on the nightstand.

The sound repeated itself. Camaro knew it: a set of picks in a lock, working the tumblers. She'd seen it done, and she'd started to learn herself. The noise was unmistakable.

A louder click sounded. The lock was open. The door would follow. Camaro used her feet to pull the bedsheets away from her body, then slowly rolled onto the floor by the bed, bringing the pistol with her. She crouched, feeling her heart against her breastbone and the rustle of her lungs.

She heard the first footfall. They were quiet steps, but she was listening for them and there was no way to hide the sound completely. She knew the tread of a boot, and these were boots, thick-soled with rubber.

Her bare feet made no noise as she crouch-walked across the bedroom to the door. She pressed against the wall and listened. Now she heard two sets of footfalls moving through the front room. They split up, one headed toward the kitchen and one angling toward the bedroom. She calmed her breathing and edged up to the door frame.

The men said nothing, but she was sure they were men. Despite the quiet, they had an unmistakable heaviness to their step. Camaro caught the whisper of a breath taken from behind a balaclava. The man was on the opposite side of the wall. Camaro shifted her grip on the .45 and waited.

The muzzle of a carbine passed through the door, followed by the long guard and the lead hand of the man wielding it. Camaro let a half second pass. The man took a short step. Camaro moved.

She grabbed the gun behind the barrel and wrenched it upward. The carbine discharged into the ceiling, a deafening report filling the bedroom like a thunderclap. Camaro jammed her .45 under the man's left arm and squeezed the trigger three times. His body muffled the gunshots.

When the man crumpled, Camaro went down with him, the carbine over her shoulder and the man's body slumped into hers. She caught a glimpse of the other gunman moving in the front room, cutting across from the kitchen. She fired twice as she fell, and saw the second gunman duck away behind the couch.

The front room lit up with muzzle flash as the second gunman opened fire. Slugs tore into the form of the dead man covering her. Camaro saw wood strip from the door frame as the man's partner squeezed off rounds in quick succession, each report landing on top of the other until she heard nothing except a bright, piercing tone drowning out every other noise.

Camaro scrambled backward, scuttling on heels and palms from beneath the dead man until she was clear of the doorway. She sprang up, blood on her T-shirt. She crouched low beside the door. Bullet holes were torn through the penetrable walls.

The blast of the second carbine died. Camaro peeked out. The top of the second gunman's head was visible above the back of the couch. She emptied the .45 in his direction. Stuffing sprayed the air, and Camaro caught sight of wet droplets like dark pearls in the light coming in from the backyard through the kitchen window.

She dropped the .45 and sprang from her position, dashing across the intervening space and clearing the end of the couch in a full-length leap. The man crouching behind the couch struggled on the floor, with blood coursing from a wound high on his shoulder, trying to fit a fresh magazine into the well of his carbine. He was buried beneath Camaro. The magazine flew away, skittering across the floor.

They tangled. Camaro reared up, knees pressed to the floor on either side of the man's waist. She saw his eyes widen before she smashed his nose beneath the balaclava, hammering down with her fists until crimson painted the slash of face still visible beneath the cloth.

The man exploded his hips, bucking her, and they rolled. Camaro tried to lock her ankles at the small of his back, but he threw her aside with enough force to send her tumbling. She hit the wall with hair in her face. She swept it away from her eyes and came up at the same moment the man did.

She jabbed, and he caught her wrist. He bent the joint at the wrong angle. Camaro went over, contact with the floor causing a shock of pain in her forearm. She was on her back again, but he was over her. She swept out with her leg, snagged his ankle as he moved. The man stumbled backward and fell.

Camaro panted as she made it to her hands and knees. She went for the man. He lashed out with a boot and struck her hard in the stomach. Her lungs emptied and she came down bodily on top of the small table in her dining area. She felt the vertebrae pop in her spine. The table's legs gave way in every direction. She was down again.

As they made it to their feet, she heard the rasping sound of the man's breath. He clawed at the balaclava and peeled it from his head. He was tan-skinned with liquid black hair. Sweat mingled with blood on his face. Both of his nostrils drained wetly red into a slab of mustache.

He went for his waist. Camaro saw a knife whip loose of the sheath. He slashed at her and she retreated, out of the dining area and into the open kitchen. He closed the distance, thrusting with the blade. Camaro twisted to let the weapon pass and brought her fist around. The blow snapped the man's head back. He collapsed against the sink, knife hand on the edge of the counter. Camaro grabbed his wrist and hammered it against the Formica. The knife fell. She kicked it between his legs. It slid to a stop by the door at the far end of the kitchen.

The man bulled into her with his shoulder. They crashed into the refrigerator and rocked it. Camaro got an elbow between them, opened a gash on the edge of his scalp. He punched her low in the stomach, and straight across the jaw. Her knees wobbled and she sank. He put his knee into her face.

Camaro's head swam. Her ears were still deaf. She saw him move toward the fallen knife. She forced life into her legs, grabbed for a nearby drawer. She dragged it open until it hit the stays. Kitchen tools inside rattled. Camaro's hand closed on the worn wooden grip of a chef's knife.

She pulled it free as the man rushed her with his blade. He cut the air when she ducked, backhanded to slash her on the return. Camaro felt sharp cold in her, followed by heat. She didn't have to look to know she bled.

He commanded the space, backing Camaro toward the end of the kitchen. Camaro shifted the chef's knife from hand to hand, watching for his shoulders to betray the next strike. When he moved, she moved. She opened up his knife arm from elbow to shoulder. The man made a single bark of pain. Perspiration soaked his face and flung away in droplets.

Camaro let him come. His blade darted in. She deflected it with the flat of her knife, pivoted, and cut him deeply across the wrist. His fingers opened. The knife fell again. Camaro saw the look of recognition on his face when she threw her weight against his, and sent him reeling backward. One foot slipped behind the other and he fell with Camaro on top. She put both hands behind the chef's knife she drove into his chest.

The knife stopped at the handle. The man grabbed for her hair. Camaro leaned against the handle protruding from his chest. The man keened when the blade shifted. He tried to roll away. Camaro took his back, coiled her arm around his throat, locked his hips with both legs. She put one hand behind his head, tucked the other under the bar of her arm. She closed the noose. The man struggled.

She held on until he passed into unconsciousness. She kept holding on until he was dead.

CHAPTER THIRTY-EIGHT

IGNACIO PULLED UP outside the house in Allapattah and into a thicket of flashing lights and emergency vehicles. There were more here than had been on the scene at Faith Glazer's apartment. He'd gotten the basics from Detective Fletcher, the cop who caught the case, but he was still taken aback by the commotion in the street.

Despite the hour, neighbors were out in force, lined up on the side of the street, held back by yellow crime-scene tape. They were ghostly in the flickering red and blue illumination. A uniformed officer lifted the tape for Ignacio to drive through once he flashed his badge. Inside the circle of trust, he killed the engine and took a deep breath.

He stepped out into the humid night. He wore no hat when the sun was down. He looked at the gathered people, then toward the cop who had let him in. "Everybody inside?" he asked.

"You looking for Fletcher?"

"She's the one."

"I think she's around back with the lady."

Ignacio took a step toward the house. Someone called out, "Hey! Hey, cop!"

"Calm down over there," the uniformed officer said. "I told you I'd run you in if you kept yelling."

Ignacio looked. He saw a young man in his early twenties, hair falling around his ears and onto his neck. He had a sharply pointed beard. "There something you want?" Ignacio asked.

"Yeah. I'm wondering when you're gonna do something about that chick."

"I'm going to tell you one more time—" the uniformed officer began.

Ignacio held up a hand. "It's all right. I'll talk to him."

At the police line he stayed an arm's length away from the young man, who glared at him with dark eyes. "You folks gonna cover it all up?" the young man demanded.

"Cover all what up?"

"Hey, man, we heard the shooting. She killed somebody in there."

"We're looking into it."

"Start by looking into whatever she's up to. She's some kind of survivalist or something. Back at Christmastime, she beat David Rosales down the street so bad, he had to come home from the hospital in a wheelchair."

Ignacio shook his head to clear it. "Listen, it's late. I don't know who David Rosales is."

"He lives two doors down, man! Don't you people know anything? She beat him bad."

"You know this for a fact?"

The young man glanced toward the ground and moved his feet. "Not exactly. But she had a beef with him, and then he turned up wrecked. She took his car apart, too."

"Why would she do that?"

A woman nearby spoke up. "Rosales was beating on his kid. She knew about it."

"Sounds like you knew about it, too."

"Yeah, but I never attacked nobody. You seen what she's got out back? She's out there on her patio getting ready to kill someone."

"That's right," the young man interjected. "She's dangerous."

"Uh-huh," Ignacio said. "Sorry."

"Sorry? She went and *killed somebody,* bro," the young man said.

"You know, speculation like that causes panic," Ignacio said. "You don't know what went on in there. I don't even know what went on in there. So until we ask questions and do our investigation, nobody knows for sure. I'm sorry one of your neighbors was assaulted, but I don't see how that has anything to do with anything. It could have been anyone."

"It was her!" the young man said. "She's crazy."

"Calm down," Ignacio said. "I'll look into it. Okay? I'll look into it."

"Yeah, you do that, asshole."

"Hey, watch your mouth," Ignacio replied. He gestured sharply with his finger. "I'm still a cop, and this is police business. You don't like it, go home."

No reply came. Ignacio walked away. "Sorry about that," the uniformed cop called after him, but Ignacio said nothing.

He was one step inside the front door when he saw the bodies. The house was as he remembered it from the one time he had visited before. It was small, but good enough for a woman living alone. Everything blended into everything else, with the back of the front room letting into a dining area, which in turn let into the kitchen. Only the bedroom was offset with a door. One body lay there. The other was in the kitchen. Empty shell casings were everywhere, and blood. A whirlwind had passed through, and left death behind.

Crime-scene technicians took photos of splatter on the walls and floors and marked out every expended shell. Tags were appended to bullet holes in the shredded couch, the floor, and the cheap wooden paneling. No one paid Ignacio any mind as he negotiated the front room for a better angle on the action. He saw the two dead better. Both of them wore black, one had a balaclava still in place, the other had discarded his, or maybe the EMTs had taken it off.

A blonde woman appeared from the bedroom. She was in a linen pantsuit that looked freshly pressed. She spotted Ignacio immediately. "Detective Montellano?" she asked.

"That's me," Ignacio said. He reached for his hat and instead touched his bare brow. "You're Fletcher?"

"Kate Fletcher. Pleased to meet you. I don't get to see you daytime guys very often."

They shook hands. Fletcher's palm was dry and cool. She was younger than Ignacio by twenty years, but he saw lines creeping into her face. They were mostly hidden by makeup, but eventually they would be impossible to disguise. He had similar lines himself. "Thanks for calling me," Ignacio said.

"It wasn't my idea. It was hers."

"Camaro Espinoza?"

"Our woman of the hour."

"Where is she?"

"Out back with my partner. We needed to clear the scene for the techs. Medics have been in and out, checking on her."

"She's hurt?"

"Not really. Bumps and bruises. Cut on the arm. But these two...She killed the hell out of these two."

Fletcher indicated the bodies with a wave of her hand. Ignacio looked at them again. The way they slumped in ugly, boneless heaps on the floor. One had been shot repeatedly. The one in the kitchen seemed almost as if he'd fallen asleep in an uncomfortable position, a knife protruding from his chest. "Who are they?" Ignacio asked.

"No idea. They aren't carrying ID and they didn't identify themselves to Espinoza, which isn't surprising. They had a rental car they left on the street like they owned the place. Came in through the front door. She managed to disarm one and kill him with her gun. She fought it out hand-to-hand with the other one until she got a knife into him and strangled him to death."

Ignacio made a face. "Yikes."

"Yeah. She probably didn't need to bother. The stabbing looks like it would have done the job all by itself."

"Don't play with sharp objects."

"They picked the wrong house, that's for sure. She has an arsenal in her closet, a couple of knives, and a pistol for carry. If you look out back, she has a whole gym setup that looks like Bruce Lee meets Rocky. I'm all for empowered women, but she's something."

"You don't know the half of it. Can I talk to her?"

"Sure. What's your take on this?"

Ignacio paused. "I can't say until we get more info on our two shooters here. You mind passing anything you find out my way? I'll keep it to myself, and if it turns out to be connected to something I'm working, I'll let you know. But tell me if these guys have any tattoos on them that might be Armenian, or if either one of them turns out to be from Armenia."

"What's the connection?"

"Honestly? I have no idea. But when I find out, you'll be the first to know."

They parted. Ignacio went out onto the back patio through a door in the kitchen. He found Camaro sitting on a weight bench while an older man in a loose suit stood over her. They weren't talking. Camaro rubbed the knuckles on her hands, one followed by the other, while staring into space. She had a fresh dressing on her arm. When Ignacio appeared, her gaze flicked over him without her expression changing at all.

Ignacio extended a hand to the detective. "Hey, you're Shane Abbott, right?"

"Yeah, that's right. You're Montellano?"

"Nacho. Call me Nacho."

"Sure, sure. We met a little while back when we were working both ends of that Haitian thing."

"Oh, yeah, I remember. Nice to see you again."

"Same here. You just show up?"

"I got here as fast as I could. Your partner gave me the rundown inside. Hell of a night."

Abbott cast a frowning look at Camaro. "I was having a great conversation with Ms. Espinoza about it."

"She's not a talker."

"I got that."

"Can I get a few minutes with her? Afterward I promise I'll be out of your hair."

"Take your time."

"Thanks."

Abbott went inside. Ignacio stood in silence, looking down at Camaro, until finally she said, "What?"

"I thought we had an agreement about not killing anybody."

"They came into the house. I didn't have a choice."

"Maybe you could have left somebody alive to question?"

"That wasn't on the table."

Ignacio nodded. He wandered the patio. He touched the worn equipment and took in the weights. He passed under the pipe in the ceiling, grabbed it with a hand, and yanked. The metal didn't shift. "You got a real setup here," he said. "This where you trained Faith?"

"Yeah."

"Hey, what is this thing? I've seen it in a million kung fu movies. It's like some kind of wooden scarecrow."

"It's called a *muk yan jong*. It's a Chinese practice dummy."

"I didn't know you did all that kung fu stuff."

Camaro shrugged.

"I guess they do a little of everything in those cages where you fight. Got to hurt, punching this wood."

"It hurts to punch anything."

"True enough."

"You want to talk about my equipment all night?"

"No, I'm just warming you up."

"I'm warmed up."

"You got some people on the street talking about how this isn't the first time something like this has happened around here. You know I'm not gonna bother you about it, but there are a lot of cops around, a lot of detectives, and one might listen."

"You can charge me for it if you want."

"I would have charged you by now if I was going to. Besides, Rosales isn't dead, so it's not my department. But you might want to take it down a notch if you want to live in this city. When you're dropping bodies in your house..."

"I didn't choose what happened tonight."

"I believe it. But you and I both know this isn't a home invasion. I saw the guns on the floor in there. High-tech and high-powered, exactly like the kind Serafian had in his place. Those guys were kitted out like commandos. They weren't kids looking to grab some stuff they could sell and maybe introduce themselves to the lady of the house."

Camaro didn't answer. She rubbed her knuckles. Ignacio saw that each was marked with light but visible scars.

"I'm trying to put this all together. It has to do with Faith, that much I know for sure. Once we find out who these guys were, everyone will know. And I mean *everyone*."

"How many people are in this?"

"Too many. I got a guy from the FBI who specializes in terrorism, I got a lady agent from the DEA who I can't figure out at all, and I've got my own department wanting to clear the case as fast as possible. I figure I got a couple of days, tops, before my captain tells me to hand this off to the feds. They're all over Faith. Now they're gonna be all over you."

Camaro glanced toward the darkened backyard. Ignacio saw something unpleasant pass across her face, but he didn't think it had to do with the dead men inside. It was a melancholy look he hadn't seen before.

"I didn't do anything," Camaro said.

"Not this time, but how far do you want them to dig? They're going to wonder about you. They're going to ask questions about how you got mixed up with Faith Glazer in the first place. And if they ask *too* many questions, they might start asking me about how we go back."

"Are you afraid?"

"Hell, yes, I'm afraid. I'm sticking my neck out for you. It doesn't take a master detective to figure out I've done it before. So we have to make good on this as fast as we can. Otherwise it's turtles all the way down."

Camaro seemed to consider this. She stared at the concrete at her feet. She lifted her gaze to Ignacio's. "So it's 'we'?"

"I don't think there's any other option. Eight to five says the two dead bodies in there are Armenians. I don't know what they want or where they came from, but that's my gut talking. And if it turns out they *are* Armenian, this means the same people after Faith are after you. Maybe because they think she told you something, or you're involved somehow."

"Involved in what? If I'm going to be in this, I need to know."

Ignacio checked the back door. Neither Fletcher nor Abbott appeared. "All right, I'm gonna tell you like they told me. And then we're gonna fix this."

157

CHAPTER THIRTY-NINE

IT WAS QUIET in the house. Ignacio was gone, and with him the other detectives and all the technicians and uniformed cops. The bodies had been zipped into rubber bags and carted off. Only the bloodstains remained, and the tattered carcass of her sofa, the remnants of which were scattered over every surface in the room.

Camaro waited until she was absolutely certain no one was coming back. While the cops were there, she was dressed in sweats and bare feet. Now she changed into jeans and a T-shirt worn a little too long to hide the .45 on her hip. She nestled the karambit in its place in her left boot. She swept her hair back into a ponytail, checked herself in the mirror one time, and left the house.

The morning sun was intense as it cleared the ocean and lanced across the low-lying expanse of Miami. The night's humidity worsened as the air heated. The whipping wind on her arms as she rode her bike kept sweat from her bare skin, but she felt the heat on her back.

She rode to the hospital. Inside it was twenty degrees colder than it was outdoors. She didn't need to ask for directions. She made her way to Faith's room directly. Questions churned in the back of her mind, driven by things Ignacio had said when they were alone.

She opened the door to the room and knew immediately Faith wasn't there. A different scent lingered in the air, a tang of age and infirmity. She saw the old man lying in the bed where Faith had been. He was asleep, monitored by three different machines and fed oxygen through a tube in his nose.

Camaro headed down the hallway to the nurses' station. A round-faced Asian nurse spotted her. "May I help you, miss?"

"Down the hall," Camaro said. "A patient. Faith Glazer. Where was she moved?"

"Ms. Glazer? She wasn't moved. She was discharged."

"On her own?"

The nurse nodded. "Her injuries weren't life-threatening, and the doctor felt she was able to care for herself."

"When did this happen?"

"Last night. Is there something I—"

Camaro walked away. She took the stairs instead of the elevator, stalked across the lobby, and burst out into the parking lot. Back on the bike, she skidded the rear tire pulling away, and headed south once she hit the road.

It took too long for her to reach Faith's apartment. She rolled into an open spot next to Faith's car, sitting undisturbed in its place. Camaro crossed the lot. The police tape on Faith's door had been torn down and was hanging in streamers from the frame. The door itself had been replaced. Camaro banged her fist on it.

No one answered. Camaro tilted an ear toward the door, but there was no sound. She tried the knob. It turned in her hand.

She drew the .45 and held it low, ready. She stepped to one side, bumped the door wide with her left hand. The front room was visible, furniture still overturned or destroyed. No one had done any cleaning. The new door had yet to be painted, the wood bare.

"Faith?"

Nothing disturbed the silence. Camaro glanced around the edge of the door, got a snapshot of the hallway and the dining area. No one.

It took seconds to clear the kitchen. In the bedroom, the closet was open. Camaro remembered seeing luggage in there before, but now those bags were gone. Faith's things were scattered, and it was impossible to tell what was missing and what was not. She cleared the bathroom.

159

Ignacio answered the phone right away when she called him. "She's gone," Camaro told him without preamble.

"Faith?"

"She left the hospital last night, and her apartment is abandoned. It looks like she packed some things and left. Her car's still parked outside, so she had to have taken a cab."

"Or a Lyft," Ignacio said. "I'll see what I can scare up on my end. But if she left last night, she has hours of head start on us. She could have gone to the airport easy."

"I'm going to look around some more," Camaro said. "I'll call you back if I find something."

"Hey, don't touch anything, okay? If she's gone, that means Mansfield and Pope are right behind her. They'll want to know why you were there and what you were doing. If you don't want to answer those kinds of questions, don't give them a reason to ask."

"I can handle it."

"Sure, sure. Keep me posted."

They ended the call. Camaro cast her gaze around the room, looking for something she hadn't seen before. She turned in a full circle. She stopped. "Goddamn it," she said.

She prowled the apartment. It was all the same. In the dining area she looked at the fallen pictures, punched out of their frames. Something itched at the back of her mind. She turned away, went to the front room, scanned the empty walls and the broken leavings of Eduard Serafian.

"To hell with this," Camaro said to no one. She left.

CHAPTER FORTY

FAITH USED MAKEUP to hide the worst of the bruises, and a large pair of sunglasses completed the disguise. She took a room on the third floor of the Avalon Hotel, with a view of Ocean Drive and the beach beyond. Two large beds took up most of the space. The desk was a miniature, but it was possible to sit and look out the window at the same time. Faith didn't mind the imposition.

She had unpacked her suitcases and made use of the room's dresser and closet. She did not want to live out of bags. She stowed the cases in the closet and put a heavy backpack on the foot of one of the beds. She extracted a laptop and an external DVD-R drive. She set up on the desk, attached the drive. She returned to the bag.

Inside she had thick binders of printouts, all on green-and-white-striped paper of the sort fed through an ancient dot-matrix printer. The printer and the workstation where she produced the printouts were buried deep in the bowels of M&I Bank and Trust in an area no one seemed to frequent for any reason. She'd been shocked to discover that the equipment still worked, even the decrepit PC. Getting access to the files she wanted was easier from that terminal, and didn't leave the footprints her personal machine did.

The printouts went into one of the drawers, beside her underthings. She shut them away. Back at the computer, she logged in to the hotel's free wireless internet and turned on a virtual private network to disguise her IP address. When that was done, she accessed a cloud storage site through an account not in her name, and scrolled through the files she had there. Everything in the printouts was replicated electronically, shuttled through the ancient bank workstation that time forgot, processed by her laptop before being squirreled away online.

She had two more backups, each on a different cloud storage service. These she never accessed using her own machine, even with the VPN active. To reach those, she needed a third party's internet access. Even a public library's computer would do.

She opened one of the files at random, copied a section of data from it. She pasted these numbers into a new spreadsheet. None of it was anything a layperson would recognize. Strings of numbers and attached dollar values. Faith knew what they meant, and she knew she wouldn't have to explain anything to the person she was about to contact.

The spreadsheet went into an encrypted archive. She attached it to an e-mail sent via an anonymous remailer. In the body of the e-mail she wrote, "I know what you're doing. Here is proof. Answer me with a post on r/movies and you'll get the password. You will not find me. Don't look."

Faith considered the words. She excised a sentence before putting it back. She tinkered with the wording, but decided it was better as it was. She sent the e-mail. She took a long, shuddering breath. She closed the laptop.

When she got out of the chair, her legs trembled. She walked to the window and looked out on the beach. It was easy to tell the tourists from the locals as they walked through the Art Deco District. The tourists had to take pictures of everything, and half the time they were sunburned and unhappy-looking. The locals moved past the old hotels without sparing them a glance. They'd seen them so many times the buildings were simply a part of the landscape. As Faith watched, she saw a man and a woman snap a selfie across the street from the Avalon. The picture would be terrible. They should wait until dark, because that's when the district came alive.

She went to the backpack, deflated and empty without its cargo. She unzipped one of the front pockets. Her hand closed around the grip of her Glock. She brought it out, and for a while she did nothing but stare at the ugly, functional blockiness of the weapon. Nothing had changed about it since the night she killed the man. She hadn't even reloaded it. The police returned it to her in a plastic bag. The first thing she did was throw the bag away and put the slide of the gun against her nose to smell the spent gunpowder. The scent was powerful, acrid. It brought memories of the moment the man died.

Faith looked at the bed. She stowed the gun under the pillow, thought better of it. She remembered how it had fallen between the bed and the wall when the man came for her. She opened the drawer of the nightstand to reveal a Gideon Bible with a green leatherette cover. She took the Bible out and put the pistol in. She dropped the Bible on the floor and kicked it under the bed. She looked at the gun one last time before she shut the drawer.

The DO NOT DISTURB door hanger was on the inside of her door. She put it on the outside before placing a call to the front desk and saying she was not to be bothered by anyone, including housekeeping. She was trying to get some rest before a big day with clients, she said. The man on the other end of the line didn't seem to care one way or another. She hung up satisfied.

She lay down on the bed and tried to put her forearm over her eyes. It hurt too much. She cupped her hands over her face instead and saw shadows. After a while she wept, and when she was done, she rolled onto her side and slept.

CHAPTER FORTY-ONE

IGNACIO'S PHONE RANG. He answered. "This is Reggie Silva from forensics," said the man on the other end.

"Silva," Ignacio said. "Hey, you're not related to Don Silva, are you? Worked homicide for thirty years?"

"Yeah, that's me. I'm his son."

"I don't even want to know how old you are. I'll only feel like I'm a hundred. Say hello to your old man for me."

"I will. Hey listen, Detective Fletcher asked me to call you if I got a hit on one of her DBs from last night."

Ignacio started. He gripped the phone tighter. "You did? Tell me the guy's Armenian."

"How did you know that?"

Ignacio pushed his mouse and stirred his computer to life. "What's the guy's name?"

"Michael Bamanian."

"Bamanian? Where'd you get the hit?"

"Through the Department of Defense. The guy's an immigrant from Turkey. Came over in the '90s and joined the army. Get this: he was Special Forces. I'll bet he got up to all kinds of stuff over there."

"Over where?"

"You know... Over there."

"Sure, sure. Is he local?"

"He is. Got his Florida driver's license about six years back when he left the service. You should be able to take it from there."

"I'm already on it. Hey, thanks, Reggie. You're all right."

"Take care, Detective."

Ignacio called up Bamanian's record. He saw a photograph of the man. Bamanian had square features and a nose that looked as though it had been pounded into his face. His hair was cut military short, and he glared at the camera as if he were about to lunge.

A search for additional records called up the man's service history. Some of it was freely accessible by law enforcement. Chunks were missing, with a notation to contact a representative of the United States Army for information. "Black bag," Ignacio muttered to himself. The man had time in Iraq and Afghanistan, along with several other ports of call. He'd been pretty much everywhere the military put a boot down.

He went further. Calling up employment data via the Social Security Administration, Ignacio saw that Bamanian had been self-employed for the entirety of his six years in Florida. His business was called MB Security and was a sole proprietorship. Digging into the state's records gave Ignacio still more information, this time about employees of MB Security. Bamanian never had more than six people working under him at any given time. Ignacio chased down the employees he found, but none of them was Eduard Serafian.

He rubbed his eyes. He felt pressure in his temples. When his phone rang again, he jumped.

"Detective Montellano, Homicide Unit."

"Montellano, this is Special Agent Mansfield."

Ignacio looked skyward and gestured with his free hand. The supplication did nothing. "Agent Mansfield. What can I do for you?"

"I thought you should know Faith Glazer checked herself out of her hospital room last night against medical advice."

"Did she? That's terrible. I didn't know."

"I'm in her apartment right now. She left the door wide open. There's no sign of her."

"I don't know where she might be," Ignacio said. "No one called me. I haven't heard anything."

"Detective, did you discuss with anyone the details we shared with you the other day?"

Ignacio planted his feet firmly on the ground and straightened up before he spoke. "No, sir, I did not," he said.

Mansfield paused. Ignacio waited. "Okay," Mansfield said. "I wanted to make sure. Because we made our move and it seems to have spooked Glazer into running. I should have expected it, but I honestly didn't think she'd break. I suppose killing someone can make you do a lot of crazy things."

"That's true," Ignacio replied.

"I only ask about outside parties being made privy to our investigation because one of the neighbors recalls seeing a woman stop by Glazer's apartment this morning. I think you know what I'm going to say next."

"Camaro Espinoza."

"Normally I'd assume this is a harmless coincidence, and it's a friend meeting a friend, but when I made a call to your department to get some information about Ms. Espinoza, I found out she murdered two people in her living room last night."

"'Murder' is a strong word," Ignacio said. "It's more like self-defense."

"Are you working the case?"

"No, but I have an interest. A guy tries to kill Faith Glazer, two other guys try to kill Camaro Espinoza. Maybe it's a coincidence."

"Coincidences have a tendency to turn out to be connections in my experience. I'd like to know if you know where Camaro Espinoza is right now."

"Honestly? I have no idea. I haven't talked to her since last night."

"This is getting ugly, Detective. People are dying. If you know something, I need to know it."

"Believe me, the very first thing I'd do is tell the FBI everything. If this has to do with terrorism, then it's way above my pay grade. But it'd be nice to know the whole story."

"You'll be briefed when the time is right. First let's concentrate on finding Faith Glazer and Camaro Espinoza. Get in contact with me or Special Agent Pope the minute you learn anything."

"Yes, but—"

"The *minute,* Detective. We don't have time for games."

"No, sir. No games. I'll be in touch."

Ignacio hung up the phone. He picked it up again and dialed Camaro's number. "I haven't found her," she said when she answered.

"That's not why I'm calling. Well, not completely. Listen, we need to get together somewhere. Somewhere we're not gonna be noticed."

"You know Club Deuce in South Beach?"

"That place is a dive."

"Meet me there in an hour."

"Keep a low profile," Ignacio said. "They're watching for you now."

CHAPTER FORTY-TWO

THERE WAS NOTHING new about Club Deuce. It looked as though it had been built in the '50s or '60s and put in suspended animation for the next few decades. It had a double bar with ashtrays scattered on them, pool tables, and lots of neon. Mirrors on the wall made the place seem marginally larger than it was, and everything else was painted flat black. The only concession to modernity was an ATM tucked beside a door violated with a garish *Reservoir Dogs* poster.

Camaro sat at the far end of one of the U-shaped bars, close to the wall. She had the bartender line up three shots of whiskey. A cold beer stood ready to quench the fire. When she saw Ignacio enter, she downed the first shot, and sipped from her beer. She waved him over.

"Little early in the day to be drinking the hard stuff," Ignacio said when he sat. The bartender approached. "I'll take a club soda. With lime."

"I drink because it makes other people interesting," Camaro told him.

"I'm flattered."

"No, not you."

"Okay, then."

"What do you have?" Camaro asked.

"I have a name for one of the goons who busted into your place last night: Michael Bamanian. He's an Armenian who came here twenty years back and went into the army. Some of the stuff he was into, we'll never know. But lately he's been working private security."

"For who?"

168

"That part comes next. But I'm willing to bet this guy Bamanian brought over some of his Armenian buddies to do jobs off the books. These security guys, they have up-front clients, but they take money on the side. Maybe they hire out as muscle. Anywhere there's some cash in it. And these people like Serafian, who don't have any history at all? They are definitely in business for hard money. No credit cards, no paychecks."

Camaro downed a second shot. She chased it with beer and thought, watching the bubbles rise in her glass. "Okay," she said. "How does this fit with Faith?"

"I'm not sure, but I have ideas. Faith, she gets a look at some financial records she's not supposed to see. She does something she shouldn't. Maybe she makes copies. Maybe she tries to blackmail somebody over it. That's the hazy part. What she doesn't know is, the people she stole from, they have tabs on her already. They decide to take her out."

"That's why Serafian searched her place," Camaro said. "To find what she had."

"Yeah, but even I know somebody like Faith isn't gonna hide information on a secret disc or something. She might have a hard copy somewhere, but it'd be in a safe place. Everything else would be somewhere she could get at it, but no one else could. Because she's one of those computer nerd types, right? I don't even keep files on my computer at home. It's all in the cloud thing."

"The cloud thing," Camaro repeated.

"You know what I mean. Or maybe you don't. You know anything about computers?"

"I know you have to replace them all the time."

Ignacio sighed. The bartender brought him a club soda and put it on a square of napkin. A slice of lime was run through with a toothpick festooned with little plastic streamers. Ignacio pulled the slice free and squeezed it out. He pushed the crushed lime down to the bottom without thinking about what he was doing. Then he remembered Camaro doing the same thing. "This is not the kind of work I'm cut out to do," he said after he drank.

"People are dead. It's your job to find out why."

"Yeah, I know. But usually it's real simple. Guy kills his girlfriend. Girlfriend kills her boyfriend. Junkies fight over who gets the last hit. Gangbangers shoot it out for a corner somewhere. This kind of stuff is like Eliot Ness or something."

"Who's Eliot Ness?"

Ignacio covered his eyes. "I am so old."

Camaro prodded. "I'm kidding."

"Don't kid. I'm not in any shape for it."

She downed her last shot. Her stomach felt like a simmering flame. She drained her beer and motioned to the bartender for another. "So what do we do?"

"You don't have *any* idea where Faith might have gone?"

"I didn't know her that well. And you said it yourself: she could be anywhere. She didn't have to stay in Miami. But..."

"But what?"

Camaro shrugged. "It's something somebody told me once. People like to stick with what's familiar. They go back to the same places again and again. The same people. Sometimes all you have to do is knock on a few doors and there they are."

"Sounds like somebody has some experience with this."

"Some. But I'm a charter-boat skipper, okay? I'm not a detective."

"That kind of thing might work with someone who doesn't know you, but not with me." Ignacio saluted her with his glass. "Cheers."

The bartender brought Camaro a fresh beer. She pushed bills across the bar. "Keep an eye out for me," she said to Ignacio.

"Yes, ma'am."

"These people tried to kill me," Camaro said. "They'll try again."

"I believe it."

"So what do we do about it?"

"We find Faith and we figure out what the hell is going on. And I mean *for real*. Everything so far has been guesswork. And it has to be done pronto. Which is more for you than me, because nobody's tried to kill me in the last twenty-four hours."

He raised his glass again. Camaro put her hand over it and pushed it to the bar. "You're going to need something stronger than that," she said.

"I'm on duty."

"We both are," Camaro said. She picked up her beer. "Cheers."

CHAPTER FORTY-THREE

CARLOS LORCA WAS a Colombian. He had never thought of himself as anything else. He had no desire to be anything else. He was Colombian, and Colombia was where he would live and die. He had never been outside the borders of his country.

He stood in the brilliant green field and looked at the coca plants growing in perfect cultivated rows under the bright yellow sun. There were periodic rains to refresh these lands, and with the climate so regular it was possible to grow coca all year long. His first job as a little boy was to harvest the leaves of plants exactly like these. Now he was content to let others do the work.

Behind him were open-sided tents where the hardest work was done: sorting product and ensuring that it was ready for the next step. That was done a half hour's drive away, in buildings disguised with camouflage netting, known only to Lorca and a handful of other men. The transformation of leaf to cocaine was something akin to magic, at least to Lorca's eyes. The money that came from its manufacture was as magical as the rest.

It was quiet, with none of the workers talking to one another during the height of the day. There were sounds of nature, of animals who didn't care for the doings of human beings, but nothing betrayed a hint of civilization. He liked it here, much better than in Barrancabermeja. The city was dirty and noisy and crowded, and even money and influence couldn't shut out completely what transpired in the streets.

He heard the swishing of boots in the grass and turned toward the sound. Daniel Parilla was a young captain, and the closest person to Lorca besides his wife. "Daniel," Lorca said, "you don't look happy."

"I received a disturbing telephone call, General."

"Disturbing how?"

"Word from Miami."

"From Kaur?"

"No. From someone else."

Lorca's brows knit. "Tell me."

Parilla took a breath. "The initial contact came yesterday. An e-mail to one of our accounts. The person who wrote it said he had information we wanted. He asked us to communicate with him via an online bulletin board. Our people reached out."

"And?"

"This person, whoever he is, knows our operation. He has access to files taken from the bank in Miami. He shared a sample in a direct message, and the numbers check out. He says he knows exactly how the money is going into our accounts and exactly how it's being cleaned. He also says he's willing to destroy all his records if we agree to a deal."

Lorca looked away. He watched the bowed forms of white-clad workers in the field filling woven baskets with coca leaves. "Blackmail," he said simply.

"Yes. One million dollars deliverable to an overseas account of his choosing. But it doesn't stop there."

"He wants more?"

"He's offering us more."

Lorca turned back to Parilla. The man shifted on his feet. They both wore green fatigues, but without insignia. Parilla's cap was pulled low over his eyes. His fatigues seemed wilted.

"If there is more to this, I must know everything," Lorca said.

"This man with our information, he says we have a problem. One which will pay much more than a million dollars if corrected. But his price is another million."

"Two million dollars."

"Yes."

Lorca shook his head. "This isn't a man. It's the woman. Unless she made a deal with someone else, this is entirely her doing. Kaur hasn't managed to contain her, and now she's made her way back to us. You can't say she isn't brave. I would skin my own brother if he took two million dollars from me. And now we're expected to hand it over without argument?"

"I'm sorry, General. If I could—"

Lorca waved the words away. He turned his back on Parilla again, and stood watch over the field for several minutes. Parilla waited in the heat. Lorca was not quick to speak. He thought instead, and each thought brought him closer to a defined conclusion. "Someone is stealing from us," he said.

"What?"

"It's the only thing it could be. This woman who has access to our accounts, she knows what goes in and she knows what comes out. Someone with this kind of access cannot help but notice if money goes missing. She's in a prime position to see everything, even those things which must remain hidden."

"What do you want me to do, sir? She says we have three days to make up our minds, and then the payment must be delivered. One million buys us secrecy, but two million will reveal the rest."

Lorca held up a hand for silence. "I want you to put our people on it and find out everything you can about this woman. There has to be more than we've gotten so far. Where is she? Who is she exactly? All of it. I want to know who I'm dealing with."

"But sir, it's all anonymous."

"Nothing is anonymous on the Internet! We pay people to find out these things, so let them earn their money for once. In the meantime, I want to hear what the banker has to say. Bring me the sat phone."

"He'll tell you nothing. Even if he knows the woman is trying to deal with us, he won't say a word."

"He already knows we're aware of his bungling. He doesn't know how far it's gone, but he has to be frightened of what might come of his mistakes."

"I'll bring you the phone immediately."

"And Daniel?"

"Yes, General?"

"Not a word to anyone about this. Tell only those people who must know something, and even then tell them as little as possible. Containment is the issue now. We mustn't let this get out of our control."

"Yes, General. Of course, General."

Parilla walked away through the grass. Lorca listened to the footsteps recede. He clasped his hands behind his back and took deep breaths. He was calm.

CHAPTER FORTY-FOUR

SHE SLEPT ON the boat because she didn't want to stay in the house. She made certain her gun safe was secure, checked all the doors and windows, locked herself out, and drove her truck to the marina. Behind the wheel of the big red crew cab she felt embraced, and the steady flow of air-conditioning kept off weather that grew stickier by the day. It could not help but rain soon, and it would be torrential.

The boat had a small bathroom with a shower. Camaro washed and changed into fresh clothes. She had already thrown away the bloody T-shirt from the night before. Sitting in the galley area, she removed the dressing on her arm and checked the stitches before re-dressing the wound. On the way she made a detour to a pharmacy, armed with prescriptions for pain pills and antibiotics. She didn't bother with the painkillers, but the antibiotics were essential.

There was little in the way of food on board, so she went to a nearby diner and had a plate of scrambled eggs, sausage, ham, and bacon, along with a short stack of pancakes. When she was full, she went to a small family-owned grocery store half a block away and bought provisions for the boat. Back in the galley, she stocked the tiny refrigerator and the cabinets.

It was early afternoon when Ignacio called. She sat in the fighting chair on the afterdeck and took the call. "How are you holding up?" Ignacio asked.

"I'm fine. You don't need to worry about me."

"Okay."

"You got something?"

"Yeah. Bamanian left a pretty easy paper trail to follow. I told you he was doing private security work? Well, I got an address and an appointment to talk with someone over there. Seems like no one knows the man's dead, which works to our advantage."

"They won't know to hide everything," Camaro said.

"You got it. I'm gonna head over there today and put the question to them. I'll figure out who Bamanian was working for in a hurry."

"You hope," Camaro said.

"Well, yeah. There aren't any guarantees."

Camaro looked out over the marina. It was still, the shapes of a dozen boats shifting subtly in the water. The ocean was never totally calm. Not even here. "I want to come."

Ignacio didn't answer.

"I said I want to come."

"I heard you. I'm wondering how badly I want to get into trouble."

"Where's the trouble? I'm an interested client. I have a security issue to take care of. Somebody broke into my house and tried to kill me."

"That's very funny," Ignacio returned. "I'm talking about me being a cop and you being a woman with a stack of bodies on her resume."

"Is that still bothering you?"

"Are you kidding? Did you miss the part about me being a cop?"

"Not every cop goes nuts when bad guys die."

"You know that from long experience?"

"I've been around."

"I'm not sure I want to take this relationship to the next level."

"We're not going out on a date. This is life-and-death stuff."

"Okay, listen: I'll agree to let you tag along, but I'm the only one who talks. You said yourself you're not a detective, so don't make a career change while I'm doing my thing. This is my favor to you, because I don't like the idea of people I know getting rubbed out on my watch."

"I feel loved," Camaro said.

"One more thing," Ignacio added. "I need you to look the part.

Detectives do their jobs, it's jackets and ties. Or at least ties. So I can't have you looking like you just came in from cutting bait."

"I know how to dress myself."

"I didn't say you couldn't. I'm only saying maybe you can be a little less...you. Know what I'm saying?"

Camaro sighed. "Tell me where you want to meet."

"Bamanian's office is on Biscayne Boulevard south of El Portal. I've got an appointment for two o'clock. Can you make it in time?"

"Is this where you ask me how long it takes a woman to get ready?"

"No judgments. Can you make it?"

"Sure. But I'm telling you right now I have a charter tomorrow. I have to keep paying the bills. We have to work around it."

"Do what you have to do, and I'll do what I have to do."

"See you at two."

Camaro ended the call. She spent a few more minutes watching the quiet in the marina. She left the fighting chair and locked up the cabin and disembarked. Once she was in her truck, she drove to Bayside Marketplace. She parked in a spot far away from the mall entrance, back where the summer crowd thinned out and she could see all sides of the vehicle.

She went to three shops. She bought a rose-colored jacket and skirt with a pearl blouse and a subtle bra. The second shop got her shoes to match. In the third shop she bought makeup that cost too much. The salesgirl had tried to get her to find the perfect shade of lipstick and eye shadow, but Camaro picked what looked the best at a glance and moved on.

The mall had a family restroom as big as her living room. She locked herself in and stripped off her jeans and shirt. She put her gun and karambit on the counter by the sink before changing into the new outfit. The shoes had a small heel and weren't perfectly comfortable. She forced herself to stand in them while she applied makeup in the mirror. She poked herself in the eye once with the eyeliner.

When she was done, she examined herself. She fluffed her hair and let it fall around her shoulders. She tried pulling it back, but decided against it. She turned left and right and shook her head. She put the gun on underneath the jacket and parted with the karambit, stuffing it into the plastic shopping bags with everything else.

She headed out past a waiting family of three, and consulted a map before zeroing in on a hair salon near the heart of the mall. "Do you want any particular stylist?" the girl at the desk asked.

"Anybody who can see me now."

"I think Bailey can. Right over there."

Bailey looked like a teenager and had hair shot with pink. She had gauges in her ears, and the piercing in her nose matched two in her lower lip. She enthused over Camaro's hair. "Do you want me to cut it shorter? Give it more volume?"

"I need to look like I work in an office," Camaro replied.

"Okay, but I think I'm going to leave it long. It's too good to shorten."

Camaro was patient for over an hour. She was styled and shampooed and blow-dried, and Bailey put something in her hair smelling of apples. When Camaro looked at herself, she saw someone else behind lipstick and blush. "Good," she said.

"Job interview?" Bailey asked.

"No," Camaro replied. She got up and paid and left Bailey a 30 percent tip.

CHAPTER FORTY-FIVE

SHE SAW IGNACIO'S car in the parking lot of the building on Biscayne. She checked her watch. It was ten minutes before two. She killed the truck's engine and got out. As she approached Ignacio's car, he put down his window. He had his air-conditioning at full blast. "You been here long?" Camaro asked him.

"Me? No. I'm waiting for a friend of mine. You might have seen her around. She dresses kind of rough, jeans and boots. Maybe you spotted her somewhere?"

Camaro rolled her eyes. "Go ahead and laugh."

Ignacio chuckled. "You look great. Get in. I want to go over my game plan."

She got in on the passenger side. It was frosty. Ignacio turned the blower down two notches. "You trying to hang meat?" Camaro asked.

"I don't like sweating. I'm a big man. Big men sweat."

Camaro looked through the windshield at the three-story building. It had stucco walls with a pinkish look about them, and green eaves. There was an insurance company on the first floor, and an HVAC business. She scanned the windows of the upper floors, but they were impenetrable in the bright afternoon sun.

"Second floor, in case you're wondering," Ignacio said. "I swung by there about an hour ago and had a peek. Everything seems normal. Nobody's trying to run. Or at least the receptionist is in."

"So how do you want to do it?"

"Like we talked about: I take the lead and you follow. I'll introduce you, but I won't give them a name. You keep quiet and listen. They probably won't even notice you're there. You pay attention to anything out of the ordinary. People acting like they have something to hide. Maybe something that shouldn't be there."

"Like what?"

"It could be anything. This is what being a detective is all about: noticing details."

Camaro nodded. She saw a car pull up and a man in a golf shirt get out. He went into the insurance company's office.

"I figure we'll be in and out fast unless I can get them to give up something without a warrant. Some people, they clam up when the cops come and you have to get a writ for everything. Other people, you play them right, they tell you more than they should."

"What if we get separated?" Camaro asked.

"If that happens, *do not* go breaking into anything or talking to people you shouldn't. And try not to snap somebody's arm. Or neck."

"I'll do what I can, boss."

"Good. Let's do this."

They got out of the car together. Camaro stumbled once in her shoes. She saw Ignacio notice. They took the stairs to the second floor, passed a law office and a chiropractor before reaching the door to Bamanian's business. The stenciling on the door simply said OFFICE. "Great name," Camaro said.

"Lot of thought went into that one," Ignacio agreed.

She let Ignacio lead. The office was larger inside than she expected, with a reception area and outlets in three directions, two with closed doors and the other open. Camaro heard a radio playing somewhere deeper in the place. They were listening to KISS 99.9.

Ignacio showed his identification to the young woman behind the high reception counter. She had the same olive complexion as Bamanian, and the same extremely dark hair. They may have been siblings, or close cousins. Her gaze flicked from Ignacio to Camaro to Ignacio again. Camaro felt herself recede from the receptionist's perception, like an object in eclipse.

"Detective Ignacio Montellano," Ignacio announced. "I have an appointment with Todd Tate for two o'clock."

"You're right on time."

"I try to be."

"I'll let him know you're here."

She got on the phone. Camaro stepped away. The waiting area had four chairs, a small table wedged between them. A stack of old magazines waited for the bored. Camaro looked at the walls. The pictures hanging were all abstract pastels. She suspected that they were bought in volume for offices exactly like this one.

Ignacio moved behind her. He spoke in a low voice. "Very nice. Keep it low-key."

"Who is this Tate guy? He doesn't sound Armenian."

"He's not, as far as I know. Ex-marine, has some commendations. Nothing weird about him."

"You think he knows what Bamanian was into?"

"We'll find out."

"Detective!"

Camaro saw a man appear in an open doorway. He wore his sleeves rolled up and a red and gold Marine Corps tie with a crisp white shirt. His hair was thinning heavily, but he cropped it as short as Bamanian had.

Ignacio stepped forward with his hand out. "Mr. Tate," he said. "I'm Detective Montellano and this is my associate. I wanted to ask you some questions."

"Something to do with a client?"

"I think so. Could we talk in your office?"

"Sure, sure." Tate paused on Camaro before moving on as the receptionist had.

"Thanks for agreeing to see me," Ignacio said.

Tate led them through a small warren of offices until they reached one marked with his name. The radio that Camaro heard was on the windowsill. "I only wish Michael was here to take your questions."

"Michael?"

"Michael Bamanian. He's the majority partner in the business. I'm a recent addition."

They went in. Camaro stopped at the door. "Do you have a ladies' room?" she asked.

Ignacio shot her a look. "Of course," Tate said. "Right down the hallway. There's a watercooler outside the door. You can't miss it."

"Thanks," Camaro said. She shrugged at Ignacio and left him behind.

She heard them talking as she walked down the hallway. Bamanian's place had five offices, three of which appeared to be occupied and two devoid of anything save a desk. There were not even chairs for those desks. She stopped to glance around a corner toward the receptionist, but the young woman didn't look her way. Camaro moved on.

Bamanian's office had his name on the door in gold paint. She entered and left the door open just a crack.

He had a flag framed on his wall, but it was one Camaro didn't recognize—a tricolor of red, blue, and orange stripes, arranged horizontally—and pictures from his service days. It was easy to recognize him, even though he didn't have his mustache in all the photos. She had clung to Bamanian while he suffocated. She had felt his last heartbeat.

His desk had a fancy pen set and a leather blotter. His filing cabinets were locked and secured with a steel clasp from top to bottom to keep the drawers from being forced. He had a computer and a printer-fax combination tucked away in the corner of his work space.

Camaro checked the desk drawers. They were unlocked, except for the lap drawer, and Camaro had no blade to pry with. She cursed under her breath. She found a drawer stacked with invoices. She put them on the blotter and turned to the computer. It was secured with a password.

She went back to the invoices. Each was tagged with a date and an account number, the name and address of the responsible party

183

neatly printed. Camaro paged through twenty invoices before she realized what she saw. She backed up and checked again. She took the top sheet, folded it into fourths, and put it in her jacket pocket. The rest of the invoices went back in the desk.

At the door she listened for anything different. Ignacio and Tate still talked. She let herself out and went into the restroom. She stayed inside long enough to flush the toilet and wash her hands. In the hallway again, she poured herself a paper cone of water.

She crumpled the cone and tossed it into the trash. Tate emerged from his office. "Oh, there you are," the man said. "I was checking on you."

Camaro put on a smile. "Sorry I kept you waiting."

"Not at all. I was talking to your partner. You are?"

"Detective Amado," Camaro said. She offered her hand. They shook.

Tate laughed quietly. "I don't meet too many women with your kind of grip."

"I work out."

"CrossFit?"

"Right."

Camaro saw Ignacio standing at the office door, his expression dark. "I was about to tell Mr. Tate the bad news," Ignacio said.

The man turned from Camaro. "Bad news? I thought this was just routine."

"About that," Ignacio said. "Actually, come back to your office. You better sit down."

CHAPTER FORTY-SIX

THEY SAT IN Ignacio's car. "'Detective Amado'?" he said. "What did I say? What were my exact words?"

"What did you want me to do? He needed a name. I gave him one."

"And what happens when he mentions it to someone else? I should never have brought you along."

"Why? So you could give him your hankie and let him cry into it? He didn't tell you anything."

Ignacio scowled. "Comforting victims' friends and loved ones is part of the job."

Camaro looked through the windshield. Heat shimmered on the hood. "I didn't sign up for that. I want to know who my problem is."

"I sense a dead person in my future."

"You have a better idea?"

Ignacio made an aggravated noise. He hit the steering wheel. The horn chirped. He shook his head. "Listen, I represent law and order, okay? So long as you play in my yard, I have no problems, but if you commit a crime with my foreknowledge...you get what I'm saying?"

"You knew what you were getting into."

"That's what they're going to say at my internal affairs review."

"What do you want me to do?" Camaro asked.

"Give me a second to think."

"While you're thinking, look at this."

She gave him the invoice. Ignacio unfolded it on the steering wheel.

"They billed a bank," he said. "So what? And you know this is theft, right? You take things that don't belong to you, it's a crime. Remember what I just said about crimes?"

"Forget that. You didn't know about it. When you were talking to Tate, what did he tell you about their client list?"

"He said it was mostly corporate accounts. Secure facilities. Background checks."

"Nothing about banks," Camaro said.

"No, nothing about banks. Maybe he forgot."

"Then he's an idiot. This is one bill, but there are tons more. I went through a whole stack of invoices, and there are a bunch for this same bank, and this same guy, going back a year. Maybe more than that, if I kept looking. Bamanian had everything locked up, but he left this stuff where anyone could find it. That invoice is from a week ago. Look at the amount."

"I'm looking. Okay, that's a lot of bread. Are they all like this?"

"The amounts go up and down, but they're never cheap."

Ignacio scratched the back of his neck. "The feds told me this was all about banking. Dirty money goes in, and it comes out the other end of the hose perfectly clean. Faith Glazer got hold of that information and started parceling it out in pieces to the FBI. Maybe she was trying to win a good citizen award, or maybe she was looking for a payoff. Either way, she had access to things she shouldn't."

Camaro shifted in her seat until she faced Ignacio. "They find out she's got information. They can't go after her directly without letting anyone in on their secret. They need someone else to handle the hard part."

"Right. And they have a relationship with Bamanian already. He's an outside contractor. He'll do the job without even knowing what it's for."

"Plus he's got these Armenian assholes working for him, so when the bank decides to take it to the next level, they hand that off because they know he'll handle it," Camaro said. "They subcontracted the whole thing. Maybe Serafian was only supposed to watch her, but he had a screw loose they didn't know about."

"Yeah," Ignacio replied. "He snaps. Oh, man."

Camaro let the silence grow inside the car. The engine hummed. The air conditioner whirred. She was cold. "Can you get these guys?"

"I might. I can get a warrant to search Bamanian's records. We already know what we're gonna find when we look, so we won't have to try too hard. This guy Tate, he's all right. He probably doesn't know anything about what Bamanian did on the side. He won't try to destroy evidence, and even if he does, there have to be backups. Afterward all we have to do is walk right up to this guy... Brandon Roche? This guy Roche at M&I Bank and Trust. He'll have to give us something, or we'll link him to three deaths."

"So how do you want to do it?"

Ignacio waved the invoice. "The first thing I do is send you home. I appreciate what you did in there, but this has officially become too hot to handle. It's bad enough I'm gonna be explaining who Detective Amado is, but now I have to keep the feds from stealing my case. They want the bank. That's fine. I want the guy putting killers on the street. The bank's not my area."

"I have to do something," Camaro said.

"Do you hear what I'm saying? You've done enough. This is not gunning down people in the Everglades and walking away. This is some serious shit—pardon my language—and if you get caught up in it then it's *federal* time. You want to do federal time? They have holes so deep you won't even remember your name by the time you get out."

"You need to stop treating me like I'm somebody you have to take care of."

"I'm not... Listen, right now you're in a good spot. You're clear of anything that went down with Faith, and it's self-defense for the two guys you wasted in your house. But what are you gonna do next? Kill some guy in his office at the bank? It's not gonna happen. From here on out it's boring stuff like handcuffs and court orders.

Go clean up your place. Or, better yet, *move*, because your neighbors hate you."

Camaro frowned. She opened her mouth to speak. Ignacio's phone rang.

"Hold that thought," Ignacio said. He answered. He listened. "Yes, Agent Mansfield, I'm all ears."

CHAPTER FORTY-SEVEN

LAWRENCE KAUR LAY in bed staring at the ceiling. The sun was over the house and headed steadily west, where daylight dissolved into the element of night. He reached for a tumbler of whiskey on his nightstand. "You really ought to try this," he said. "I've been drinking too much of it. It'll be gone soon."

Roche sat up and pulled back the sheets. He sat on the edge of the bed, staring out at the ocean. His back was dark from the sun, a long scar along the line of one shoulder blade, but the muscles underneath were still taut. Neither of them was a young man anymore, but they hadn't lost everything. Roche had the stamina of someone twenty years his junior. "We're wasting time," he said without looking back at Kaur.

Kaur drank. He made a satisfied sound. He sat up. The silk sheets pooled around his waist. He touched Roche's back. "It's going to work out."

"You don't know what I know," Roche said. "If you did, you wouldn't be so sure."

"Then tell me."

"I thought you wanted me to handle it."

Kaur let it go. He left the bed and fished for his boxers on the floor. He put them on and his robe and slippers. He took the empty whiskey tumbler to the bar. The bottle of Macallan sat apart, mostly empty. He weighed the bottle in his hand before opting not to pour another drink. He rinsed the tumbler and set it aside. Roche still sat on the edge of the bed. "It's always been my policy to let you handle the things you're best at doing," Kaur said. "Maybe I leaned on you too heavily sometimes. That's my fault. But if you need to put some of the burden on me, do it. I'm ready for it now."

Roche glanced at him. "How much do you have put away? And I don't mean the funds I took care of for you. How much else is there?"

"Enough. We could take it and disappear. Maybe we couldn't live like kings forever, but if we picked the right country and we invested wisely... there's a lot of opportunity available."

"Investments," Roche said, and he laughed. "No matter where we go, you still try to make deals."

Kaur sat beside Roche on the bed and put his hand on Roche's bare thigh. Naked, Roche was defiantly hairy, his chest a thicket of darkness. He wore a gold medallion engraved with the face of some Southeast Asian figure Kaur never could remember the name of. He leaned close and kissed Roche on the ear. "Money is what keeps us safe and happy," he said. "It's nothing more than that."

"I don't believe you."

"Then don't believe me," Kaur returned. "You want me to admit I like the game? Yes, I like the game. It takes skill and time, but when you get really good at it, there's nothing like it. I couldn't make you understand."

Roche sat still until Kaur became uncomfortable with his stillness. After a long while Roche turned his head toward Kaur. He looked at Kaur with dark eyes. "I think it's time to admit the game is over. It's only a matter of time before Lorca realizes the situation is out of our control. The best we can hope for is to move before he does. Do you understand what I'm saying, Larry? *Listen* to what I'm telling you. Bamanian screwed us. He screwed us both. He missed with the woman and he missed with the other one, too. And he got himself killed in the process. It won't take a master detective to link Bamanian to me, and I am the only thing standing between you and the law."

Kaur tried to smile, but Roche didn't. Kaur frowned instead, and brushed a lock of Roche's hair from his forehead. "Then we'll leave. Once we know there are no other options, we'll go. It'll be the end."

"I've spent years protecting you, Larry," Roche said. "You know if there was more I could do, I would do it."

"I know. We've been playing a long game here. My father played it, and now I'm playing it. But I think even he knew it wouldn't last forever. These things have a limit. And as much as I'd like to pretend otherwise..."

Roche took Kaur's hand. "I'm glad you know it now."

Kaur shook their clasped hands. "Who knows? Maybe you can still kill those two before it gets any worse."

Roche rose sharply from the bed. He ran his hands through his hair and stood naked in front of the windows. "That's exactly what I'm talking about! I'm out of cards to play, Larry. We missed our window of opportunity."

"So Bamanian didn't work out," Kaur said. "There have to be a dozen other contractors like him. A hundred! Get one of them to do the job. It doesn't matter if it's not as neat as we'd like it. Tell me how much they need and I'll make sure they get paid. They take care of our problem and everyone walks away happy."

Roche's face fell. His cheeks were shadowed with a day's beard growth. Hair fell across his forehead again. "No. Our priority needs to be shutting down the operation without undue exposure. Not to the FBI, not to Lorca or the local police. Get things in order and be ready to move when I say. It's the only way I can be sure to keep you alive."

CHAPTER FORTY-EIGHT

CAMARO DROVE IDLY for an hour or more after leaving Ignacio at Bamanian's office. She was cruising through commercial areas and shaded streets, listening to BIG 105.9 at low volume, her mind a hundred miles away.

There was anger. It came first. There was frustration. It passed. Now there was a sense of something about to happen, an expectant quality Camaro could not name.

She stopped outside a bar in a strip mall, its windows blacked out, neon beer signs fighting against the day. She went inside and breathed the unmistakable stink of stale brew and cigarette smoke. Scratchy rock played from speakers in all four corners of what was essentially an open space crowded with places to sit and two pool tables. A few die-hard drinkers were there early, some against the short bar smoking and nursing beers.

The bartender looked her up and down. He wore a black vest over a Victory Motorcycles T-shirt, and a cross the same silver as his hair dangled from a leather thong. He was broad and strong, and his beard was white, too. A second cross glinted in his ear. "You lost, miss?" he asked.

"Huh?" Camaro asked.

"There's a nice tapas place a few blocks east of here."

Camaro shook her head. She took a seat at the bar. "Give me a double Jack and beer back."

The bartender's eyebrows went up. "Yes, ma'am."

Camaro thought while the whiskey poured and the bartender

192

pulled the beer. She ran her finger around the edge of the whiskey glass. She picked it up and put it back. She picked it up again and drank. She quelled the burn with beer. The bartender watched her. "What?" Camaro asked him.

"Bad day at the office?"

"You could say that."

The bartender leaned against his side of the bar. "Business types tend to steer clear of here. We're more a leather and jeans kind of place."

"Okay, leather and jeans. Give me another."

He poured. Camaro didn't knock it back immediately. She had more beer. In the mirror behind the bar she saw herself in the suit jacket, hair and makeup done just so. The floor of the place was dirty and the vinyl of the stool on which she sat was split, the stuffing coming out. Miami had holes like these all over. She had lost count of them.

"Hey, honey," said an old man farther down the bar. "You got a cigarette?"

"I don't smoke."

"Pretty thing like you ought to get your lips around something."

Camaro gave the old man a black look. He and another decrepit drunk enjoyed the joke. "Sorry," the bartender said.

"Comes with the territory."

"I get the feeling this ain't your usual look," the bartender observed. "Am I right about that?"

"Leather and jeans are all right."

The bartender shot a finger gun at her. "Called it. You dressed up for a job interview or something?"

"Or something. Are you bored?"

"Why do you ask?"

"Because you're still talking to me. Whatever your name is."

"It's Amos."

"Camaro."

"No shit? Good to meet you."

They shook hands over the bar. Camaro raised the glass of whiskey and watched lights dance in the liquid before she polished it off. "Another," she said.

"You driving?"

"Yeah."

"Maybe you ought to slow it down."

"Maybe you ought to mind your own goddamned business, Amos."

Amos put his hands up in surrender. "Okay, sorry. But I have the legal responsibility to make sure nobody drives away drunk."

"I'm not drunk. I'm not going to be drunk. I need to take the edge off."

Amos bobbed his head before pouring out a single of Jack Daniel's for Camaro. "Last one for a little while," he said. "If you don't mind. I don't want to see you spread out all over the road in pieces."

Camaro thought to say something. She turned her attention to her beer and sipped at it. The brand was unfamiliar, but it was cold and bubbly. She drank and she rubbed her temple softly. It felt as though something was in there, but wouldn't come out.

"What do you do?" Amos asked.

"Jesus Christ," Camaro said. "What is it with the questions?"

"It's slow," Amos replied. He smiled. "And you seem like a nice lady."

"I'm not. I'm difficult to get along with and I have an anger problem."

"Get that from a shrink?"

"It's what people tell me."

"I can see where they're coming from. But you seem all right to me. Wound up a little, like you're trying to do calculus in your head."

Camaro let the wind sough out of her. "I can't figure something out."

"Maybe you need to bounce it off someone. Hit me."

She looked Amos in the face. He had icy blue eyes. "I'm looking for a woman who has people after her. Who want to kill her. They tried once already and they'll try again if they find her. So I need to get there first."

Amos's eyebrows went up again. "Okay, that's not what I expected."

"I have special problems," Camaro said.

"You a cop? I wouldn't figure you for a cop."

"No, I'm not a cop. And I'm not a secretary or the lady who works in the cubicle next to the watercooler, okay? I saw this place and I thought maybe I could put it all together, you know? Drink. Think. You know how it is."

"I do. Familiar surroundings help people work things out."

Camaro stiffened. Her beer was halfway to her lips. She put it down. "Familiar surroundings," she said.

"Sure. If you like this kind of place, you want to be where you feel comfortable."

"People always stay close to the things they know," Camaro said. She was barely aware of Amos now. "You knock on doors and there they are."

"You want something to eat? We got a guy who can grill you a burger."

"No," Camaro said. She went for her wallet and spilled bills onto the bar. "Keep the change."

Amos swept the money into his hand. "You got what you need?"

Camaro didn't answer. She went straight for the door.

CHAPTER FORTY-NINE

SHE WAITED, REFRESHING the movie subreddit every few minutes, waiting for someone to respond. The sun was low, and the palm trees on Ocean Drive threw long shadows onto the beach. When dusk fell, all the hotels and historical buildings along the water came alive with lights. They transformed into new shapes, luminous creatures deep beneath the surface of the sea.

The reply came. It was one word: "Privately."

The sender had a throwaway account on the site, but all accounts on Reddit were ultimately throwaway. Faith sent a private message with a Skype address for them to contact. The address itself was routed through another anonymizer, and had no direct connection to her anywhere. They could look, but they wouldn't find.

It took another hour and a half for the Skype call to come. Outside it was dark. Faith had only the desk lamp burning. She was surrounded by shadows. She had a piece of masking tape over the camera on her laptop, even though the call was voice only. She answered. "I'm here."

"To whom am I speaking?"

The man's voice had a rich accent, redolent with the sound of wealth and breeding. Faith felt herself gravitate toward his tone, but stopped herself. "It doesn't matter who I am. Besides, I think you already know."

"I know of you, but I don't know you. You have precisely one minute to make your case to me. After that one minute is up, I will end this call and you will be cut off from further communication. I will then have people find you and kill you. Do you understand this?"

Faith forced firmness into her tone. "Yes, I understand. Should I start?"

"The timer is running."

"You don't know me, or what I do, but it's pretty simple: I look for problems in people's accounts. M&I Bank and Trust needed an independent auditor for a tax inquiry. They hired me and a few others. They came and went and never saw anything, but I found you. Large cash deposits to a corporate account with no other activity. No payroll. No insurance. No taxes. The bank took those deposits and put them in the laundry before they sent them on to accounts outside the country."

"You followed all of this?" the man asked.

"Yes. I saw where the money went, and I saw who controlled the cash. I found you, Señor Lorca."

Lorca laughed softly. "They call me El General here in Colombia."

"I don't know anything about it. I don't want to know. The only important thing is you have money and I want some of it. One million dollars and everything I found out about your cash flow disappears. Unless someone goes looking for it, you're safe again. But I'd recommend changing banks."

"Is this because you gave information on my dealings to the FBI?"

Faith caught her breath. "Let's talk about our deal."

"But we have no deal. You want a million dollars to hide the things you found. That is fair. A million dollars is nothing to me. However, you haven't told me anything about the second part of your offer, and your time is almost up."

"Someone's skimming your accounts," Faith said.

"Who?"

"That's what the other million dollars is for. You pay me and I'll give you everything you need to find them. It's solid evidence. It'll stand up in court."

"Courts are an inconvenience. I would rather deal with problems directly. As we are doing now."

"I don't have a lot of time," Faith said. "You need to make up your mind soon. No more than a couple of days. This information is hot, and there are people looking into it."

"Your FBI. Your DEA."

"Yes. They already know some things, and if they get to me before we make a deal, I'll have to make a deal with them instead."

She heard nothing on the other end of the line. Then she heard a musing sound. "I see your conundrum," Lorca said.

"Do we have an agreement?"

"You offered forty-eight hours to respond to your initial communication. I will take the rest now. You'll know my answer by tomorrow. And my answer, señorita, is final. There will be no more bargaining once it is given. This thing you say you will do for me, you will do. I have no patience for people who do not keep their word."

Faith's hands shook. She knotted them together. Her words caught in her throat.

"Are you there?"

Faith coughed. "I can wait. And I'll do what I say I will."

"Then it will be tomorrow. Shall I contact you the same way?"

"No," Faith said too sharply. "I mean, no, I'll send you another account to contact. We'll communicate the same way. Once we have a deal, I'll provide you with account numbers and the amounts to deposit. When the deposits are confirmed, I'll send you the information in an encrypted file. After that you'll never hear from me again."

"You've thought of everything," Lorca said.

"Okay," Faith said lamely. She smacked herself on the forehead.

"It's too bad you didn't think so thoroughly when you first started this game. It might have kept you from getting hurt."

Someone knocked on the door. Faith started. She twisted in her chair. No one called through the closed door. "I have to go," she said.

"We'll speak again soon," Lorca told her.

"Yes. Goodbye."

She terminated the connection. The knock came again.

"Who is it?"

No one replied. Faith rose from the desk and got the gun from the nightstand. She approached the door. There was another knock, softer this time.

"I don't want to be bothered!" Faith said.

Silence. Faith felt the gun waver in her hand. Her palms turned damp. Perspiration rolled down her side beneath her blouse.

She took a step closer. She looked through the peephole.

Camaro Espinoza was outside.

CHAPTER FIFTY

FAITH OPENED THE door. Camaro didn't have to speak. Faith let the gun flop to her side. She stepped back. "Come in, I guess."

Camaro shut the door behind her, turned the lock, and set the chain. Faith put the gun away. Camaro said, "You know, for a smart girl, you're pretty stupid."

Faith sat on the edge of the nearer bed. She put her face in her hands. Camaro waited and watched. Faith's shoulders shook up and down, but she made no sound. When she took her hands away, her eyes were wet and red. She had tears on her cheeks. "I had to run," she said. "I didn't have any choice."

"What did you think was going to happen? The FBI has people who'll protect you. They have that witness program. You're safer with them than you are here. It only took me a few hours to find you, and it wasn't hard."

"How *did* you find me?" Faith asked.

Camaro walked to the window. Colored lights on the Avalon spilled into the street and painted the asphalt with a glowing brush. Traffic picked up as the hour moved toward dusk, both on the road and on the sidewalks. By the time Camaro landed at the Avalon, there were easily twice as many people as when she started. It would build all night.

"Those pictures in your apartment. I didn't think anything about them at the time, but I saw a picture like it in Eduard Serafian's place. It hadn't been up as long as the others, so he must have seen yours and decided to get his own. If there was anywhere in Miami you'd go, it'd be here. All I had to do was ask questions."

"I have to move," Faith said.

"You do," Camaro agreed. "Eventually someone's going to figure out the same thing I did. Maybe it'll take a while, but they'll keep coming and coming until they find you. Or you go so far away they get tired of chasing you."

Camaro looked at the laptop on the desk, and the thick binders of printouts. "Is this the stuff?"

"That's everything," Faith said.

"Where did you keep it?"

"A safe-deposit box. But I have backups online."

"What are you going to do with all of it?"

"I'm going to buy my way out," Faith replied.

"With the feds?"

"No."

Camaro examined Faith's face. The ugliness of the bruise around her eye was still there, but she'd regained some of her color. She didn't shrink from Camaro's look. Camaro didn't speak.

"It's a better deal," Faith said to break the silence.

"How much?"

"One million for me to make the information disappear. Another million to give up the people stealing from them."

"Who's giving you the money? People at the bank?"

Faith shrugged. "I don't know a whole lot. They're Colombian. Some kind of army. I don't know how they get their money, but I figure it has to be drugs. The numbers don't tell me what they sell or how they sell it, but what else could it be? The accounts show me cash coming in. M&I Bank and Trust makes it legitimate. I saw a thing on TV about drug dealers: they have tons of paper money, but they don't have any way to get rid of it. Do you know the government catches the Mexicans taking tons of cash across the border back into Mexico every year? Like, actual *tons*. Cash is hard to move, but once you turn it into ones and zeros, it can go anywhere and do anything."

"People like this will kill you," Camaro said.

"Yeah, I know. But it wasn't them I had to worry about. It was the bank."

"The bank hired the man who attacked you."

"How do you know?"

"I have a friend who's really good at figuring things out. He followed Serafian's tracks. But how did they even know you took what you took?"

Faith looked at her hands.

"What did you do?" Camaro pressed.

"I took money from them," Faith said.

"From who? From the *bank?*"

"There's one man who handles accounts for these Colombians, and his name is Lawrence Kaur. His dad founded the bank, and when he died he handed it over to his son. These Colombians have been doing business with the bank forever. Kaur makes sure they're happy and all the money goes where it's supposed to go. When I found what I found, I thought about it and..."

"You held it over his head."

Faith lifted her gaze. "Yes."

"How did they figure out it was you?"

"That's the part I don't know. I guess I didn't cover my tracks well enough. When they hired me for an audit, they hired five other forensic accountants to do the same thing. If they worked their way through all six of us, especially after the payment was made, they might have been able to narrow it down. And they did. They found me, and they sent that...animal after me."

Camaro paced the room. It was stuffy. She adjusted the thermostat, and the vents blew fresh, cool air. "How much did you take them for? Millions? Like with these Colombian people?"

"No, no. I only asked for two hundred and fifty thousand dollars. I wasn't greedy."

"Did you promise them you'd bury the evidence when they paid you?"

"Yes. I told them, but I didn't do it. I wanted the insurance. In case anything ever happened."

"And it happened," Camaro said.

"It happened."

CHAPTER FIFTY-ONE

IGNACIO FINISHED HIS shift after his time at Bamanian's office. He spent a chunk of his time on the phone talking to an assistant district attorney. The ADA's name was Norma Singleton. He'd met her once or twice. When he asked her to keep it quiet, she agreed. "But it won't stay under wraps forever," she told him. "Eventually someone's going to notice, and it'll be your ass. I'm going to plead ignorance."

"I have plenty of ass."

Singleton didn't laugh. "You'll have your warrant by the morning."

He left his cubicle, got his hat and jacket, and headed for the door. He heard his desk phone ringing. He stopped and waited. The ringer quieted. The phone in his pocket trilled. The number was listed UN-KNOWN. He answered. "Montellano."

"Detective, it's John Mansfield."

"Agent Mansfield. What can I do for you? I'm heading out."

"Do you mind coming down to my office for a get-together? Only a few people. I think you'll find it worthwhile."

"This time of day, it'll take me about an hour to get there."

"We can wait. See you soon, Detective."

Ignacio left the building and went to his car. The interior baked, even in the fading sun. He opened the windows to air out the car while he drove, and when the heat dipped he put them up again and ran the AC. He didn't listen to the radio. He tried calling Camaro. She didn't answer. "Where the hell are you?" he asked aloud.

The FBI's field office was in Miramar on a well-maintained road lined with greenery and surrounded by grounds, like a college campus.

The building itself was a soaring construction, latticed steel and mirrored glass, engineered to seem as if it were blown gently by an offshore breeze. Ignacio had to show his identification at the gate, and again at the door. He asked for directions once he was inside. They sent him to the third floor. He made a wrong turn, and took five minutes to find his way.

It was a conference area with a long oval table and multiple flatscreen displays. One wall was glass, providing a view of the darkening grounds. Mansfield was waiting in the room along with Pope and a handful of other men and women in business dress. There were introductions all around. Ignacio did his best to commit names to memory.

"Everyone have a seat and we can get started," Mansfield said, remaining on his feet. "Unless you need something, Detective? Coffee? Juice? Coke?"

"No, thank you. I have everything I need."

"Detective, everyone in this room represents part of a coordinated task force designed to isolate and destroy certain illegal operations in the United States. Mr. Austin over there is from the U.S. Attorney's office. They have multiple indictments out for a man named Carlos Lorca Márquez, a Colombian national who has never set foot in the United States and is unlikely to. We also have indictments for major figures in his organization. This is where we want to bring you up to speed."

"So it's all about drug money," Ignacio said.

Eyes turned toward Ignacio. He felt himself color. He shifted in his seat. Mansfield nodded. "It is and it isn't. Are you familiar with Colombia's problem with right-wing paramilitaries?"

"I'm not, no."

"Most people aren't. Colombia has been involved in a civil war of sorts for fifty years. The FARC are the communist guerrillas who want to overthrow the government, at least technically, but they are generally more interested in producing cocaine and heroin for sale on the international market. The Colombian authorities are with us, working hand in glove with people like Special Agent Pope to execute Plan Colombia, an ongoing operation meant to cripple Colombia's various drug cartels and related groups from producing the crops they need to stay in business. In a sort of middle ground, you have the paramilitaries. These are people like the AUC, ostensibly dedicated to wiping out the communists, but still dirty. Follow me so far?"

"Is this where terrorism comes in?"

"We'll get to it. I'm going to let Special Agent Pope take over here."

Mansfield sat. Pope stood. She had a remote control the size and shape of a pencil, and she directed it at the displays. The screens flashed pictures of hard-looking men, maps of Colombia overlaid with colored zones and columns of numbers. "Everybody talks a good game in Colombia, but it's really about drugs," Pope said. "Everything comes back to drugs. Colombia is actually second to Peru these days when it comes to producing cocaine, but they're not out of the business. And the AUC pledged to demobilize over ten years to end that part of the conflict."

She pressed a small button on the remote. A bearded man's face appeared. He had the dead expression of a convict. When Ignacio looked at him, the man seemed to stare back.

"This is Lorca. When the AUC agreed to demobilization, that was supposed to be it. The government spent three years helping them shut down and reintegrate into society. The AUC officially disbanded ten years ago, but it was all a smoke screen, because they splintered into new groups. Some of these groups are as strong as the AUC ever was. Lorca's group is the Black Eagles. They are the worst of the worst."

"So this is his money."

Pope gave him a flat look. "That's correct. Some of the accounts we watch are associated with the Black Eagles. Before that the AUC maintained them. Faith Glazer stumbled into it, and she was quick to put two and two together. She started feeding the FBI her information. Which led to my agency and from there to everyone else in this room."

"Detective Montellano, I'm Noah Austin," said one of the men at the table.

"U.S. Attorney's office," Ignacio said.

"Right. Detective Montellano, by itself the discovery of a single account feeding into a single bank is not that big of a deal. The banking industry is riddled with corruption and money laundering schemes to a scale you wouldn't believe. But we don't think the treasure trail stops with this little bit of information. Special Agent Mansfield was brought in because the Black Eagles are a terrorist group who directly threaten our allies by destabilizing the region. Before he came on board, the number crunchers at the Bureau processed the information the informant—"

"Faith Glazer."

"Yes, Faith Glazer. They processed the information Ms. Glazer provided, and there is much more. This is a back door into a larger world. Think of it like the exhaust vent on the Death Star."

"The Death Star," Ignacio said. "And this guy Lorca is Darth Vader, I guess?"

"In layman's terms."

"I think I understand."

"But here's the thing, Detective: unless we have Faith Glazer's evidence in hand, or if we can directly link the bank to criminal malfeasance, we are not in a position to move on this case."

Mansfield spoke up. "What we're trying to ask is this: What do you have for us, Detective? Because we're running out of options."

CHAPTER FIFTY-TWO

FAITH'S EYES WERE alight. "Oh, my God," she said. "Oh, my *God*."

"This is where we are right now," Camaro said. "These people at the bank, they think you told me something, or maybe they think I was working with you all along. It doesn't even matter, because they made up their minds. I'm a target."

"Is that why you're dressed up like an insurance salesman?"

Camaro plucked at the lapel of her jacket and frowned. "I don't think they care what I'm wearing. But I'm in this. *We're* in this. You can't make decisions without affecting me. We need to resolve the problem. Otherwise more people are going to come and I'm going to have to kill them, too."

It was Faith's turn to pace the room. She stopped at the window. Camaro let her take her time. When Faith spoke again, she was calm. "I'm sorry this happened. It's not what I wanted."

"But?" Camaro asked.

Faith turned away from the window. "I have to keep going. I need the money. If you want a share, we can work it out. Tell me where to make the deposit and we'll go from there. Fix up your boat. Buy a *new* boat! Do whatever you want."

"I want to go back to my life before you came along," Camaro returned. "I tried to *help* you. I'm helping you now! Do not go down this road, because once you start running, you can never stop. Even if you find a place where you can hide, and everything seems okay, it falls apart. You'll lose it all. That's what comes next."

"I don't know what to tell you."

"Talk to the detective. Or take it all to the FBI. You have to trust someone."

"I trust you."

"No. No. I am not your spirit guide, okay? I am not your bodyguard. I taught you what I taught you so you could take care of yourself, not so I could go on taking care of you forever."

"I am taking care of myself! This is me taking care of myself. I make this deal with the Colombians and I disappear. Anyway, I don't believe you when you say there's nowhere to run. There are lots of places to run. I can go anywhere. I can do anything."

"With two million dollars?" Camaro asked. "Do you really think that's going to last forever?"

"I'm good with money."

"I can't let you go," she said.

Faith crossed her arms. "I don't think you get a say in the matter."

"I am not going to get left holding the bag for you. When the feds can't find you, they'll come for me. And when they come for me, they're going to find out things I don't want them to find out. Things that will wreck my world. I risked my ass to get the things I have! I put my life on the line. I'm not going to lose everything because some bean counter can't get her shit together."

Faith pointed toward the door. "Okay, you can go. Go right now. Don't come back."

"You're being stupid. Let's fix this."

She took a step toward Faith. Faith retreated, her back against the window. Camaro saw a stab of fear in her face. Faith pointed toward the door again. Her finger shook. "I said *go!* Turn around and go. I don't need you anymore. I don't want you here!"

Faith trembled all over now, and she hugged herself like someone taking refuge from the cold. Camaro felt something sick in her stomach. She started to speak, stopped. She started again, but the words didn't come. She stepped back.

"Are you going to go?"

SAM HAWKEN

"Do not do this, Faith."

"Will you tell the police where I am? The FBI?"

"No."

"Okay, then. We're done."

"Do you have a sister?" Camaro asked Faith.

A deep notch appeared between Faith's eyebrows. "What?"

"I asked you if you have a sister."

"Why would you even want to know that?"

"Because you need somebody right now. Someone who only wants the best for you. Someone you can believe."

A new expression dawned on Faith's face. "That's who you saw," Faith said. "In me."

Camaro didn't answer.

"I don't care. I don't care about any of it." There were fresh tears. Faith wiped at her face and sniffed. "You're not my sister. I'm not your family."

Camaro left without saying anything else. She lingered in the hall until she heard Faith lock the door and set the chain. She breathed a shuddery breath. Her throat hurt. She walked a few doors down before she stopped. She took out her phone. She dialed Ignacio.

The call went to voice mail. Camaro tried again, but the same thing happened. She waited for the tone. "Detective, it's Camaro. I need to talk to you. Call me anytime, day or night. I have a charter tomorrow. I'll be on the water for a while, but I'll be back. It's important, so don't wait. You know my number."

She ended the call and stared at the phone. She pressed the button to lock the screen. The click was final in the quiet hallway.

CHAPTER FIFTY-THREE

THE ENGINES OF the Piaggio P-180 Avanti on the worn dirt landing strip roared as the pilot tested the throttle ahead of takeoff. Lorca walked with Parilla toward the plane from a line of armored SUVs. They were flanked by five other men, all dressed in civilian clothes, as was Parilla. They carried no cases. Everything was already on the plane.

Lorca signaled for Parilla to stop before they were in the wash of the propeller. The others went on, clambering up the short set of steps into the plane. They were dark men and the night was also dark, the strip unlit by anything except moon and stars. Lorca's pilots flew in any weather, day or night, and they could take off and land on any strip, no matter how crude. Many of them had flown for him for decades.

"Listen to me, Captain," Lorca said to Parilla. "It is essential you understand what is about to happen."

"Yes, General."

"Once you land in Miami, I will make contact with the woman. I will agree to all her terms. If she is true to her word, we will have all the information we need within a day. I will have targets for you then. Some may be outside the city. Be prepared for a long stay in the United States."

"Of course, General."

"Know this: those already on the list are to be eliminated regardless. Get what you can from them, and send them on their way. Don't allow them an opportunity to escape. Be certain to get every last bit of intelligence you can."

"I won't fail, General."

Lorca patted Parilla on his cheek. "You are a good man, Daniel. Your father would be very proud. And I am proud of you, too. Everything you've done for me has led to this moment. It should have happened a long time ago, but I fooled myself into believing it would run perfectly forever. This was my mistake to make. I won't make it again."

"You mustn't blame yourself."

"Go now. *Buena suerte.*"

They parted. Parilla ran the rest of the way to the plane. The copilot drew up the steps and sealed the hatch. A few moments later the plane throttled up. It aligned with the vector of the runway. In seconds it was airborne, banking gently over the trees and the darkly verdant hills, running lights extinguished, white shape rendered a quicksilver flash in the shadows. The engine noise faded until there was only the jungle night.

Lorca walked to the parked SUVs. He climbed into the middle vehicle. Its interior lights were on. A man in the passenger seat ahead of him sat hunched over a laptop, tapping furiously on the keyboard.

"Is it done?" Lorca asked.

The man glanced up once. "We're ready, General."

"Tell the woman. We want her accounts by the time the banks open in the morning."

"Yes, General."

The man typed. Lorca leaned forward and laid a hand on the back of the man's forearm. The typing stopped. "You can follow the money wherever it goes, can't you? This is what you told me."

"There are ways, General. She will move the money as soon as it hits the accounts she gives us. She'll do her best to disguise the transfers, but I'm familiar with several people who can provide us with access."

"Hackers," Lorca said, and the word felt sticky in his mouth.

"Yes, General. They work for the highest bidder, but they are discreet. As long as we're careful not to expose ourselves too much, it won't come back to us. These transfer accounts are entirely new. Perfectly clean. I made certain there is nothing connected to the bank in Miami, nor any shell corporation previously used to move funds. Once this operation is complete, I will burn everything associated with the payoff and shift all our operations to a third set of accounts already set up."

Lorca took his hand from the man's arm. He sat back against the cushioned leather of the seat. "If I didn't hate it all so much, it would be fascinating," he said. "The money goes here, the money goes there. And all of it begins with a seed in the soil."

The man said nothing. He didn't resume typing. He looked at Lorca, a question on his face.

"What is it?" Lorca asked. "You look like a monkey taking a shit. What is the problem?"

"There will be questions. This shift will make our partners nervous. They like things a certain way. To change everything so rapidly ... it's not something they're used to. Already I'm hearing complaints."

Lorca scoffed. "They can bring those complaints to me in the jungle where the real blood is shed. This country's government is a pathetic shell, and the people who scurry to do the Americans' bidding make me sick. To them, all this is a minor inconvenience. They will have to take their payments from some other bank somewhere on the other side of the world. Who cares? To us, this is a matter of life or death. They will never understand. They have never understood."

"Yes, General."

"Go on, make it happen. Tell the woman we are ready to make a deal. No more internet phone calls. No more games. If she wants the money, she needs to take it. Tell her. She will listen."

His driver closed the open door of the SUV and got behind the wheel. The idling engine stepped up its hum and they rolled. The small convoy drove without lights. They knew where they were going.

CHAPTER FIFTY-FOUR

IT WAS DARK on the boat. Through the portholes there was only blackness. Camaro felt her phone vibrate. "Detective?" she answered.

"I'm sorry I didn't call sooner. Were you asleep?"

"Does it matter?"

"I guess not. I've been dealing with a lot of heavy things on my end. This is a lot more serious than the feds let on."

"How so?"

He told her and she listened. She thought of Faith in her hotel room. She did not speak of it to Ignacio.

When he was done there was dead quiet on the phone. Camaro heard his breathing. "What do you want to do?" she asked him.

"I don't know. I have to keep moving forward. They're giving me a gift, letting me take point on the next move. They didn't need to, but they're opening the door for me. I gotta step through."

"And I stay behind," Camaro said.

Ignacio was slow to speak. She heard something new in his voice, something like an apologia, which couldn't be put into so many words. "I should never have let you get this deep."

"You didn't *let* me do anything," Camaro replied.

"So I guess I should ask you: What do you want to do?"

"I've done everything I can. Faith doesn't want my help. You don't need me stepping in with the feds all around you. It's time for me to go back to being a charter skipper."

"Hey," Ignacio said, "you know I think you're more than that.

214

You've got heart, and you don't let anyone beat you down. That counts for a lot with me."

Camaro got out of bed. She walked barefoot into the galley and stood looking at the floating lights of the marina. Coming in at night, it was like seeing a dense collection of stars, an unrecognizable constellation, or maybe a new galaxy being born. Up close they were far more prosaic. The poetry was gone from them.

"Hello?"

"I always wondered something," Camaro said. "Why is Superman called Superman and Supergirl not called Superwoman? You ever think about that?"

"No, I never did."

"Most men don't. I'll see you when I see you."

"Camaro—" Ignacio started, but she pressed the End icon and he was silenced. She waited to see if he'd call again, but he didn't.

She went back to the bow and put on the same day's clothes in the dark. She went up to the flybridge and stoked the boat's engines. With twin diesels running, she cast off. Within a minute she was back behind the wheel, maneuvering the *Annabel* out of its slip. She navigated the confines of the marina to open water, opened the throttles, and let Miami fall away behind her.

The boat crossed into night, where there was nothing on any horizon save the flat black shadow of the Atlantic. Camaro cut the engines. She let the *Annabel* drift, listening to the lick of water against the hull, feeling the slow roll of the deck. It was calm tonight, with barely a wind. She climbed down from the flybridge and sat in the fighting chair and fell into herself.

The moon slid across the sky, silent and silver. Camaro was gone. She stared into nothing and thought nothing and was nothing except a speck in the water that would disappear if the attention of any watcher faltered for more than a few seconds. Once lost, this tiny white spot would be swallowed up by the deep blue, and even in the brightest day Camaro would be absent from the mind of the world.

She stirred when the eastern sky blushed with the first hint of false dawn. The breeze picked up, carrying a clean, raw scent. She was alone out here, utterly alone, as though she were the last woman on the face of the waters.

Everywhere she had ever gone, no matter how crowded, she had found this place. In the desert she had found it. In the forest she had found it. Here she had found it, and it was expansive and real and she could breathe. Here the quiet was palpable, a thing alive embracing her gently and smoothing the jagged edges of her thoughts.

"Shit," she said out loud. Serenity vanished.

She checked the luminous hands of her watch. She had a charter coming in before noon, another in the evening. There would be no more time for quiet or isolation. Instead there would be talk and the whirring sound of cast lines as reels spooled out. The clink of beer bottles taken from a cooler. The cry when a hook found its way into the mouth of a battling fish.

Camaro climbed to the flybridge. She checked her coordinates relative to the shore. She throttled up, brought the custom Carolina around in a long, swooping arc, turning blue water into bright white foam. She pointed the bow toward the heart of a city only starting to wake.

CHAPTER FIFTY-FIVE

IGNACIO LOOKED AT the decorations in Brandon Roche's outer office. He didn't know the exact price of things, but he recognized what was cheap and what wasn't. The paintings on Roche's walls, the vase in the corner on a teak table, the table itself with its scrollwork—they were not the slightest bit cheap.

He sat in a leather chair with brass buttons. It was comfortable and big even for a man his size. He found himself relaxing into it but forced himself to sit taller. He watched the woman behind her desk, typing on a flat keyboard that made no noise when her fingers hit the keys. Once he breathed heavily, and she glanced up. "Only a few more minutes," she said.

"Thanks." He smiled at her. He turned his hat in his hands.

The phone on the receptionist's desk made a chirping noise. She picked up the receiver and listened. "Yes, sir," she said. She looked at Ignacio. "Detective, Mr. Roche will see you now. Are you sure you don't want to leave your hat?"

"I feel good having it with me," Ignacio said.

She left her desk and opened the doors to the inner office. Ignacio stepped through into the brilliant light of a Miami midmorning cascading through the windows. He saw Roche at his desk, a stern-faced man with thick black hair swept away from his temples. His suit was perfect. "Mr. Roche?" Ignacio said.

Roche came to Ignacio and offered his hand with a smile. "Detective Montellano. Brandon Roche. It's good to meet you. Please, have a seat. Can I get you something?"

"No thanks, I'm all good."

Roche returned to his desk. Ignacio sat opposite. "What can I do for the police department today? Your call took me by surprise, especially when you said one of our contractors was attacked. And the man who attacked her was killed?"

"Yes," Ignacio replied. "She shot him to death. And a good thing, because he was a grade A wacko. But I kind of figured you'd know that, what with him working for you."

The light drained from Roche's expression. His mouth turned down, and new lines formed on his face. He had a deep voice, and his tone was flat. "What was that?"

"He worked for you," Ignacio said. "His name was Eduard Serafian, and he was an Armenian in this country illegally. Apparently he was wrapped up with some kind of revolutionary group in the home country, but that's not really why he was trying to kill the nice lady who did your books. He was a subcontractor for a man called Michael Bamanian. You know him ... right?"

Roche's brows were heavy. They furrowed together. "If you're asking me, then you already know Michael had contracts with us."

"It's a funny thing," Ignacio said. "Bamanian got himself killed trying to murder another woman. A friend of the first victim. Him and a second guy whose name we're still trying to dig up. I figure he's another undocumented alien. Armenian like the rest of them."

"I don't know anything about it. I don't ask people where they're from. In Miami they come from all over."

"That is very true. And I have to admit, the whole Armenian thing had me thrown for a little while. I couldn't figure out what the connection was. I mean, Armenians? They don't exactly have a bad reputation around here. Not like Colombians."

Roche didn't reply. He watched Ignacio and Ignacio watched him. Roche's face was very still.

"Colombians," Ignacio said again. "Old-school. Before my time. But the cops who were around back during the cocaine cowboy days?

They have some stories to tell. Crazy stuff. Shoot-outs in the street, people with their tongues pulled out through holes in their necks... wild. Working homicide is a full-time job today, but back then? I can't imagine. Can you?"

"I assume we're coming around to a point here, Detective," Roche said.

"Oh, sure, sure. Sorry to keep you. I know you're busy. I'll get right down to it: your bank is laundering money for a Colombian paramilitary running coke into the U.S. through South Florida. The bank's been doing it for years. In fact the whole bank is built on drug money from these same bloodsuckers."

The stillness in Roche's face extended to the rest of him. "I'm listening," he said.

"This is how I figure it: you find out someone's snooping where they shouldn't. A call gets made from somewhere up the food chain, maybe all the way to the top, and they put you on it. Somehow or another you figure out who's got your numbers. But you're not quite sure if you can kill her without exposing yourself. After all, she's smart, so she's probably got copies tucked away. You contact your buddy Bamanian, who doesn't mind getting his hands dirty. He puts someone on her. Just to watch and see how things pan out. The problem is, the guy who's doing the watching, Eduard Serafian, is some kind of pervert, and what starts off as a job ends up being a full-blown obsession."

"I see."

"Anyway, you decide to make your move. You tell Bamanian, Bamanian tells Serafian, and he does what he's been waiting to do all this time. Maybe he's still thinking about his assignment a little bit, but he's more interested in hurting his target before he kills her."

Ignacio stopped. He waited for Roche to respond. Roche's frown picked up slightly at one corner of his mouth. He ran a hand through his hair. He leaned forward. "Assuming all this is true—and I don't admit to anything—what evidence do you have? If this crazy man... What was his name?"

"Serafian."

"Right. If this man, Serafian, was working for a contractor who occasionally did work for the bank, shouldn't Michael Bamanian be the prime suspect?"

"If he'd kept his cool, he probably would have been. Eventually. But you told him to clean up whatever loose ends Serafian left behind, and unfortunately Bamanian decided to step in and take care of things personally. That's how he ended up dead."

Roche spread his hands. "And there's the other problem. If Bamanian is dead, you have no one to confirm Serafian worked for him, let alone anything connecting me or the bank to any of this."

"You're right. I don't."

"Well," Roche said. He stood. "If that's everything, I'd like to thank you for an entertaining story."

Ignacio rose with Roche. "Look, I may not have a paper trail leading directly to you, but I have enough."

"Enough for what?"

The sound of the receptionist's raised voice carried through the wall. The door rattled. Roche looked past Ignacio, and Ignacio caught the hint of something different in Roche's manner. "Enough to get a search warrant to look through all your records, interview employees, and what's the other thing? Oh, yeah: enough to start digging through accounts to find what Faith Glazer found. Because we know it's still in there somewhere."

"Who's 'we'?" Roche asked.

The door swung wide and hit the wall. Mansfield and Pope burst into the room in dark blue windbreakers. His said FBI in yellow letters. Hers said DEA. They were accompanied by a phalanx of agents. "Me and my friends with the federal government," Ignacio said. "You might want to call your lawyer."

CHAPTER FIFTY-SIX

CAMARO HOSED DOWN the *Annabel*'s aft deck. Water ran off through holes and merged with the sea. She had lights on against the failing day, and they cast hard-edged shadows as she worked. She heard her cell phone ringing in the cabin. She dropped the hose. By the time she reached her phone it had rung five times. "Hello?"

There was silence.

"Hello?" Camaro said again. She looked at the display. The number was listed UNKNOWN.

"Camaro." Faith's voice sounded as though it was coming from the bottom of a well. She was on a speaker.

"Where are you? What's happening?"

"I'm safe. Nothing's happening. I wanted to talk to you one more time. You know, before I go."

Camaro shut the cabin door. "Did you take their money?"

"They have everything they wanted. I destroyed my online backups. I took the hard copies somewhere to be shredded."

Camaro swung a fist in the air. "Why? If you don't have a safety net, there's no reason for them not to come after you."

"These people are businessmen, Camaro. They made a deal. They'll stick to the terms."

"No, they are *not* businessmen. Do you know anything about them? Detective Montellano told me all about it. These Colombians are butchers—that's all they are. They have a cause and the money they make selling drugs is what they use to fight a war. People with a cause can't be reasoned with. They don't think about what they do. They only know they're right, and then people die."

Faith made a sound. Camaro realized she was crying and trying to hide it. "I don't want to argue with you, Camaro. I wanted...I wanted to thank you again for what you did. I don't care why you did it. I won't try to understand. All I know is you helped me when no one else would. And the more I thought about it after you were gone, the more I realized you said the things you said because you still wanted to save me. But I don't *need* to be saved. I can take care of myself from here on out."

"Are you still at the hotel? Let me come see you. I won't try to stop you, but I want to make sure you get where you need to go. Airport, train station...wherever. Because you have their money now. They might tell you it's okay, but it's not. If they can get it back, they will. And if they can shut you up about everything you know, that's even better. Faith? Can you hear me?"

"I hear you."

"Are you still at the beach?"

"Yes. I haven't checked out yet. I'm paid for a few more days. But I'm not staying."

"I'm coming to you."

"*No.* Don't. All you're going to do is what you're doing now. I told you before, you're not my sister. We're not family. We're...I don't know what we are."

"We're friends," Camaro said.

"Do you really have friends?"

"Sometimes."

This time Camaro heard Faith sob without attempting to hide it. "I'm tired of being scared," Faith told her.

"I know."

"How do you do it? How do you keep on when you're scared? You never told me."

"You have to care more about surviving than you care about getting hurt," Camaro said. "Then you can do anything."

222

"I should go," Faith said.

"Please don't," Camaro said. "Switch hotels if you want to feel safer, but don't go tonight. There's still something I can do for you if you'll let me."

"I don't want to know."

"I won't tell you. Stay put for another day. Keep the door locked. Don't let anyone in. Wait for me. And if I can't do what I say I can do, I'll help you any way I can. I'll drive you out of town myself."

Faith didn't answer.

"Faith? Are you listening to me?"

"Okay."

Camaro realized her chest was tight, holding a breath. She let it go. "I'll see you tomorrow night. Be safe."

"I won't wait past tomorrow night."

"I won't be late."

Faith hung up. Camaro listened to the silent phone. She walked with it to the counter in the galley and slammed the phone down. She spread her fingers on the cool granite surface and stared at the backs of her hands. She nodded to herself. She picked up her phone again.

Ignacio answered. "I'm kind of in the middle of something."

"I talked to Faith."

"Wait, what? When?"

"A minute ago. And a while before."

"Hold on a second." Camaro heard the murmur of voices in the background. They faded. A door shut. Ignacio spoke again. "Were you ever going to tell me this? She's a material witness!"

"She's dealing with the Colombians. They paid her for everything she had, and in return she destroyed it all."

"This is not happening," Ignacio said. "This is *not* happening. That's evidence of an ongoing felony directly related to three homicides! And she destroyed it? All of it?"

"That's what she said."

223

"I can't go to the feds with this. They'll turn me inside out if they think for a second I was in on this with the two of you."

"I'm not *in* on anything. She made this decision on her own. I tried to stop her. All I could do was get her to wait until tomorrow night before she disappears."

"Where is she now?"

"Are you going to send someone to pick her up?"

"Of course I am. Did you miss the part about her being a material witness?"

"I promised her it would be me."

"You are climbing out on the same limb with her, Camaro. This is not what you want."

"Can we meet?"

"Not tonight. I'm going to be with the feds until morning, at least. I can forget about sleeping or eating."

"Meet me at the boat. I have a charter in the afternoon."

"How can you work when this is going on?"

"I need money. I don't have people handing it to me on the street."

"But this is important!"

"Believe me, I know. But everything stays normal. You said the FBI was all over this, right?"

"Sure. They dropped a blanket over the whole thing."

"Then they could be watching. Find out what you can. Tell me later."

"What are you going to do until then?"

"Be here."

CHAPTER FIFTY-SEVEN

THE FBI KEPT Roche cornered in his office all day. From the moment Detective Montellano entered to the time they finally released him, Roche was trapped at the bank for twelve hours. They didn't allow him to send for food, and they only offered him a chance to drink water and occasionally use the restroom.

Kaur wanted to come down from the top floor, but Roche said no. If they climbed the tree high enough, they would come to Lawrence Kaur in due time. There was no need to rush it. "I'll talk to you soon," Roche told him. "Stay far away from me for now."

He was exhausted and his stomach felt hollow. His skin itched. He wanted a shower. He parked his Audi in the drive of his house in Coconut Grove, and spent minutes draped over the steering wheel listening to the sound of his own breathing. Eventually he got out with his keys in hand. The lights inside were already on, set to illuminate when he was nearby. The doorstep was bright.

Roche went in. He heard the chirp of the alarm system and stopped. When the system was armed, the sound when he opened the door was a long tone. When disarmed, it simply beeped to indicate that a door had opened. He took an instinctive step back before he was rushed from behind.

A man in black grabbed him and shoved him into the arms of another man dressed in the same garments. They were joined by a third, and the trio manhandled Roche through the foyer and into the living room. They threw him onto the couch. One of the men searched him and found the small gun holstered on his belt. Everything was done in silence. Roche knew there was no point in calling out, or cursing, or saying anything at all.

When they finished, the three men stood over him, watching from behind ski masks. Roche looked from one to the next. Then he looked down. The buttons had popped off his jacket. He tried to straighten his clothes and tuck in his tie. His hair fell onto his forehead. He wanted to sweep it away. He didn't want to raise his hands so high.

Roche couldn't even hear the men breathing. His own lungs sounded like bellows, and his heart wouldn't slow. He swallowed repeatedly to loosen his throat. Eventually he tried to speak. "What do we do next?"

None of the three men spoke a word. "We have questions," said someone else.

At an unspoken command, the others stepped aside to reveal a fourth man in a panama shirt and khaki trousers. He looked like a young tourist, his shirt open at the throat, a gold watch on his wrist. Only his hairstyle gave him away. It didn't speak of money.

Roche squinted at the man. "I don't know you."

"No, you don't."

Roche sagged. "Lorca sent you."

"You're quick. El General, he said it was so. You and Señor Kaur have been very smart. But now I am here."

"If you want to know where the woman is, I have no idea. We lost her. Any chance we had of finding her was gone the minute her friend killed my people. Sending one team after another until someone breaks isn't going to work."

"I agree."

Roche tried not to let surprise show on his face. "You do?"

Another man entered the living room. Like the others, he covered his face, but he also wore gloves of black latex. He carried a filleting knife from Roche's kitchen. Roche felt an ill sensation.

"My name is Captain Daniel Parilla," said the man in the panama shirt.

"I don't want to know your name," Roche said.

"I know. And you don't ever want to see me. Because if you hear my name and you see my face, you know there is no way out for you. I cannot let you talk to your federal police. This is a storm you brought to your own doorstep."

The sick feeling intensified. "Look," Roche said. "This doesn't have to end badly. The FBI and the DEA are on a fishing expedition. We've already taken steps to eliminate any connection between the General and our operations. The woman doesn't seem interested in turning over what she found to the authorities, so it's only a matter of stringing the auditors along."

"And you think this will save you and Señor Kaur."

"Won't it?" Roche asked. He didn't like the sound of his own voice.

Parilla stepped closer. The man with the knife stayed in his shadow. "Señor Roche, there is a problem. It was bad enough when your incompetence exposed a business deal so old it goes back to before I was born. Your bank exists because of the General. You have this beautiful house because of his money. But you're greedy and you stole from us. Not once or twice, but again and again."

Roche raised his hands. They trembled. The other men moved forward and he put his hands back in his lap. "It can all be explained," he said.

"You will explain. You will tell me everything. And when you have finished, I will be merciful."

The three men grabbed Roche. He cried out and soiled himself as the men stripped off his jacket and tore open his shirt. The man with the knife came to him, and the cutting began.

CHAPTER FIFTY-EIGHT

CAMARO SLEPT LIGHTLY. Every small sound stirred her. Sometimes she knew where she was. Sometimes she didn't.

When morning light came, she rose and made breakfast in the galley. She went to the aft deck and looked out over the marina toward the parking lot and the road beyond. A single car sat on the road, a figure beside it, and while Camaro watched, a silver flash burst over his face, a reflection from binoculars.

Camaro crouched and scuttled into the cabin. She closed the door and waited. She peered out over the lower edge of the windows, but it was impossible to see the road from this angle. She found her phone and called Ignacio. "Where are you?" she asked when he answered.

"I'm pulling up now. What's wrong?"

"Look toward the street. There's a car parked up there. A gray sedan. The driver's out on my side with a pair of binoculars."

She listened. "I don't see anyone," he said.

"He was *right there*."

"I'm telling you, I don't see anyone. I saw a car driving away when I came up. It might have been a gray sedan. I can't be sure. Are you okay?"

"Did the FBI say anything about monitoring me?"

"No, but I'm not exactly high on the totem pole. They're letting me tie my investigation to theirs, but right now it's the guys and gals with expensive calculators doing all the work. The bank president lawyered up the second we knocked on his door. He's not talking to anyone. We sweated their security guy, Roche, all day. He's tough to read, but I'm thinking we might have an in with him."

Camaro saw Ignacio approach. She hung up the phone and left the cabin. When she looked toward the road, she saw the car and watcher were gone. The back of her neck itched. "Come aboard," she told Ignacio.

He clambered over the side. They went into the cabin together. Camaro checked one last time before shutting the door. There was no one.

"You don't have to worry," Ignacio told her. "These FBI guys, they're not interested in you. They don't have any idea you're in touch with Faith Glazer, and I didn't tell them anything."

"Why not?" Camaro asked.

"Why should I? If I tell them you're conspiring with her, they'll come down on you like a ten-ton weight and we'll lose Faith completely. If I let this play out, everything comes together the way we need it to. She talks, the feds listen. Even without her copies of the records, she can tell the accountants where to look. You know the bank has to have this buried deep."

Ignacio sat on the couch. Camaro leaned against the counter. She crossed her arms. The muscles twitched in her forearms. "I don't know if I can get her to listen to you. She's barely listening to me. If I come on strong with you there...she'll run. And I *don't* want her cuffed and dragged off, because she doesn't deserve it."

"I don't know how to put this to you, but if Faith Glazer is deliberately withholding evidence—and she is, so I don't think we can argue about it—she's committing a felony. Maybe it's not the kind of felony you're used to, because nobody gets stabbed or shot to death, but it's still the kind of thing that gets you prison time. I'm a nice guy, but I'm also a cop. Eventually I gotta lay my hands on somebody and take them to jail."

"Not her," Camaro said.

"Why stick up for her? She's the reason those two guys busted into your place. If it hadn't been for her, you'd be running charters like nothing ever happened. Do you *want* her to turn your life upside down?"

229

Camaro made fists where her hands were tucked. She felt her pulse in her temples. "I don't have to explain myself to anyone."

Ignacio leaned back. He looked thick-bodied on the couch, sturdy like the trunk of an old tree. He loosened his tie. "Maybe you don't. People help people for lots of reasons."

"What are we doing?" Camaro asked.

"I don't know, but some shrink would probably have a field day with it. Maybe it's because I can't stand to see a lady in trouble. I'm old-fashioned that way."

Camaro looked over his head and past him. She didn't raise her voice when she spoke. "If you want to help, you can come. But I want you to promise you won't take her into custody. She gets a walk. Everything she's been through . . . I'm telling you, she doesn't deserve it."

"We don't always get what we deserve."

She turned her gaze on him. Ignacio's face was stolid.

"If something goes wrong, and you need somebody to turn over to the FBI, let them take me. I'm not afraid."

"You're not afraid of anything."

"Faith thought that, too."

"Was she wrong?"

"Yes."

"When do you want to meet?"

"My charter ends at nightfall."

Ignacio slapped his knees. "So it's decided. You want breakfast?"

"I ate."

"You want to watch me eat breakfast?"

"Why?"

"Maybe I like an audience. I want eggs with hot sauce," Ignacio said. "Lots of eggs. Lots of sauce. What do you say?"

"Are you going to want to talk?"

"Not if you don't."

"I don't."

"Then we won't. Come on."

CHAPTER FIFTY-NINE

LAWRENCE KAUR TRIED to reach Brandon by phone all night, but no one answered. He left a dozen messages, and sent twice as many texts. He used the encrypted e-mail account they agreed to utilize only in case of an emergency. No response came by morning. Enrique cooked a breakfast that Kaur didn't taste at all. He stared at his phone as the battery slowly ran down, waiting for a notification to tell him all was well.

He had an early meeting with his attorney, but it would still be a few hours. Already the FBI had petitioned the court for a warrant to search his home. Delaying tactics put it off for a while. The attorney told Kaur he was insulated: whatever they found they would never use. His attorney didn't want to know if there was anything to find. "What I don't know, I don't have to lie about in court," he said. "That's the best way to handle it."

It was unspoken between them: Roche had to be sacrificed. He was on the front lines of this thing with Faith Glazer. The leads came directly to his office. Brandon knew this might happen. Kaur knew it, too. They never discussed it openly. Now Kaur wished they had both been more careful. Anything to keep Brandon Roche clear of what might come. What had come.

"Not hungry today, sir?"

Kaur saw Enrique standing over him. "I'm sorry. What?"

"You barely touched your breakfast, Mr. Kaur. Is there something else you prefer?"

"No, no. Don't bother. I've eaten everything I can. I'll make up for it at lunch."

"I'll take your plates."

"Thank you. And when you're done cleaning up, take the rest of the day off."

"Are you sure, Mr. Kaur? Your lunch?"

Kaur looked toward the ocean. "I'm sure."

He waited until Enrique was gone. He called Roche again. As it had before, the phone went to voice mail, but now it didn't even ring first.

He got up from the table and adjusted the belt of his robe. The ocean remained, steadily rolling in, unchanging. The sun turned the water brilliant, clear blue. Groundskeepers raked the beach every night. Not a thing was out of place.

His phone vibrated on the table.

Kaur jumped an inch at the buzz. He grabbed the phone with both hands. He had a text notification. He opened the app.

Brandon Roche looked directly into the camera. He had a cut over one eye, and severe bruising on his face. He was stripped to the waist, and was soaked in perspiration. His medallion was missing, and there was a red line on the side of his neck where the chain had been yanked and broken.

The message app vibrated. A new photograph arrived. Men in black, only their arms visible, held down Roche on his couch. His chest was covered in long, straight slashes, none too deep, but all bleeding freely.

More pictures followed, the progress of torture advancing in each shot. Once, Kaur caught sight of the knife, an expensive Wüsthof filleting knife, the silvery flat slimed with red. Roche's face drowned under a mask of blood.

The second-to-last picture showed Roche's throat cut. The final photograph was vile: they had pulled his tongue through the incision in his neck, so it lay on his chest.

Kaur put his hand on the edge of the table and hunched over. He covered his mouth, but it was too late, and he vomited on the floor. He heard Enrique running from the kitchen. "Mr. Kaur! Mr. Kaur, are you okay?"

His stomach heaved on nothing. He spat thick saliva. His throat tightened. He heaved again. "I'm fine," Kaur managed to say. "I don't need any help."

"I'll send someone to clean up."

"Whatever. Go. Go away!"

Enrique retreated. Kaur sucked air, his stomach settling until there were no further rebellions. He gripped his phone and left the breakfast room, sweeping through the house and up the stairs to his bedroom. He tossed the phone on the bed and went to the nightstand.

In the drawer was a 9mm automatic that Brandon had encouraged Kaur to learn how to use. Kaur had fired it once, and only once, before putting it away. He laid the gun by the phone. He raided the cavernous walk-in closet. He piled clothes on the bed to await suitcases. Those were in a closet in the hall. He got them and opened and stuffed them, paying no attention to order or wrinkling.

The suitcases full, he dressed in a salmon-colored golf shirt and linen pants and loafers with monogrammed socks. His underwear was also monogrammed. He dressed quickly, catching sight of himself in the full-length mirror in one corner. He was pallid, his face damp and feverish. The clothes were grotesquely casual.

He put his phone in his pocket and grabbed the gun. It didn't fit in his other pocket. He tried stuffing it in the front of his pants and pulling his untucked shirt over it, but its shape was too obvious. He put it at the small of his back and examined himself in the mirror. Anyone looking would know in a second what he had underneath his clothes. "To hell with it," he said.

His phone used a charging station by the bed, but the station was too bulky to carry. Kaur searched drawers until he found an adapter. He wadded up the wire and jammed it in an empty pocket.

Kaur had a suitcase in each hand as he deserted the bedroom. He nearly collided with a woman in a tan dress and white apron. She squawked, "Mr. Kaur, where are you going? I saw the mess downstairs. Do you need a doctor?"

"Liza," Kaur said, breathless. "I'm taking a trip. If anyone asks, I left early this morning and no one saw me go. Do you understand? No one saw me go. I didn't say where I was headed."

"I don't understand. Do you need me to call a car?"

"I'm taking my own car this morning. Not a word to anyone, Liza. *Nothing.*"

Kaur pushed past her and fled down the hall. He took the stairs two at a time and nearly fell down the steps. His loafers made hollow sounds on Italian marble in the foyer. He muscled his bags through the front door. A Porsche waited in the drive.

It took a minute to load the car and another thirty seconds to secure himself behind the wheel. He pushed the ignition button. Nothing happened. He pushed it again. Silence.

He searched himself. The keyless ignition fob wasn't there. Kaur hit the steering wheel. "Shit!" he shouted.

Liza stood at the open front door, wringing her hands. Kaur got out of the car. "I need my key ring. My *key ring*, Liza! Hurry!"

The woman scurried away. When she returned, Kaur ripped the ring out of her hand and returned to the car. This time the engine started when he pressed the button. Kaur saw Liza's distraught face before he disengaged the brake and slammed the car into drive. He left skid marks on the brick drive, and accelerated away as fast as he could.

CHAPTER SIXTY

IGNACIO WAS ON his way to the bullpen when his phone rang. He was trapped in congestion. He answered hands-free. "Detective Montellano speaking."

"Detective, it's John Mansfield. Where are you right now?"

"I'm stuck on the Dolphin Expressway. There's an accident and we're down to two lanes."

"When you get a chance, grab an exit and head to Coconut Grove. Brandon Roche's residence."

"What's happening there?"

"Roche is dead."

Ignacio gripped the steering wheel. "Say again?"

"Roche was murdered sometime last night. Miami PD already sent a detective, but I asked them to defer to you since you're working with us. It's a mess here, so be ready."

"How bad are we talking?"

"I've got people puking their guts out right now."

"I'll be there as soon as I can."

The call ended. There was silence in the car.

Ignacio pressed a button on the face of his phone. "Call Harley."

"Calling Harley," the phone returned.

He got voice mail. "This is Coral Sea Sport Charters," Camaro's voice said. "Leave your name, a number, and information on your charter request and I'll get back to you inside twenty-four hours."

Ignacio hissed with disappointment as the tone sounded. "Camaro,

I don't know when you're going to get this, but we need to move on your girl now. Brandon Roche was murdered last night. Call me as soon as you can, okay?"

He ended the call. He looked at the clot of traffic ahead of him and leaned on the horn. He thought to curse, but didn't.

"Serafian tries to kill Faith," Ignacio said out loud. "Faith kills Serafian. Roche tells his people to move on Camaro. Camaro kills them. Faith disappears. Roche doesn't have any plays left. Roche dies. Roche dies."

Traffic crept forward. Ignacio rubbed the back of his neck. He sweated despite the AC.

"Roche dies," he said again. "Who kills Roche?"

He called Mansfield back. "Are you on your way?" Mansfield asked.

"I'm getting there. Listen, who's working the scene?"

"Detective Pool is here."

"He looked through any security video Roche had in the house? A guy like him, he had to monitor himself day and night."

"It's the first thing he checked. All the hard drives were pulled. We're canvassing the neighborhood right now, trying to grab any footage we can from security cameras at other residences."

"I don't get it," Ignacio said. "All this time it's been Roche, and probably his boss, behind everything going down, and then he gets himself offed? Who's the new player?"

"Do you want my hot take?" Mansfield asked.

"If you want to share."

"I'll forward some photos if you want to see right now, but I'm thinking Colombians. Pope thinks the same. It's classic, all the way down to...well, you'll see."

Ignacio honked his horn again, put on his signal, and forced his way between two cars in the next lane. A swarm of protest honks burst behind him. He waved through his back window. "So Roche and Kaur try to clean up their mess, and now the Colombians are doing the job for them," he said. "Except Roche and Kaur *are* the mess."

236

"It fits, but I don't want to jump to any conclusions. That's why I want you to work it. If M&I Bank and Trust were doing business with the Black Eagles, it stands to reason they were in deep with other groups, foreign and domestic. These banks can't help themselves. They go wherever the money is. What we're seeing here might be another set of players entirely."

"What about Kaur?"

"My people hit his house as soon as we found out about Roche. Kaur already cleared out. His housekeeper says he was in a panic about something. Which he probably is. The question is whether we can find him before these people do."

"You want me to cover that end?"

"No, I want you on Roche. You did a good job for us, and you're going to get the credit you deserve, but it's time for the Bureau to step up."

"What about Faith Glazer? Even with Roche and Kaur out of the way, she has to be a target. I don't want another body on my hands."

"We'll find her. I have people going over every part of her life with a fine-tooth comb. We're on top of it."

"Yeah, like you were on top of the bank guys. Why wasn't anyone watching them?"

Mansfield cleared his throat. "That was an oversight."

"Well, I hope you tighten things up, because it seems like we're running out of people to arrest."

"Let me worry about that."

"I see my exit."

"I'll be waiting."

Ignacio hung up and shook his head. His mind moved too quickly. He reached out. His finger hovered over the phone. He stopped himself. She'd call when she called. "I hope you catch a lot of fish today, lady, because I got a serious problem on my hands," he said to no one.

He made it to within a few yards of the exit, yanked the wheel to the side, and pulled onto the shoulder. He pressed the accelerator, rushed down the edge of the road, tires grinding on pebbles and grit and broken glass. More people honked as he streaked past. Ignacio paid them no mind.

CHAPTER SIXTY-ONE

HER PHONE PINGED when the *Annabel* came within signal range. Camaro stood on the flybridge with the throttles open, hair streaming in a twenty-nine-knot wind. A few of her charter party were on the afterdeck, and a few were in the cabin. The sun was directly in her eyes, dazzling even though she was wearing sunglasses. She played her voice mail.

When she was done listening, she called Ignacio. He answered. Camaro heard the sound of men speaking in the background, a deep-voiced babble of people at work. "Thank God," Ignacio said. "Are you back?"

"I'm coming in. It'll be a little while longer. What's going on?"

"All hell is breaking loose. Roche is dead. Kaur is missing. The feds are in control of everything."

Camaro watched the Miami skyline draw closer. Tall buildings gained definition.

"Are you hearing me?"

"What about Faith? Do they know anything about Faith?"

"Give me a second."

Through the phone, Camaro heard a car door open and close. "Listen, I'm leaving Roche's place right now. I need to be at the medical examiner's office for the postmortem on Roche, but there's time for us to meet. We can get Faith and put her in protective custody before anything else happens. Roche's people were dangerous, but whoever did him took it to a whole new level. I don't want to see your girl carved up."

239

"Meet me at the marina in an hour."

"You have people with you?"

"They're off as soon as I get there. I don't host parties."

"Ditch them as soon as you can. It's go time."

Camaro didn't say anything right away. She pushed the throttles farther forward. The engines picked up. "I'm trusting you," she said at last.

"I won't let you down."

She ended the call. Down on the afterdeck, two men exploded with laughter. The *Annabel* danced on the swells, cresting one after another. The ride smoothed at a lower speed, but Camaro notched the throttles again anyway. The *Annabel* topped out at around forty knots.

"Hey, Skipper!" shouted one of the men on deck below. He held up a can of beer. "What are you drinking?"

"I'm driving," Camaro replied.

"Come on! One beer!"

"Another time. Hold on."

She pressed the throttles to the stops. The men stumbled as the boat surged underneath them. Camaro waited for their complaints. They fled to the cabin instead.

She saw the marina when the sun was almost down. She throttled back and hoped no one had thrown up in the cabin on the way in. She entered the maze of boats, careful on the controls. She spotted Ignacio waiting dockside. He waved as she drew close, but he didn't smile.

The charter party emerged from the cabin as she tied up the boat. They were green and unsteady. "Have a nice night," Camaro told them.

"Took it a little rough coming in, huh?" one of the men asked.

Camaro started to answer. Ignacio interrupted. "How about you cut the lady a break and head on out of here?"

"Who are you?"

Ignacio showed his badge. "I'm the cop who's going to bust somebody for DUI if they're not careful leaving the parking lot. So say night-night to your captain and enjoy the rest of your evening. Okay?"

The charter party left without further complaint. Camaro regarded Ignacio from the deck. "I could have handled it," she said.

"You don't have to do everything alone. That's what friends are for. You ready?"

Camaro pulled the .45 from where she had it holstered under the edge of her shirt. She press-checked with her right hand before she put the weapon away. "I think so."

"You worried you're gonna have to kill someone tonight?"

"Aren't you?"

"It's definitely been on my mind. Let's get Ms. Glazer before it comes to that."

They left the boat behind. Ignacio paused at his car and seemed about to say something.

"What?" Camaro asked.

"You want me to drive?"

"I'll drive myself."

"You ever let anyone drive?"

"Depends."

"I'll follow you."

She led the way. The V8 Hemi under her truck's hood rumbled like the *Annabel*. Camaro looked straight ahead and didn't listen to the radio. She felt pressure at her back, propelling her forward. Occasionally she glanced in the mirror. Ignacio never fell far behind.

When they turned onto Ocean Drive, they had to slow down while tourist traffic crept along the lit Art Deco faces against the sea. Camaro found a parking spot, and Ignacio slotted in at her rear bumper. They convened on the sidewalk across from the Avalon. "Nice spot," Ignacio said. "I wouldn't mind hiding out here."

People streamed in and out of the hotel. Camaro watched them. No one seemed to care if she and Ignacio were there. "We go in, we get her, we come right back out again," Camaro said. "I put her in the truck. We'll go wherever you want, but promise me it'll be somewhere safe."

"I promise."

"Let's do it."

They crossed the street against traffic and mounted the steps to the lobby. Cuban music livened the atmosphere. It was possible to look away from the signs of modernity and imagine everything was now as it had been then. Camaro and Ignacio went to the stairs and ascended.

She stopped at Faith's door and knocked. "Faith," she said, "it's Camaro."

Ignacio waited beside her. "I don't hear anything."

Camaro knocked again. No one answered. She drew her gun.

"Let me," Ignacio said. He stepped in front of her and pounded on the door. "Ms. Glazer, this is Detective Montellano of the Miami Police Department! We talked before. Open up right now."

The chain rattled. The lock turned. The door opened. An old man with a towel wrapped around his waist looked out at them. His skin hung from a frail body. He spotted Camaro's weapon and raised his hands. The towel fell to the floor. His hair everywhere was white. "I give up!"

Camaro pushed past the old man. "Faith? Faith!?"

"Where's the lady who was here?" Ignacio asked the man.

"Lady? I'm here with my wife. She's downstairs."

Camaro cleared the room. Her pulse raced. "There's no one else here. All her stuff is gone."

CHAPTER SIXTY-TWO

CAMARO SAT IN a wicker chair next to a rubber plant in the lobby of the Avalon. The music washed over her. She had her elbows on her knees, and looked at the waxed lobby floor. Her mind was blank of everything except an image of Faith framed by the window in her room.

She heard Ignacio approach. "Okay, I have units patrolling all over, looking for any sign of her, plus cops talking to every hotel in the district. If she switched rooms at the last minute, we'll find out fast. In the meantime, I don't think there's anything else we can do here."

Her watch said it was a little past eleven. The night on Ocean Drive was only now getting started. "She said she'd wait for me," Camaro said without looking up.

"Maybe something spooked her. Maybe she wasn't totally honest. You said she took money from Kaur and she took money from the Colombians. She was a busy girl. I wouldn't put much trust in her."

Camaro straightened up. She looked at the smiling, oblivious people. She looked at Ignacio. "You don't get it."

"No, I get it. Sometimes you want to believe in somebody so much, you don't think about what they do wrong."

"I can find her," Camaro said.

"I think it's time for you to go home and get some sleep. I already kept the ME waiting for hours. I have to get back. And any minute now Mansfield and Pope are going to be on me about what's happening here. I have to work out my story."

"Tell them the truth."

"Oh, I think we're past that now."

243

She stood. "Okay, I'm going."

"You need anything, call me."

"I won't."

Camaro walked out of the lobby and crossed the street and went to her truck. She popped the locks, stood with her hand resting against the metal frame of the truck. All trace of the day's fire had fled from it. The night was a sweaty layer on her skin. She glanced back. Ignacio was nowhere to be seen. She got in and started the engine and pulled away.

She headed for the marina, but stopped along the way to buy tacos and a fifth of Jack Daniel's. Both came back to the truck with her in brown paper. They rode in the passenger seat. The scent of tacos permeated the cab.

The marina was still at midnight. A light was on in the office, which meant the marina manager was in. She parked and walked down the wooden dock, boots hollow on the planks. The *Annabel* was dark.

She stopped, the fifth of whiskey in one hand and the sack of tacos in the other. Something seemed to brush against her shoulders—the light touch of a feather, or a breath of wind. She turned in place, looking back toward the road. The parking lot was empty except for her truck and the marina manager's ancient blue Caddy. Camaro watched until a minute turned into two minutes.

She dismissed the sensation with a shake of her head. She passed along the dock to the *Annabel*.

The blast leveled the *Annabel* at the waterline, the entire structure of the boat transformed into an expanding hail of shredded plastic, resin, glass, and chrome. A pressure wave lifted Camaro off the dock, propelling her over the water in night turned to fiery day. Her lungs compressed, and all the oxygen burst out of her. She was suspended in midair for less than a heartbeat before she crashed hard. The warm water of the marina smashed into her like a solid object before it sucked her beneath the surface.

Salt and wet covered her. Reflexively she inhaled, her lungs empty.

Water rushed in and she choked. The darkness illuminated from above; flickering oranges and reds played over the surface as the remaining chunk of the *Annabel*'s hull rolled in place and began to sink. Floating debris slopped heavily in the backsplash from the detonation.

Camaro clawed at the water, chest convulsing. Her eyes burned and her skin stung from a hundred angry cuts. The surface receded the more she strove for it. She kicked, trying to free her feet from her boots. Her brain struggled for focus. She allowed herself to sink as she loosened her heavy boots. They slipped from her and she was lighter. She tried for the surface again. One hand broke into air. Her head and shoulders followed.

She vomited seawater before she took a real breath. She was in the middle of the marina's open straightaway, ten yards from the *Annabel*. What remained of the *Annabel* above the water was ablaze. Parts of the dock were alight.

She struck out for a retaining wall lined with old radial tires. She clambered up, using the tires as handholds, until she made it to the top and flopped onto her back. She coughed violently, bringing up more fluid. Someone yelled, but she didn't understand what they said. Consciousness flickered. One moment she was aware, the next was blackness, only to return to heat and pain and light.

A figure stooped over her. She saw the face of Dallas, the marina manager. He shouted in her face, but his voice was unintelligible. Camaro thought she heard the word "ambulance."

CHAPTER SIXTY-THREE

IGNACIO WATCHED BOMB techs work side by side with the crime-scene investigators. Divers were in the water. They had nothing yet. The night was alive with strobing lights, and the section of dock where the *Annabel* once berthed was brilliant with floods.

He heard Mansfield before he saw him. Mansfield and Pope were together. They always seemed to be together. "I have a forensic team flying in from Virginia," Mansfield said by way of greeting.

"Not much to find. Camaro Espinoza's boat's in pieces, and the bomb guys haven't found anything left of the device."

"That's what our people are good at: finding things that are hard to come by."

"Like Lawrence Kaur?" Ignacio asked.

Mansfield's face clouded. "We're working on it. Like I hear you've been working the Art Deco District for Faith Glazer. When were you going to clue us in about that?"

Ignacio shrugged. "I didn't think it was worth mentioning unless it panned out."

"Everything is worth mentioning," Pope said.

Mansfield put his arm around Ignacio's shoulders. "Why don't we take a walk, Detective? You and me."

They moved away together and drifted up the angle of the parking lot toward the road. Ignacio saw an unmarked federal SUV sitting where Camaro had told him she was watched. He glanced back. The teams still worked.

"Nacho," Mansfield said, "you like to be called Nacho, right?"

"I think Detective Montellano is good for right now," Ignacio answered.

"Okay," Mansfield said. "Detective Montellano. You are a good cop. People say excellent things about you, and you've never gotten yourself into any trouble too severe. These are great qualities to have in a working partnership, because solid cops are trustworthy. Reliable. They know what to do, and they listen when they're told."

Ignacio didn't reply. They kept walking until they reached the road.

"We have a little bit of history, you and me, and that's fine," Mansfield continued. "I have no cause for complaint. But I feel like something different is happening here. Like your focus isn't on the team goals. I've done some asking around, or rather, Special Agent Pope has, and we've discovered you and this Camaro Espinoza have something going on together."

"I don't know what you mean," Ignacio said.

"Oh, come on, Detective. It's common knowledge. Starting about a year ago you began keeping tabs on her. Where she goes, what she does. There's even some talk you might have gotten her out of a couple of jams. Now, I'm not saying you're sleeping with her—"

"I'm not sleeping with her," Ignacio interrupted. "It's not like that."

"Okay, what is it like? Because when this business started, you stepped in as soon as you knew Espinoza was involved. And you were on the scene after she killed Bamanian and his man. Now you're here. And if that's not enough, there are people—and these are your colleagues, mind you—who saw the two of you together in the Art Deco District. So don't kid a kidder. What's really going on?"

Mansfield didn't rush him. "She's a friend," Ignacio said.

"How serious of a friend?"

"I already told you we're not sleeping together."

"But you want to."

"No, I don't want to! She's good people, that's all. And it happens she's friends with Faith Glazer. That's how she got caught up in all this. The same people who killed Roche and probably killed Kaur are after

247

her, too. Don't you see what's happening? They're cleaning up. Your accountants aren't going to find anything because Roche and Kaur already closed the door. They were the last people you could talk to outside of Faith Glazer, and she's gone, too."

"You know Espinoza is a killer."

"She was a soldier."

"No, I mean she's killed people in the United States. Recently. It was all aboveboard as far as the legalities go, but the woman is dangerous. And given everything else going on, I'd like to know more about how she got involved with Glazer in the first place."

"You can't be serious. You think Camaro is in with *them?* They blew up her boat! They tried to gun her down in her own house! If anything, she should ask you where you've been all this time. People are dying all over the place, and I don't see a lot happening to fix the situation. What's the next crime scene I have to visit? Who's gonna be dead then?"

"There's no need to be combative."

"You know what? I *am* going to be combative. I played nice cop with you from the beginning, and all that's happened is whatever case you're putting together is falling apart one body at a time. So from here on out, I think I'm going to look after my duty as a Miami police detective and deal with things the right way. You can follow my lead for a change."

"You don't want to do that, Montellano."

"If you don't like it, you can talk to my captain. I'm done."

He walked away. Mansfield called after him, "You still need us, Detective. Whatever you think, this is still a federal case. Anything you do to jeopardize our investigation can be used against you. We could have your badge."

Ignacio stopped at his car. "You want my badge? Come and take it."

He got behind the wheel. His headlights washed over Mansfield at the edge of the road. He drove away.

CHAPTER SIXTY-FOUR

THE MACHINE NEXT to her bed made noise until Camaro silenced it. Now it monitored her quietly, counting heartbeats and checking her blood oxidation levels. Ten minutes past every hour, a nurse came in to take her blood pressure. They gave her something in an IV drip and she fell asleep several times. She did not want to sleep.

Ignacio was there when she opened her eyes. He stood at the foot of her bed, hat in his hands. She didn't say anything. He spoke first. "Hi."

"How do I look?" Camaro asked.

"Not bad, actually. It's like you got run over by a truck only one time, instead of twice." He smiled at her, but his expression faltered.

"They'll try again."

"I know. Once they find out they missed, they'll come around."

"Where's my gun?"

"It's in evidence. You're not gonna get it back for a while."

"I lost my knife."

"You'll get another one."

Camaro lifted her hand. It trailed tubes, and clear liquid flowed into a vein. Whenever they changed the bag of saline, she felt a new, cool flush under her skin. "They're going to get Faith," she said. "Wherever she went, they'll find her. She's not the kind of person who can hide like she has to."

"Not like you," Ignacio said. He pulled a chair away from the wall. He sat down with a whoosh of exhalation. "Boy, am I feeling rough right now. But this is what happens when you get to be my age and pull an all-nighter. I'm not built for it anymore."

249

Camaro turned her gaze to the ceiling. The panels above her head were spotted with a thousand tiny holes, and little hints of shine flecked here and there, as if seashells were shattered into the mix. She studied the ceiling for a while and realized she was getting woozy again. She didn't remember when they had given her the last dose.

"They tell me you should be good to go in a little while. Maybe you can get out tonight. That'd be nice, huh?"

"Sure."

"I guess, uh, I guess you had insurance on that boat, right? I mean, it was all paid up and everything?"

"Yeah."

"So you can go back into business before you know it."

Camaro looked at Ignacio. Her lids were heavy. "I don't know if that's what I want anymore."

"Don't go making any decisions right now. You're not up to it."

"You don't get it," Camaro said. "I came here to be safe. That was the whole point. No one knew me, and I could...live. But that's not how it worked out. It never works out. It's time to go."

"Where?"

"I don't know. Somewhere. I don't have anywhere to be."

"You have family in California, right?"

Camaro nodded but said nothing.

"You could move out that way. California's a nice place, I hear. You still have beaches and there's plenty of sunshine. You won't miss Miami at all."

"Would you go?" Camaro asked him.

"It's different for me. I've been here a long time. I've got roots."

"Roots," Camaro repeated.

"Well, as good as that kind of thing gets, anyway. People know me. I know them. I could always put in for retirement, because I got my twenty already, but what's the point? I'm no good at fishing and I don't like to be alone."

Camaro smiled despite herself. "Being alone isn't the worst thing in the world."

"For some people. But I think you need people more than you let on."

Camaro's smile melted. "I don't like being analyzed."

"Sorry. It's part of my job."

"It's okay. Don't do it again."

Ignacio clicked his tongue. He looked around, still playing with his hat. "So what do you want to talk about? Maybe someone has a deck of cards. What do you think?"

"Why do we have to talk about anything?"

"Sure. Sure, sure. Why don't you rest? I'll be right here."

She felt her eyelids grow heavier. It was as though she were already asleep, though she knew she wasn't. "Go home," she said.

"Maybe later."

Camaro sank into a complete darkness with no moon or stars. It was as black as the depths where the swordfish hunted, but there was no sound, no space. Even underwater there was the pulse of the sea. Here she heard nothing and saw nothing. She drifted alone. From time to time she stirred, but the black had an inertia, and it held fast to her.

She tried to form some conscious memory of being awake and alive, but it was difficult. Swimming up through the turgid darkness was as arduous as making it to the surface of the water in the marina as the *Annabel* burned. Except here there was no visible surface, no defining line between sleeping and wakefulness.

Camaro opened her mouth and said, "I am alive." The words were silent.

Time had no meaning here. All was stopped. She heard the murmur of hushed voices, and the flow of moving air, and then Ignacio speaking. "She's waking up."

"I'm waking up," Camaro mumbled, and this time she heard herself.

Someone touched her face. "Can you open your eyes?"

Camaro obeyed. A nurse shone a light into each pupil. The intensity was painful after the void. The light went away. Camaro focused on the nurse. "I'm fine," she said.

"I think so," the nurse said with a Haitian accent. "I'll tell the doctor how you're feeling. She'll be in after a while. Rest."

She left and Camaro saw Ignacio standing by the wall. "I have to get out of here," Camaro told him.

"I'll take you home."

CHAPTER SIXTY-FIVE

KAUR TOOK A room at Fontainebleau in Miami Beach. It was on a high floor by request, and he asked the front desk to make his registration under another name. Passing two folded one-hundred-dollar bills across the marble counter made any problem disappear. He tipped the bellhop to make him go away. He made sure all the locks were secure and the curtains drawn over the view of the beach in the brilliant afternoon sun.

The room came equipped with a small bar stocked with bottles of brand-name alcohol. Heedless of the cost, Kaur made himself a drink, and another, and another. He got into a hot shower, stayed there until his fingers turned to prunes. His hands still shook.

He let afternoon turn into evening and evening into full night. He used a prepaid phone he had bought on the way to the hotel. It was still in the plastic shell, and it took wrangling to get it out. The phone worked when he tested it. He made certain the GPS was turned off. He dialed an international number.

A man whose voice he didn't recognize answered. The connection was scratchy. "Who is this?" the man demanded.

"It's Kaur. *Mr.* Kaur. I need to speak with him."

A pause. "Is your line secure?"

"It's as secure as it's going to get. This isn't my phone. I'm not calling from work or home."

Another pause. "Wait at this number."

The man hung up. Kaur listened to dead air before returning to the bar. He could have used some ice, but he didn't want to leave the room.

It took almost half an hour for the call to come. Kaur cleared his throat. He answered. "This is Mr. Kaur."

"Señor Kaur," Carlos Lorca said.

"I'm calling to ask you to call off your people."

"I'm afraid I don't know what you mean. My people? All my people are here, with me."

"Now, I know—" Kaur started. He checked himself, continued in a softer manner. "I got the messages from your people. I know they killed Brandon. I know it was a warning. I understand what it means. Now, please…call them off."

"Mm," Lorca said. "I see why you are frightened. The way Señor Roche died was so terrible. Yes, I know all about it. I have seen the pictures, of course. I am told he was very cooperative at the end."

"Then why did you have to kill him!?"

Lorca tutted. "Please calm yourself, señor. I understand the two of you were very close. In my country we look at such things a different way than you do in America. Here we do not trust a man who lies with another man. If he cannot be true to the laws of nature, how can he be expected to attend to his responsibilities as a businessman? You see where the breakdown of trust begins. I was assured by you all would be taken care of, only to discover this was not the case. You and Señor Roche planned to escape together and leave me exposed."

"I would never. The evidence they're looking for is gone. Without the testimony of the woman, the accountant, and the information she stole, they have nothing. They can make life difficult for a while, but eventually they'll go away."

"They will *never* go away. Once they smell blood in the water, they will circle and circle until they find their meal."

Kaur's knees were unsteady. He sat on the end of the bed. He pressed the phone to his ear so hard it hurt. "You have to listen to me. This is my business. I know how to keep the situation in hand. My attorneys are hard at work resolving the issue. These are the very best lawyers in Miami. They know these sorts of cases backward and forward. You have nothing to worry about."

"Where is the woman?"

"I don't know!"

"Then how do you know she won't give you up to the government?"

"I . . . Look, I don't know what you want me to say. When things cool down, we'll find her. She can be neutralized."

"It has already been done."

Kaur froze. He waited, but Lorca said nothing else. Kaur could not even hear Lorca's breathing on the other end of the line. The connection popped and sizzled like hot fat.

"I can tell you are surprised," Lorca continued.

"Is she dead?"

"It's only a matter of time. I simply did what you should have done in the first place and paid her a sum which made betrayal an unwelcome option."

"We paid her a quarter of a million dollars!"

"And I paid her *two million* dollars. Two million dollars for the information in her possession and the destruction of all copies."

"You'll never be able to hold her to it. These blackmailers, they'll come at you again and again. We knew it was a possibility. That's why we decided to finish her off."

"And this, too, I have foreseen. Soon there will be no loose ends left to tie. None whatsoever."

The words hung over Kaur's head. "You don't have to kill me," he said.

"Give me a reason not to."

"I'll do whatever you want. I'll give you anything you need. Name it."

"Should we begin with the money you stole from me? Plus interest?"

"You know?"

"Yes."

Kaur didn't hesitate. "It's yours. All of it. It'll be in your accounts by the end of the week."

"This I would like to see," Lorca replied. "Goodbye, señor. Sleep well."

The line went dead. Kaur felt sweat prickle on his flesh. "General Lorca? General, are you there? Listen to me, General!"

He tried the number he'd called before. No one answered. He tried three more times.

Kaur slipped from the end of the bed onto his knees. He buried his face in his hands and folded over until he was curled on the carpeting. He cried, his body racked with shudders. The phone didn't ring.

CHAPTER SIXTY-SIX

IGNACIO TOOK CAMARO home. Her clothes were stained and torn. They were still damp from the water in the marina, and they smelled of diesel and smoke. The stink was almost overpowering in the confines of Ignacio's car. Camaro said nothing about it, and Ignacio didn't either.

He parked at the curb directly in front of the house and leaned over to examine it from his seat. "Looks like no one's home. You want me to go in and check it out? Our people already swept the place while you were laid up, but I can always make sure. You don't have to go in by yourself."

"I'll be fine," Camaro said. "I need a shower and fresh clothes. Real food."

"You can always stay in a hotel somewhere. Grab some things and get out. I can wait."

"No. Thanks. I'll be okay."

"All right. I'll swing by tomorrow to check up on you. Call me if you need to."

"No phone," Camaro said. "It went in the drink."

"Oh, yeah. Right. Maybe I should grab one for you? There's a 7-Eleven right down the way."

Camaro shook her head and opened her door. "I'll figure it out for myself. Don't worry about me."

"It's my job to worry."

"Not about me. See you."

She got out and walked up the uneven concrete to the front door. Her keys were in her pocket, unscathed. They jingled in the dark, surprisingly loud. She paused once to look back. Ignacio waved before he drove away.

Camaro turned on the porch light, and then the light in the front room. Yellow illumination spilled over the disaster left behind. The floor dusted with white fluff, the scent of spent gunpowder in the air.

She locked the door behind her and went straight to the bedroom. She stripped off her old clothes and threw them in the trash. Under a hot stream in the shower she felt a deep ache in her muscles and the bruising on her body that over days would turn many colors. She wrapped a towel around her head and another around her body when she got out. She opened the bedroom closet.

The gun safe was undisturbed. Camaro opened it. She took the first pistol off the upper shelf, a 1911 Mil-Spec, unloaded. Boxes of ammunition were stacked at the bottom of the safe. She grabbed a brick of jacketed hollow-point .45 rounds and brought them to the bed. She dropped the .45's magazine. The weapon took seven rounds in the magazine and one in the chamber. Camaro lowered the hammer and set the safety before she put away the ammo and locked the safe again.

She kept the pistol with her while she blew out her hair, stopping here and there to listen for any change in the sounds of the empty house. When her hair was dry, she brushed it before dressing in sweats and a T-shirt. She left the bedroom.

Wood scraped concrete on the back patio. Camaro stopped halfway to the kitchen and listened, the gun in her hand. The sound didn't repeat. Camaro crouched, weapon compressed ready. She stole toward the kitchen, waited a beat, crept ahead. She tilted her ear toward the closed door to listen, but heard nothing.

She unlocked the door. The click of the dead bolt seemed loud, but Camaro knew it was barely audible. She eased the door open, filled the space with her body. The patio was darkened, every light out. She saw the shapes of the heavy bag and the *muk yan jong*. She saw another silhouette move, black against gray. She brought the .45 up. "Don't move or I'll kill you."

"Camaro. It's me."

Camaro reached for the light switch inside the door. The patio flooded with light. Faith was there, her hands raised.

"It's me," she said again.

Camaro looked past her into the yard. Nothing moved. She lowered her weapon. "What the *hell* are you doing here?"

"Oh, my God, look at you!"

"Forget that. What are you doing here?"

"You didn't come. You said you'd be there, but you didn't come. I took a cab to the marina. You know, where you told me you kept your boat? I saw what happened there. I thought I'd come here and wait."

"Get inside."

Faith came in. Camaro doused the outside light. She locked the back door, left the kitchen, and crossed the front room to kill the rest of the lights. She was aware of Faith moving around in the dark.

"Sit down," Camaro told her.

Faith did as she was told. Camaro took a seat in the chair. Faith had the couch.

"Why did you leave the hotel?"

"I thought someone knew I was there."

"Who?"

"I don't know. It could have been people from the bank, or people from Colombia."

"How would the Colombians have any idea where to find you? Weren't you careful?"

"Yes, but there are ways to find anyone. No matter how careful you are, there are people who can find things out. I'm not a hacker, I don't know all the tricks. I'm pretty good at some things, but not everything."

"And now you came here, which is the first place they'll look for me after they find out I'm not in the hospital anymore."

"*You're* here."

"That's because I can take care of myself! You... You're..."

Camaro didn't have to see her frowning to know it. "Say it," Faith told her. "Go ahead and say it. Because I'm hopeless."

"That's not what I was going to say."

"I don't know why I even came here. I was worried about what happened to you. I wanted to *help* you. But you don't need help from someone like me. You don't want it."

Camaro put her hand on her face. She pressed her thumb and forefinger to her eyes until she saw colors in the dark. "It's not like that."

"It's not? Do you even know yourself at all?"

Camaro didn't answer. "I want to take you to the police," she said instead.

"I can't. I did the deal with the Colombians. I destroyed everything."

"Did you?" Camaro asked.

Faith was quiet.

"Did you?"

Faith didn't speak.

"Faith," Camaro said.

"No. Not everything."

CHAPTER SIXTY-SEVEN

IGNACIO PULLED UP in front of the house but didn't get out. Camaro saw his hardened face clearly from the front window of the house. She had the 1911 in her hand. Faith was on the couch. "Okay, he's here," Camaro said. "When I go to the door, I want you to step up right behind me. I'll open the door and we'll move out together. Don't get more than an arm's length away."

"Do you think they're out there?"

"Do you want to take the chance?"

"Okay."

"Here we go."

They did it the way Camaro said they would. Camaro went to the door and Faith followed. Camaro went out and didn't stop to close the door behind her. It stayed open as Faith hurried to keep pace. They crossed the unprotected space of the lawn. At the car, Ignacio popped the locks. Camaro moved to the rear door and opened it. Faith ducked inside. "Lie down on the seat," Ignacio told her.

Camaro shut Faith in. She looked both ways down the street before she got in beside Ignacio. She held her weapon in her lap. "Okay, let's move," she said.

Ignacio accelerated away from the house. "People are going to rob you blind," Ignacio observed.

"Anything they can take, I can replace."

"Why aren't there any other police here?" Faith asked.

"What I'm doing isn't exactly approved by the powers that be," Ignacio explained. "Anything I do, my department is going to tell the

261

feds, and I want to keep you safe and secure until I'm a hundred percent sure it's going to be all right. I don't need anybody else getting blown up on my watch."

"Okay, but shouldn't there be more police?"

Ignacio glanced at Camaro. She shook her head.

"Where exactly are we going?" Ignacio asked.

"Miami Station," Faith said from the backseat.

"A train station? Are you kidding me?"

"It's the best I could do on short notice."

"She can use her laptop to get the bank records," Camaro said. "And *only* her laptop. Anyone using another machine would never be able to break the encryption."

"How's that?" Ignacio asked.

"She explained it to me, but I don't get it."

"Can I sit up?"

"No," Ignacio and Camaro said at the same time.

Ignacio scanned the mirrors. Camaro glanced through the rear window. Morning traffic was light. "I think we're good," she said.

"I don't like it," Ignacio said. "I should never have let you go back to the house. There's a hundred ways they could trace you. No one has to camp out in the street to watch, not if they have the gear they need. They might already know Faith was there."

Camaro looked back again. She saw an SUV three car lengths back. A woman drove. "Why wouldn't they rush us?"

"Would you go busting in if you weren't sure what was up? Especially after what happened the other night with those two Armenians?"

"No."

"I rest my case."

It was no more than twenty minutes from Allapattah to Miami Station on a bad day. The vehicles following them came and went. Camaro saw no similarities among them. Only a few tailgated. Most kept their distance.

"The station," Ignacio said.

She saw the building. It was low and old, looking as though it had gone up in the '70s, Amtrak logo prominent on its face. Most of the space around it was given up for parking no one used at this time of day. Only a handful of cars parked close by. Across the road there was a power station, huge gray transformers behind chain-link fencing. The other nearest building was a warehouse almost a hundred yards distant. "It's wide open," Camaro said.

"Good for seeing who's coming," Ignacio said.

"How do you want to play this?" Camaro asked him.

"She's safer in the car. You take the key and go. I'll cover from out here."

"Faith," Camaro said.

The key had a round plastic head with a locker number stamped on the end. The teeth were hidden behind a loose sheath of thin metal. The key weighed almost nothing. Ignacio pulled up in front of a door marked BAGGAGE CLAIM. "Okay, you're on. I'll keep the engine running."

"One minute," Camaro told him.

"Go."

Camaro swung out of the car and onto the sidewalk. She stuffed the .45 in the back of her jeans as she reached the doors. She stepped inside and icy air spilled over her. The morning glare was shut out, replaced with the sallow glow of fluorescent lightbulbs. Camaro saw benches and a revolving belt like an airport baggage claim. A small snack shop operated in the far corner. The ticket counters were open. On two walls were dark blue lockers made of high-impact plastic.

She counted off numbers until she found the right one. The key fit. Camaro twisted it. The catch released. The door swung wide. She saw the messenger bag. She stopped long enough to unzip the bag and see the laptop. She closed the bag, put the strap over her shoulder, and let the locker's spring close the door.

It was twenty feet to the doors. Camaro walked directly toward them, not looking left or right. She pushed the bar when she reached the doors and passed outside. Humidity and heat crashed into Camaro's face.

It was ten feet to the car.

Tires screeched, shattering the quietude of the parking lot. Camaro looked past Ignacio's car, saw vehicles streaming in, black sedans and SUVs, from two sides. She swept the bag backward with her right hand to clear her weapon. She drew. Ignacio was already out of the car with his gun.

Black vehicles skidded to a halt, forming a solid wall. Men and women in tactical gear leaped out with carbines, shotguns, and pistols. The letters FBI were emblazoned on their body armor.

A white man in a suit stepped out of one of the cars. A smartly dressed black woman was with him. Camaro didn't lower her weapon. Ignacio stood where he was. "Stand down," the man said. "We're in charge here now."

CHAPTER SIXTY-EIGHT

CAMARO WAITED IN the small interrogation room. The four walls were bare. The little table, especially designed to force questioner and questioned together, was cheap, the plastic coating of the tabletop peeling at the edges. She hadn't replaced her watch, shattered by the blast wave from the boat. She had no idea of the time.

The door opened. The black woman entered. "I don't know if you know who I am," she said. "My name is Trina Pope, and I'm a special agent with the Drug Enforcement Administration."

Camaro watched Pope sit down. Pope had a small leather binder that she unfolded on the table. Inside was a slim pad of notepaper. She had a fountain pen in her jacket. Up close it was possible to see the perfect cut of Pope's outfit, the richness of the fabric. She smelled faintly of perfume.

"I know who you are, of course," Pope said. "Your name is Camaro Espinoza, and until recently you were a fishing boat captain."

Camaro made no reply.

Pope frowned. "Look, if you want to do the hard-ass routine, that's your business, but I can tell you right now no one does hard-ass better than me."

"Okay," Camaro said. "I want a lawyer."

"You don't need one. You're not under arrest. Brandishing a firearm at a federal officer is something we can charge you with, and it *would* stick, but we're not going to bother. Everything you say here is completely voluntary, and if at any time you want to stop talking and leave...there's the door. Of course, then I do have to charge you with something, and it starts all over again."

Camaro didn't move.

"I'm glad we understand each other."

"When I get out of here, I want my gun back, and I want whoever's watching me to back off. In that order."

"Who says anyone's watching you?"

"You're either watching me or you're watching the detective. Somebody had to tell you we were on the move with Faith."

Pope leaned back in her chair. She regarded Camaro with hooded eyes, her expression studied. "We were keeping an eye on your house in case someone wanted to take another shot at you. People willing to blow up a custom boat like yours, right out there in public...they're the kind of people who don't take failure lying down."

Camaro looked at Pope's hands. The woman had the pen in her left hand, but she hadn't written anything yet. The notepad was unmarred by so much as a pencil mark. "What exactly do you do?" she asked Pope.

"I handle major international cases. My area of expertise is South America. Colombia, specifically."

"So you know all about these Black Eagle guys."

"I do."

"Then tell me: If you knew how dangerous they were, why didn't you try to help Faith before it got ugly? Why would you let her dangle?"

Pope made a small, squiggly line in the upper left-hand corner of the notepad. "Sometimes you have to leave out bait to catch the big fish."

"Are you?"

"Am I what?"

"Are you going to catch the big fish?"

A slow smile spread over Pope's face. She had strong-looking and prominent teeth. "I think you have other things to worry about."

"Like what? You said I'm not under arrest."

"You willfully withheld information from a federal investigation and interfered with the protection of a material witness to an ongoing crime. And you killed two people. Let's not forget that part."

"I've never killed anyone who didn't need to be dead."

"I see. Is that how it went down in California? Oh, yeah, we know all about it. You went out to California to see your sister because she was mixed up with some bad people. Next thing you know you're running around shooting up the place. The only thing that kept your behind out of jail was a federal marshal who claimed you were officially deputized at the time you gunned down...how many?"

"I lose count."

Now Pope laughed. "You lose count. Now that's funny. Well, honey, Uncle Sam keeps records, and he accounts for every time someone loses their life, whether it was self-defense or plain old murder. So when I looked through your file, I saw someone who's been very busy, going all the way back to her service days. Got yourself a Silver Star, too."

"I didn't kill anybody for that."

"First time for everything."

"Do you have any actual questions, or are we gonna shoot the shit all day?"

Pope laughed again. "Oh, my, my. Okay, if you want to get started, we can get started. Why don't you tell me how you got involved in Faith Glazer's business in the first place?"

Camaro glanced toward the door. "Maybe I ought to make you arrest me."

"Do you want me to? I'll read you your rights now."

"What's going to happen to Detective Montellano?"

"He's in with Special Agent Mansfield. They're having a little chat like we are. You ought to be glad you're not a part of his situation, because if *you're* in trouble, Detective Montellano is in a whole world of hurt. It's one thing when you're a private citizen and you make some mistakes along the way. It's something else if you're an officer of the law. Judges and juries don't look kindly on misconduct."

Camaro looked at Pope's hands again. Pope wrote MONTELLANO on her notepad.

"You ready to start for real now?" Pope asked.

"Go ahead."

CHAPTER SIXTY-NINE

"I LIKE YOU," Mansfield told Ignacio.

"I like you, too," Ignacio lied.

"No, I mean it. You have a great record, you're popular with your peers. Sure, you pissed me off the other night, but in the end you brought us Faith Glazer, so it all works out."

They were in a conference room to one side of the bullpen. At one point the room was half filled with filing boxes, but in the past year it was cleaned out. Though the carpet was still marked with dirt and flecked with random bits of paper confetti, it was as squared away as anywhere else in Homicide Unit.

Ignacio sat at one end of the conference table, and Mansfield sat on the edge of the table itself, his arms crossed casually. The positioning made Mansfield seem much taller than Ignacio, and Ignacio was forced to look up. This was not accidental.

"I'd like to take you back to something we touched on before," Mansfield continued. "And that's this Espinoza woman. I understand you have a lot of respect for her, and she's a friend, but she doesn't seem like the best match for a cop with your background."

"I don't follow," Ignacio said.

"Okay, let me put it to you this way: she's a murderer and you put her type away. Those two things don't seem compatible."

"I put bad guys away. She doesn't qualify."

Mansfield bobbed his head. "Right, right. But here's a thought, and hear me out: What if she isn't everything she says she is? What if there's more to her involvement in all of this than she's saying?"

"That's bullshit, pardon my language. You saw her boat. You know what happened before."

"Of course it's bullshit. I don't know what I'm talking about. But how well do you really know her? And how do you know when she came out of the train station she wasn't going to kill you and Faith Glazer right there on the spot?"

Ignacio sat back sharply. "What the hell are you talking about? She's helped me *and* you every step of the way!"

"She kept Glazer's location a secret from everyone, even knowing there was a federal investigation underway. You already told us she allowed Glazer to cut a deal with a major South American drug connection, and *now* she hands the woman over to you with the only remaining evidence that could aid the governments of the United States and Colombia in the prosecution of a terrorist army? Whose side is she on? Really. Whose side is she on?"

Ignacio fumed. He looked away from Mansfield. When the silence grew too great, Ignacio said, "She's on Camaro's side."

"Right. Whatever works for her. If it's good for her to help Glazer, she helps Glazer. If it's good for her to help you, she helps you. And if she had the fear of God put into her by the Colombians who nuked her boat, what makes you think she wouldn't turn on you in a heartbeat?"

"You're not going to get me to say something to incriminate her," Ignacio said.

"No?"

"No. She's a victim in all of this, as much as Faith is. Now maybe she's not all touchy-feely the way you'd like her to be, but that doesn't mean she'd kill me. I know she's a little out there, but she has *reasons.* She doesn't do anything without a good reason. I know her well enough to know that for sure."

"Okay," Mansfield said, and he put up his hands. He moved from the table and pulled out a chair. He sat and looked at Ignacio over the scratched wood of the tabletop. "So let's talk about you. Let's talk about how you're going to avoid charges of obstruction, aiding and abetting a fugitive, and criminally negligent behavior."

"No jury in the world is ever going to believe that."

"My jury will. And the U.S. Attorney knows how to work the system. We can get any kind of conviction we want. This is a post-9/11 world, Detective. That's how the game is played now. Make America great again."

"Look, you got everything you wanted. You have Faith Glazer, you have a way to recover all the information from the bank, and pretty soon you'll have the guy responsible for laundering all the cash. You'll go after your Colombian connection, and everybody's happy. Why do you need to come down on me?"

Mansfield's eyes hardened. "Because I don't like being played, *Ignacio*. And neither does Special Agent Pope. That's why. You worked this fast and loose with your friend Camaro Espinoza and your ideas about who gets to know what and when. I don't like it."

"I'm sorry. I did the best I could."

"I'm sorry, too. Because I really do think you're all right. Confused, but all right."

"So that's it?"

"Is what it?"

"The scolding is over? I can get back to work?"

"No, you don't get to skate after something like this. Sure, you'll both probably get out from under it eventually, and the police department might even keep you on after all the money you cost them, but it'll take some time."

"Jesus, you really are a prick," Ignacio said.

Mansfield chuckled. "That's what my ex-wife always says. But this has nothing to do with me. This has to do with respecting the institutions of government. No one makes their own rules. Not even you."

271

CHAPTER SEVENTY

A STORM LAY flat and black against the line of the sea, darkening the water as it rolled ahead. Lightning popped inside the roiling mass of clouds, illuminating swirling pools of onyx. Kaur sat on his bed in the hotel room, drank the very last of the alcohol from the bar, and watched the approaching front through bleary eyes.

He thought he might have slept for a little while, but he wasn't certain. There was so much drink in his system that he couldn't stand without supporting himself. Sometimes he couldn't sit up under his own power. All the while the storm advanced, until it covered the horizon from end to end, and even the bright sunny beach was reduced to shadows.

Kaur cried. He tried not to, but it was impossible to stop. He thought of Brandon Roche, and his imagining of Roche's last moments was enough to get the tears flowing. And when he didn't cry for Brandon, he cried for himself because there was no alternative.

He blinked. Heavy raindrops whipped against the tall windows. He'd slipped away again. The storm had leaped ahead, encompassing the whole of the sky. Now when lightning crackled, it was immediately followed by a profound boom of thunder. The hotel was lit inside and out. The beach chairs were all abandoned, umbrellas scattered by the wind.

The rain began to beat against the glass. Kaur turned toward the phone by the bed. He reached for it and swayed before he got his hand around the receiver. He dialed for an outside line. He called 911.

"This is 911 emergency," said a female voice. "Do you need police, fire, or ambulance?"

"I need to talk to someone in the police department," Kaur slurred.

"I'm sorry, sir. What did you say?"

"My name is Lawrence Kaur and I need to speak to a detective. Can you contact him for me?"

"Sir, this is a line for emergencies only. Do you need emergency assistance?"

"His name is Montellano! I'm not sure what his first name is. Get him on the line for me."

The dispatcher didn't speak right away. "I'll see what I can do."

"Sure."

She put him on hold. Kaur did not know 911 put people on hold. He waited and watched the storm intensify. This had been coming for days, even weeks. A cleansing storm. This was his moment.

A different woman came on the line. "Who is this?" she asked.

"My name is Lawrence Kaur. I want to speak to—" Kaur stopped as his throat spasmed. He bent over and vomited on the carpeting. His feet were splattered.

The woman didn't hang up. "Lawrence Kaur," she said.

Kaur spat out the last vile mouthful. "I want to speak to Detective Montellano."

"Detective Montellano is on administrative leave. My name is Special Agent Pope. If you really are Lawrence Kaur, I need to speak with you. Your life is in danger."

Kaur fell back onto the bed. He looked up at the spinning ceiling. "I know, I know. They killed Brandon. They'll kill me."

"Where are you? I can send someone to get you."

"I'm in a hotel. In Miami Beach."

"Which one? What room?"

Kaur told her. It felt like expelling something awful, like vomiting, but with a sudden peace at the end. "Come and get me. You have to save me."

"We can get someone to you soon. Whatever you do, do *not* leave your room. Don't call anyone else. Stay where you are and stay safe."

"I can," Kaur said tiredly. Consciousness began to fade again. "I can."

She said more, but Kaur was gone, the receiver in a slack hand. He slept despite the thunder and the blasts of lightning. He drifted in dreams filled with half-understood words and malformed shapes. A dream like the storm clouds, full of hidden depths that were only illuminated by intermittent flashes.

He heard waves in the dream. Strident, continuous waves, rolling over and over and crushing him. His eyes flickered. He was back in the room. The storm still punished the hotel. Crashing waves became knocking. Kaur convulsed and smelled his regurgitation. He'd thrown up again, in his sleep.

Knocking came at the door once more. Kaur levered himself off the mattress, his robe wet and reeking. The spaces between his toes were caked. He made it to his feet and got his balance against the window.

"I'm coming," Kaur said. "I'm here."

He put one foot in front of the other, but still weaved on his way across the room to the door. He fell against it, pressed his forehead to the smooth, cool wood. His stomach rebelled, but nothing else came up.

Kaur unlocked the dead bolt. He turned the handle and opened the door.

The dark-faced man on the other side shoved the door against him, and Kaur reeled. He toppled onto his back. The man entered, followed by others. They fanned into the room, leaving only the first to stand over Kaur as he moved himself on heels and palms away from the door, which closed itself silently.

"Please. Don't," Kaur said. He raised a hand.

The man took a pistol from inside his jacket and shot Kaur. The bullet passed through Kaur's palm, but he felt only an instant of pain

274

before the impact smashed him against the floor. His vision swelled with blackness. His head lolled. He saw some of the other men watching him. He tried to look back toward the man with the gun, but his neck muscles wouldn't obey.

He did not feel the second bullet.

CHAPTER SEVENTY-ONE

CAMARO DIDN'T KNOW the name of the FBI agent driving the car. No one had introduced him, and he hadn't bothered to introduce himself. They went in silence through the driving storm, Camaro in the backseat. They were headed directly into the front. The windshield was almost impossible to see through, even with the wipers at full tilt. Other cars along the way looked as though they were drowning.

They skimmed the coast, passing through Miami Beach. Outlandishly expensive houses and condos were wind-lashed and gray under the unforgiving sky. Camaro tried to keep track of their turns. They took a bridge across water she thought might be Sunset Lake.

The agent took her farther, navigating close streets with beautiful homes on both sides. Their owners were huddled away now, shrinking from the storm. Everything seemed deserted. The Ford sedan carrying them was the only vehicle on a road scattered with fallen branches.

Another short bridge took them into a new area, no less wealthy. The houses here went for millions, even though a solid hurricane blow could flatten them all. The agent took a right turn, slowed along a stretch of high greenery that hid a lot from the street. They came to a complete stop in front of a wrought-iron gate.

The gate had an intercom mounted next to it. The agent didn't open his window. He made a call on his phone. "Yeah, it's Mills. I'm out front. Open it up."

No one came to open the gate. It swung wide of its own accord.

The agent, Mills, pulled through an arch in the green and onto an oval drive surrounded by palm trees. The house was white as bone in the darkness, windows glowing yellow from the inside. A two-car garage let out into the drive, but both doors were closed. No other vehicles were parked outside. Someone opened the front door. Camaro saw a man silhouetted in golden light. He had a shotgun on a shoulder sling.

Mills parked directly in front of the house. He turned around in his seat. "All right, this is it. We're gonna get out and we're gonna walk straight in. Don't slow down, don't look around. Once you're inside, stay clear of the windows and only go into areas you're given permission to use. Got that?"

Camaro looked at him.

"Okay, you got it. Let's go. I'll get out first and open your door. Wait for me."

Wind and rain blasted through the driver's-side door when he opened it. Camaro watched Mills hurry to her side of the car. He opened her door and waved her toward the house. The man with the shotgun stepped back to allow them entry.

The ten feet from the car to the house was enough to soak Camaro to the skin. She entered a broad foyer painted stark white, the floors a matching shade of marble. The man with the shotgun closed and locked the door behind them. "Pouring, huh?" he said.

"I didn't notice," Mills said. He took off his jacket and shook it out. He had a holstered Glock 22 under his arm. "This is Camaro Espinoza. Ms. Espinoza, this is Deputy U.S. Marshal Romero. He's part of a two-man detail protecting the house. Whatever you need, he's the one to talk to, but when he tells you to do something, you listen."

"Nice to meet you," the marshal said.

"Where's the other one?" Camaro asked.

"Marshal Stanley's out back," said Romero. "Somebody has to walk the grounds. Poor bastard. It'll be my turn next. Hey, Mills, you sticking around?"

277

Mills shook his head. "I have to keep moving. We're still looking for our guy. Might have some activity on that."

"Does he get a cell or a safe house?"

"Depends on what he has to say, I guess."

Camaro looked deeper into the house. She saw open stairs going up, chrome, steel, and wood, beyond that a formal living room, white on white, with only the furniture providing splashes of color. The walls displayed perfect, balanced artwork. She heard rain drumming on the roof. At the far end of a long hall, high glass windows let in dingy sunlight. "How large are the grounds?" she asked.

"About half an acre," Romero answered. "Big house, though. Six thousand square feet, give or take. Four bedrooms. You have three to choose from."

"Why three?"

Footsteps fell on the stairs. Camaro turned. She saw Faith on the landing.

"One of them's taken," Romero told her. "Unless you want to bunk with Ms. Glazer."

Camaro looked at Mills. "We shouldn't be here together. She should be somewhere on her own. It's too easy for them if we're together."

"Relax," Mills said. "We have the situation under control. And we don't have unlimited resources, so you go where we can put you. Better to have both of you where we can keep an eye out."

Camaro saw a look pass between Mills and Romero.

Faith came all the way down. "I could use some company," she said.

"See? There you go," Mills said. "It's all good. Settle in and enjoy yourselves. The kitchen's fully stocked, and if Romero thinks it's okay, you could even send out for Chinese."

The agent and the marshal shook hands. Mills let himself out. Romero paused at the door long enough for Mills to drive away before he secured the entrance. He turned to Camaro and Faith. "All right," he said. "The arrangements are pretty straightforward. You have full access to the second floor. Special Agent Mills probably told you about the windows. If you want to come downstairs, make sure one of us is with you. The kitchen's enclosed, so you don't have to worry about being seen when you're cooking. Dining room's off-limits."

"Anything else?" Camaro asked.

Thunder made the whole house tremble. Romero looked up and grinned. "And no dips in the pool."

CHAPTER SEVENTY-TWO

JOHN MANSFIELD DROVE with the storm at his back. He would be lucky to beat the rain.

His phone trilled. He pressed an icon on his car's dash screen. "This is Special Agent Mansfield," he said.

"It's Trina."

"Everything okay?"

"Everything's fine," Pope said. "What's the status on Kaur? It seems like the storm is slowing everybody down."

"We're on it. I expect to have him in custody before I make it back to my office. How are things going with the Miami cops?"

"As well as you'd expect."

Mansfield checked his blind spot. An Audi was a white lozenge in his mirror, hugging him closely. He signaled, but the Audi didn't fall back. He cursed and wobbled the steering wheel until the Audi's driver got the picture. Mansfield changed lanes. The engine of his BMW hummed.

"Is there a problem, John?"

"No, no. Florida drivers. Anyway, about Montellano: it's a shame he has to be sacrificed, but that's how these things go. The Bureau probably won't ask for his head, but I imagine he won't have too many promotions in his future. You cut corners, you get into trouble. Everybody knows the drill."

"Your man took Camaro Espinoza out of here a little while ago."

"Good. We're keeping her at the 27th Street safe house for now. It's all been arranged."

"The 27th Street safe house?" Pope asked. "Sunset Islands?"

"That's right. We grabbed it up from a big embezzlement case last year. Nice house. She should be comfortable."

"How long will you keep her?"

"Until we're sure she's not a target anymore. The same goes for Faith Glazer. The two of them are walking around with huge bull's-eyes on their backs, and I don't think we can afford to have more people getting killed on our watch. We don't have Montellano to dump it on if things go wrong from here on out."

"Sounds like you have it under control."

"Were you worried?"

"I always worry. It's how I know when there's a problem close to me." Mansfield frowned. "Problem?"

"I'm working on resolving it. You have enough on your plate. Working late?"

"Yeah, I'm headed into the office."

"Staying there awhile?"

Mansfield frowned again. "Are you thinking about stopping by?"

"I might. If not, have a good night."

"Will do."

The call ended. Mansfield waited until he heard the double beep confirm it. He allowed himself to hum a little as he drove. He was nearly there, but the storm had caught up to him. Rain spotted the asphalt and splattered the black lacquer of the BMW. Mansfield put on his headlights and touched the wiper controls. He glanced over and saw the Audi pacing him again. He shook his head.

His phone rang. Mansfield made an exasperated sound. "Yes, who is it?"

"Do you wish for me to use names on the phone?" asked the man on the other end.

"This is the wrong number to call," Mansfield told Lorca.

"I wanted you to know it's done. We've concluded our business with Mr. Kaur. You can tell your people to move at any time."

The storm picked up. "So he's dead?"

"You have to ask this question? And you are half a million dollars richer. Thank you very much for your cooperation."

"Listen, I hope your boys did a good job of covering up the transfer. People are watching."

"People close to you?"

"I don't know. I took precautions on my end, but you're compromised. I don't want any of this coming back on me."

"Special Agent Mansfield, you are a humorous man," Lorca said. "You worry about things you shouldn't, and you forget things which are most important."

"Like what, exactly?"

The Audi came abreast of him, its interior dark, the windows showered with rain. Mansfield wanted to curse out loud. He gave the driver the finger instead.

Lorca continued. "What is important now is you take the steps necessary to close out our dealings. I did not pay for one man's death. I paid for a resolution. And remember: you came to me. I did not come to you."

"I know how it happened," Mansfield said. "And I also know if you're paying so much to everyone else, there's no reason you couldn't pay a little something to me. So long as you know I'll spill everything if it serves my interests to do so. I'm not spending the rest of my life in prison for a million dollars."

"Our agreement was for five hundred thousand."

"Now it's for an even million."

Lightning arced across the sky. For a moment the road was lit as brilliantly as midday. Thunder hammered Mansfield's car. Lorca's voice was the quiet in the storm. "Are you threatening to expose me, Agent Mansfield?"

"I'm in a position to do a great deal of damage."

"I don't think so. If you thought you had a chance to hurt me, you wouldn't have cut a deal for yourself. So the Glazer woman has a copy

of the information she failed to destroy. It's meaningless if she's eliminated. Your government can attempt to turn numbers into convictions
without her testimony, but I assure you it will be more difficult than
you imagine. Or perhaps not, since you decided to take my money.
And if those numbers should disappear..."

"I told you before, I can't get access to that. It's in the hands of our
forensic accountants. I'd never be able to delete everything, and that's
assuming I could penetrate all the safeguards to get to it. You'll have to
find some other way."

"So your...bonus is for nothing at all."

"Maybe you want to look at it that way. If there's nothing else, I'd
like to go back to work. The more normal things appear on the surface,
the better it'll be for both of us. I have to continue to work the case.
And Special Agent Pope is not going to drop it, not even if you offered
her as much as you paid Faith Glazer. My part is done. All that's left is
for you to deposit the next half million."

"I suppose it is time to say goodbye, Agent Mansfield," Lorca said.
"I have enjoyed our time working together."

Lorca terminated the call. Mansfield found himself gripping the
wheel with both hands so tightly his knuckles bled white. Fresh sweat
was in his pits.

His turn was up ahead. The Audi had fallen back. He forced his
limbs to relax. By the time he reached his office, he would be as calm
as a breezeless sea.

The Audi moved up again. It honked its horn. Mansfield turned his
head. His window shattered.

CHAPTER SEVENTY-THREE

IGNACIO STAYED AT his desk long after the captain told him to go home. He busied himself at his computer going over open cases, double-checked reports on the last five cases he had closed. They had told him he was on administrative leave. He had no business doing anything at all. He didn't want to go, and he did not want to drive in the storm. Every time the captain left his office, he threw darker and darker looks Ignacio's way.

Someone touched him on the shoulder. He jumped in his chair. "What the—?"

Pool smiled down at him. "Gotcha. What are you still doing here?"

"Getting everything neat for whoever takes my caseload."

Pool pulled up a chair. "That would be me. Things went sideways with the feds, huh?"

"Yeah. And Captain Palmer is going to throw me out of here any minute, or have some unis drag me away."

"Why stay? From what I hear, it's a huge mess anyway."

"I don't like letting things go, I guess," Ignacio said.

Pool clapped him on the shoulder. "Sometimes that's exactly what you have to do. Go home. Forget things for a while. When you come back, it'll all have blown over. I promise."

Ignacio smiled a little. "Maybe so. All right, I'm out."

He gathered his things and put on his hat and headed for the door. He was halfway to the elevator when he heard Pope talking to someone. He spotted her standing near the drinking fountain, phone pressed to her ear. He stepped out of sight and listened.

She was talking to Mansfield. He heard the man's name. Ignacio listened to their conversation end, and heard her low heels click on the floor toward the elevator. He waited until he heard the elevator come and go before stepping back out into the hallway. He stood still, his mind working. He went to the stairs.

By the time he reached the ground floor, he wheezed with the effort. He opened the stairwell door and peered out. Pope was nowhere around. He stole down a side hallway. At the end, a large glass window impregnated with wire above a small counter with a bank teller's slot and a sliding security drawer. A uniformed cop was on the other side of the glass. Beyond was a broad room filled with shelves and boxes and trays. Ignacio didn't recognize the man. His name tag said STRICKLAND.

The cop looked Ignacio over. "Something I can help you with?"

Ignacio stepped up to the glass. "I'm Detective Montellano, Homicide Unit."

"ID?"

He slapped his breast and felt the void where his identification had been. His badge was in Captain Palmer's desk, along with his weapon. "Oh, man, I left it on my desk. Look, call up to Homicide Unit and ask for Detective Pool. He can vouch for me."

Strickland gave Ignacio a sour glare, but picked up the phone. Ignacio watched him dial out. Strickland turned his back on Ignacio while he talked. Strickland hung up. When he turned around his demeanor had shifted into something friendlier. "What can I do you for, Detective?"

"I wanted to know if a weapon had been checked in. Belongs to Camaro Espinoza. It would have come down a few hours ago."

"I recognize the name. It's not in evidence. One of those federal folks turned it over."

"That's right. It was only confiscated temporarily. They asked me to return it to Ms. Espinoza."

He thought Strickland would balk. He didn't. "You'll have to sign for it."

"No problem."

Strickland retrieved the .45 from somewhere in his lair. The 1911 was in a plastic bag. A separate bag held the magazine. Strickland took a few moments to note the numbers on the bag in a ledger. He filled out the top half of a form he passed through the teller's window. "Sign the bottom."

Ignacio signed with a flourish, and passed the form back. His mouth was sticky.

The gun went into the security drawer. Strickland shoved the drawer on his end and it popped out on Ignacio's. Ignacio gathered both bags. "Much obliged. Talk to you another time."

"Stay dry," Strickland said.

Ignacio stopped at a trash can and stripped the weapon and the magazine of their plastic bags. He threw away the bags, loaded the .45, and stuck it in his waistband. He went out of the building and into the rain.

Behind the wheel of his car, he leaned over to unlock the glove compartment. He found a .38 revolver inside in a leather hip holster, along with an ID wallet. He checked the weapon to ensure it was still loaded.

Rain gusted as he started the engine. He pulled out of the parking lot as the downpour sheeted over the street. He muttered to himself, "You are not doing this. You are not a stupid person. Everything is not all right."

He directed his car toward the coast. The Sunset Islands were a small quartet facing the water directly. The 27th Street safe house, Pope had said. The storm would be even worse once he got there. In his mind he turned over the things he'd say and the things he'd do. He tried to lead himself away, back to his empty house and the long hours of administrative leave open to him. He returned again and again to the water's edge, and the multimillion-dollar houses abutting it.

Traffic moved sluggishly in the rain, as if everyone had been beaten down to the three feet in front of their bumper. Ignacio wanted to hurry. He couldn't.

CHAPTER SEVENTY-FOUR

THE STORM SHOWED no sign of moving on. Camaro and Faith sat on a large bed in the biggest of the bedrooms, curtains drawn and the curved eighty-five-inch 4K UHD on the wall showing the Weather Channel. The front was enormous, covering Miami in a blotch of green extending completely across the metro area, with still more out to sea. The woman reporting promised the storm wouldn't end for hours.

Faith didn't talk. Camaro didn't either. Thunder rocked the house every time a massive flash of lightning exploded outside. Twice the lights flickered. Camaro felt Faith tense up when it happened.

"It's only a storm," Camaro said.

"I don't like it. I came to Miami because it was supposed to be sunny all the time."

"There has to be a storm eventually."

The Weather Channel moved on to other regions. Camaro tuned out. She listened for the sound of the marshals downstairs. They didn't talk much, but when they did speak, their voices rang off the marble floors and the stretches of blank white wall, carrying all the way up to where Camaro sat with Faith. They complained about the weather and having to go out in it. They discussed who would make dinner. A phone rang after a while. Camaro left the bed.

"What is it?" Faith asked.

"Quiet."

Camaro slipped out of the bedroom and to the end of the hall, where the stairs led down. It was easier to hear there. Sound carried up the staircase so clearly that she might as well have stood beside Romero while he took the call. He was on the phone for less than two minutes. Afterward he spoke in low tones to Marshal Stanley. Camaro heard everything. She went back to the bedroom and closed the door.

"Something's wrong," Faith said.

"Yes. The banker's dead. Kaur. They found his body."

Faith hugged her knees. She seemed shrunken on the bed. "That means I'm the only one left."

"I don't know how safe this place is," Camaro told her. "These people..."

"It's my fault. I didn't go when I had the chance."

Camaro walked to the window. She eased back the curtain despite the rules. From here she saw the pool and dense foliage closing in around it. A path led to what was probably a private dock. The pool glowed blue, lights burning beneath the surface. More lights marked out the path. Through the greenery Camaro caught a glimpse of something burning near the water. There were no real shadows. "You came back because I said you should," Camaro said when she stepped away from the window.

"What do we do?"

"We need to—"

The doorbell chimed. It was shocking, even with the storm crashing outside. Camaro heard Romero and Stanley talking again, their voices muted through the closed bedroom door, followed by the distinct rack of a shotgun slide. She felt the muscles in her back tighten. She hurried to the door and cracked it open. Faith turned off the TV.

Someone's voice, broken with static, came over a speaker. Camaro heard Ignacio's name. "Close the door and stay," Camaro said to Faith. "I'll be right back."

Camaro heard Romero talking on his phone. Camaro reached the stairs, eased down the steps to the landing, and crouched to see the front door. Romero and Stanley were there with their weapons.

Stanley caught sight of her. "You," he said. "Upstairs."

"Is it Detective Montellano?"

"How did he find this place?"

"You have to ask him. Is he coming in?"

"We're working on that."

"Let him in."

"I said we're *working* on it. Go upstairs."

Camaro came down the rest of the way. Marshal Stanley slung his weapon, an M4 carbine, and reached for her. She stepped clear of his grasp. He reached for her again and found her out of reach. "Don't put your hands on me," Camaro told him.

Stanley started to speak. Romero ended his call. "He's coming in," Romero said.

Romero pressed a button on a panel by the front door. There was a muffled buzz. The three of them stood in the foyer, unspeaking. A pair of headlights washed across the front of the house. A few moments later, Romero opened the front door with his shotgun held low. Stanley covered him.

Ignacio came in from the pouring rain, jacket soaked, water running from the brim of his hat. He saw Camaro. Romero pushed him against the wall. "Get your hands up there. Doug, secure the perimeter."

Romero searched Ignacio while Stanley put on a dark blue rain slicker with US MARSHALS emblazoned on the front and back. Stanley paused on the doorstep to look at all of them before he moved out into the storm and closed the door behind him.

"Service weapon?" Romero asked Ignacio.

"Right hip."

"Then what's this?" Romero asked. He pulled Camaro's .45 from the small of Ignacio's back.

"That's mine," Camaro said.

"Nope. It's mine. What are you thinking, Detective? You think we're going to have a shoot-out in here?"

"Are you carrying that shotgun for fun?" Ignacio asked.

"Shut up. Put your hands down."

Ignacio pulled himself off the wall and straightened his wet jacket. He looked at Camaro. "You okay?"

"I'm fine. You should not be here."

"No, I shouldn't. But I had a bad feeling."

Romero brought out his phone. He showed it to Ignacio. "Call this number. You and Espinoza take it in the kitchen."

The marshal pointed. Camaro and Ignacio went.

"Faith's upstairs?" Ignacio asked her on the way.

"Yes."

"How is she holding up?"

"She doesn't like the storm."

They entered the kitchen. It was large and glossy, with granite countertops and stainless steel appliances. A rack over the central island dangled pots and pans, all looking untouched. A magnetic strip on the wall held a selection of expensive knives.

Ignacio's phone rang. He put it on speaker and held it between them.

"Hello? Is this Detective Montellano?" a woman asked.

"Yes. Who is this?"

"This is Special Agent Pope. We have a situation, Detective."

Ignacio passed a look to Camaro. "I had a feeling."

CHAPTER SEVENTY-FIVE

"I DON'T UNDERSTAND," Ignacio said. "Mansfield is dead?"

"Do I need to repeat myself?" Pope asked. "Yes, he's dead. His car was run off the road. He survived the crash, but they executed him behind the wheel."

"What the hell is going on?" Camaro asked.

"Who is that?"

"Camaro Espinoza."

"So you *are* at the safe house."

"Yes, ma'am, that's where we are."

"I don't know whether to be happy or angry. This afternoon I got a call from Lawrence Kaur. He'd holed up in a hotel and was drinking himself stupid. He was sure Lorca's men were onto him. He had nowhere else to go. I told Special Agent Mansfield, and he said he'd put his people on it. Later they found Kaur dead. Shot twice in the head. Turns out Mansfield didn't report the call from Kaur for more than two hours. That was plenty of time for Lorca's hitters to seal the deal."

"Mansfield told them where to find Kaur," Camaro said.

"He really was an asshole," Ignacio said. "Pardon my language."

"I should have been ready for it," Pope continued. "We picked up activity in some accounts linked to Lorca. Nothing we could ever say for certain are his. Otherwise his assets would be frozen, but enough for us to keep an eye on. A payment was made fifteen minutes after I talked to Mansfield for half a million dollars."

"This kind of thing doesn't come out of nowhere," Ignacio said. "Didn't anyone have an idea about Mansfield?"

SAM HAWKEN

Pope was slow to speak. "I had an idea. The further we got into this, the more things stacked up. I moved on it too late."

"Go on."

"There's more," Pope said. "Additional activity. Payments going out fast and furious. Lorca's buying targets. He started with Kaur, but he wants to close out all the books."

"Faith," Camaro said. "Me."

"Maybe even Detective Montellano."

"I'm starting to think I should have stayed home the night Faith killed Serafian," Ignacio said.

"If Mansfield took Lorca's money, what's the point of killing him?" Camaro asked. "And why go after us now? It's over. We don't have anything."

"Carlos Lorca wants to send a message. He wants to make sure it's loud and clear."

Camaro straightened. She looked toward the kitchen door and saw Romero there. "We don't have enough cover here. There's two marshals, and that's it."

"Reinforcements are on the way. But we have to assume Lorca's hitters are already en route. Detective Montellano, it's good you're there, because we need everyone out of that house, and we need all the guns we can get."

A sound like the collision of two mountain ranges burst over the house. The lights in the kitchen flickered and died. There was no sound except the storm. Camaro caught Ignacio's wrist in the dark. "The power's out," Camaro told Pope.

"Shit. You need to move. We have a rally point half a mile from the house. Romero and Stanley can get you there."

"It's no good to move. There's limited visibility and no real cover on the street. If they took down one car, they can take down another. We don't know how many they have and we don't know how they're armed. It's better if we stay put and let your people come to us."

"I think we know what we're doing," Romero cut in.

292

"Marshal Romero is right," Pope said. "This is what he does. You're exposed. A moving target is harder to hit than a sitting one."

Camaro saw Ignacio's profile in the dark. He spoke. "I'm sorry, but I'm with Camaro—I mean *Ms. Espinoza*—on this one. We're armed and locked in. We'll get backup when? Twenty, thirty minutes?"

"I'm not arguing with you. Marshal Romero?"

"I'm here."

"Get them out of there. These people coming at you know their business."

"We'll handle it, ma'am."

"I'm on my way."

Camaro turned to Romero when the call ended. "Give me my weapon," she said.

"You're a civilian."

"It's my ass. I want my gun."

"I'd let her have it if I were you," Ignacio said.

Romero grunted. He moved in the shadows. Camaro put out a hand. He pressed the .45 into it. She chambered a round, set the safety, and put away the weapon. "Okay," she said.

"We move in two," Romero said.

"No."

"Look, goddamn it, we are in charge here. We *move* in *two*."

Ignacio checked his weapon. "I think we're gonna stay here."

Romero turned toward the door. "Doug!"

Stanley appeared. "What's going on?"

"We're moving out. Bring the witness down."

"Don't," Camaro said.

"We do not take orders from you!" Romero shot back.

"And we are *not* going to expose ourselves out there!" Camaro shouted. "If you want to get cut to pieces, that's your business, but we're not moving. We stay, and we take them."

"You are insane," Romero said.

"I know you already checked this place out," Camaro told him.

"You know we're open to the water and the street. They could come either way, but there's a clear field of fire all the way across the pool area, and we can hold them out front if we keep the drive open."

"Luis?" Stanley asked.

Romero shook his head. "Goddamn it, now *I'm* the crazy one. Okay, you want to seal it up, we can seal it up. Nobody gets inside. Detective Montellano, we can use your car to block the gate. If you don't mind getting wet again."

"So I don't get dead? Sure, I'm cool with it."

They moved out of the kitchen. Romero and Stanley conversed in low tones. Camaro saw movement on the stairs. "Faith, go back up," she said.

"I want to know what's going on."

Ignacio headed for the front door. Camaro cut Faith off before she reached the bottom step. "People are coming. I need you to listen to me. Go upstairs and find the smallest corner you can find. Stay there until I tell you it's okay to come out."

"What are you going to do?"

"I'm going to take care of this."

Romero headed for the dining room. "I'm going to cover the back. Doug will handle the front. I want to—"

The tinkling of breaking glass was almost too tinny to be heard under the boil of rain. Camaro saw the marshal silhouetted against the weak light from the windows at the far end of the house. A perfect line of blood, solid black to the eye, jetted from the side of Romero's neck. He collapsed to the floor all at once. A dark pool spread on the white marble.

Faith screamed. Ignacio said something that sounded like a curse he'd never use. Stanley shouted Romero's name. Camaro surged forward and drove Faith to the floor as the front door disintegrated into a shower of splinters, bullets shredding through Stanley. More bullets struck the far wall with the rattle of stones in a tin. Stanley fell on his face.

Camaro didn't hear any reports. The attack was silent.

"Detective!" Camaro shouted. Faith writhed under her. Camaro had the .45 in her hand. Her pulse pounded in her temples. Her vision was limned in silver. She was hyperventilating. "Detective!"

"I'm here!"

"Can you see them?"

Ignacio crawled toward a window near the door. He peeked through. "Yeah, I see them. Two coming up fast."

"It's happening," Faith said.

Camaro ignored her. "I'm gonna move. Get Faith upstairs."

"They're all around the house, Camaro. You need someone behind you."

"We don't have time to negotiate," Camaro said. The pool of blood forming around Stanley touched her boot. "If we don't get this right, we are going to die. Right here, right now."

CHAPTER SEVENTY-SIX

IGNACIO AND FAITH went up the stairs. Camaro crawled into the kitchen and came up against a double oven with the .45 in her hand. She heard nothing but the constant white noise of the rain.

The kitchen had two ways out. One went to the foyer, the other opened onto a hallway running lengthwise along the edge of the house. Camaro moved, crouching as she went into the darkened hall, where high windows let in the slightest trickle of light. She saw other doors along the way—the laundry room, a utility closet, a half bathroom—and passed them. Somewhere ahead she heard the muffled sound of two men speaking Spanish.

Camaro crossed a game room with a billiards table and a pinball machine, the latter a standing statue of dead metal with the power out. She went on. At the rear of the house was a large diamond-shaped area scattered with love seats and chairs. The back wall was a cathedral of glass. Big-screen TVs were at both ends of the room, and there was an unnecessary fireplace.

Two men in black stood outside the twin doors opening onto the pool area. As Camaro watched, one of them used the butt of a carbine to smash a larger hole in an already broken pane. Camaro raised her weapon in both hands as the man reached inside for the knob. He opened the doors. The pair came in together. Camaro squeezed the trigger.

The lead figure took two in the chest and toppled against his partner. The second man's carbine discharged. Camaro saw no flash and heard nothing but the thud of a suppressor. Bullets skipped off the marble floor and ricocheted into a glass coffee table. It collapsed into fragments.

Camaro left her position, moving perpendicular to the second gunman as he struggled underneath his dying companion. She fired twice more. Glass fell. Blowing rain passed through the open doors, soaking the floor and mingling with blood.

The second gunman made it to one knee and opened fire. Camaro hurled herself down, skidding across the slick marble as the carbine coughed and chopped. A picture took three rounds and jumped off the wall. Bullets cut through the back of a leather-upholstered chair, rocking it on its legs. Camaro scrambled on elbows and knees, belly nearly touching the floor.

She reached a spot behind a side table decorated with a vase and a single flower. The gunman tracked with her, squeezing off bursts. She fired again, and the man wrenched violently to the side. Bits of bone and tissue splattered the glass behind him. He went down and didn't move.

Camaro got up. She dashed to the dead men. She searched one with her free hand. They wore tactical vests with pouches for extra ammo and holsters for a sidearm. Her fingers brushed across the hard plastic handle of a sheathed field knife as the sound of cracking wood carried through the house. The front door was down.

The knife was in her hand now, blackened blade in the shadows. She heard the rush of boots, and a gunman with a shotgun ran into sight. Camaro fired at the same time he did. She felt a hot burning in her arm. Her shots went wide. A tall sheet of picture window disintegrated.

She spun on the balls of her feet and dove through the open doors, into the rain. The gunman came after her, the bellow of his shotgun swallowing up the metal noise of the slide racking with every shot. Camaro got to her feet and sprinted along the edge of the pool toward a line of palms and bushes, gunfire chasing her through the downpour. She cleared the lead edge of the greenery, tucked into a fall, and shoulder-rolled into cover.

The shotgun didn't speak. Camaro risked a peek and saw the gunman reloading. She pointed and fired. He ducked away. Camaro's gun went dry. She dropped it in the bushes and moved. She bled from wounds in her side, leg, and arm. It was difficult not to limp. Soaking plants whipped at her while she ran.

The middle steps to the private dock were ahead of her. She stopped at the edge of the foliage and crouched. She heard one man yelling to the other in Spanish. She understood some.

"Come back inside!"

"In a moment. One of the bitches is out here."

She went low out of the bushes and onto the rain-slick wood. She ascended the steps until she was able to raise her head enough to see over the line of the top stair. Both men were out in the rain, one armed like the two dead, the other with the shotgun. They said more, but Camaro couldn't catch the words.

She panted from exertion and pain. She felt hot blood where it mixed into cooler rain. The knife was half a pound in her hand, the ridges on the handle locked inside her fist.

The man with the shotgun ventured away from the house. His companion called after him one more time, but the gunman waved it away. He rounded the pool, weapon up, scanning the rainy twilight. Camaro retreated into the undergrowth with the knife still ready. She heard the creak of wet boots on concrete by the pool. His head appeared at the top of the steps, followed by the rest of him.

He stopped. Camaro held her breath. Lightning arced overhead, a latticework inside a jet-black cloud. Thunder slapped down on them like an open hand. The man with the shotgun flinched. Camaro came off the ground. Eight feet separated them. Camaro crossed it in two steps. The gunman's eyes shimmered wide and white. His shotgun swung Camaro's way. She weaved under it, drove it upward. The weapon detonated between them. Camaro's vision stung with bright light and flecks of burning gunpowder. She was deafened.

She stabbed the man in the side twice, the point going in under the ribs. The air went out of him. They careened toward the pool. He struck Camaro in the face with the hot barrel of his weapon. They tumbled over together.

The knife fell. Camaro grabbed the shotgun in both hands and twisted, seeking leverage with toes and knees. The gunman tried to work the slide, but Camaro ripped the weapon from his hands. She flung the shotgun away. It clattered across the concrete before vanishing into the pool.

They rolled. Camaro looked for a way onto his back. Their skulls cracked together and the man's bloody spit drooled across Camaro's mouth. Wet strands of hair stuck to her face and obscured her vision. She let him take her over, shoved her arm underneath his, forced her head into the gap it made. He tried to crush her. She slithered out of his grasp, greased by the rain, and mounted him from behind.

The man tumbled again, as violently as an alligator feeding. They came to rest at the edge of the pool. Camaro had her arm around his throat. She had his legs trapped by hers. He lurched until his face dangled over the water. Camaro reversed her grip, fastened her hands at the base of his skull, and levered downward.

He thrashed. Camaro's breath came in gulps and bursts. The muscles in her arms screamed, pushing down and down until the gunman's face was against the water. Under the water. Bubbles surged to the surface around his head. His movements turned to panic. She held on until he was still.

The other one hadn't reemerged. Camaro couldn't see him through the windows. She rolled away, sucking air, and pushed hair from her face. Her hand found the bloody knife. She got to her feet again. She ran toward the house, conscious of every yard. She didn't know how many there might be. Three were down and one was up, but there could be two or three or four more.

The diamond-shaped room was empty when she reached it. Camaro stepped over the dead men, pausing long enough to loot one body of its pistol, a heavy 9mm automatic. She ventured farther into the house. She heard screaming. A man's voice, followed by a woman's voice. A burst of shouted Spanish. A .38 snapped like a string of firecrackers, six rounds quickly.

Camaro ran to the stairs and covered the landing. No one. She mounted the steps, turned, and crouched to take in the top of the staircase. A man with a shotgun was there. She shot him three times in the chest and face.

Camaro entered the upstairs hallway. An identically dressed gunman came at her, weapon up. She flung the field knife when he pulled the trigger. He fired into the ceiling, the handle of the knife jutting from the exposed flesh of his neck. He sank to his knees. His carbine hit the floor. He reached to pull the blade free, spat up black blood in the shadows of the hallway. The knife made a wet sound coming out. He fell.

The report of a gunshot followed, but there was no bullet. Camaro left the dead man behind. She found the bedroom where she had sheltered with Faith. She saw the last of the gunmen in the center of the room. Faith was on the floor. The gunman clutched Ignacio to him. He was almost completely shielded by Ignacio's wide body.

Camaro came into the room and pressed the 9mm out. The gunman held an identical automatic to Ignacio's head. Camaro saw the shape of Ignacio's .38 on the floor. "Detective," she said.

"Stay back," Ignacio said. "Don't."

Camaro ignored him. She spoke to the gunman. "Your friends are dead. You kill him and you're dead."

"We exchange. Your life for his."

"My life's not worth anything."

"El General, he disagrees. And I can see you are wounded already. Don't be foolish."

"Camaro," Ignacio said. "Walk away. He can do what he wants with me. Pope's people are coming. They'll get him."

"You shut up!" the gunman shouted in Ignacio's ear. He looked at Camaro. "He doesn't know what he's talking about."

"It's true. It's over."

"Then I have nothing to lose." The gunman pressed his pistol harder against Ignacio's temple. Ignacio's face was a tight mask.

Camaro took a sharp step forward.

"Don't!" Ignacio managed.

"Drop the gun," the man told her.

"No."

"What's wrong with you? Everyone will *die*. Him. You."

Faith stirred on the floor. Camaro didn't look at her. Her aim wavered. Her arm ached. Droplets fell from her, but she didn't know if it was water or blood.

"Do you hear me!?"

"I'm not dying today," Camaro said.

"You stupid woman!"

Faith rose to one knee. Camaro saw a wet, dark stain on her clothes. Faith faltered. Camaro held her breath. The man with the gun saw nothing.

Camaro saw his finger tighten on the trigger. Faith lurched ahead and caught him low with her shoulder, 120 pounds directed in a single movement. The gunman exclaimed. He lost his grip on Ignacio and slipped sideways. Ignacio fell to the floor.

Camaro triggered her weapon. The gunman's chest burst open. Camaro fired again and again and again. His automatic flung into the air. He crashed backward over the corner of the bed and onto the hardwood. His foot snagged on the bedspread and twitched.

Faith fell to her hands and knees, coughing. Camaro stepped forward. Ignacio reached for her, but his fingers only brushed her leg. "Camaro," he said.

The gunman was still alive with five rounds in him. Camaro shot him twice through the cheek.

CHAPTER SEVENTY-SEVEN

SHE PACKED EVERYTHING, but even so, there were only a few boxes. Everything fit easily in the bed of her truck. She had her bike on a trailer in the street. The house was bare of anything that might be considered hers. Camaro stood in the front room looking over the place. She nodded to herself. She went out.

The landlord was there. He was an older man, close to seventy, and frail. He accepted her keys without enthusiasm. "Goodbye, Ms. Espinoza," he said.

"Goodbye."

She went to her truck. Once she backed out of the driveway, she lined up the trailer hitch with the bike hauler and got out to make the connection. She saw two cars cruising up the street. Ignacio was behind the wheel of the first. Camaro expelled a sharp breath. She got back in the truck.

Ignacio headed her off. The second car blocked her from behind. Camaro smacked the steering wheel with the heel of her palm.

She put down her window. Ignacio got out of the lead car. He came over to the truck. "No *adiós?*" he asked.

"I didn't see the point."

"Sure. Right."

"So..."

"Yeah. Okay." He glanced toward the white dressing on her arm. "How's that healing?"

"Fine. How about you?"

"I didn't get shot."

"That's not what I meant."

"Yeah," Ignacio said. He looked toward his feet. "Yeah."

Camaro saw movement in her side mirror. Special Agent Pope got out of the second car. "Am I under arrest or something?" Camaro asked.

"No. But people are concerned about you."

"I've been on the road before. I can be on the road again."

"And you aren't coming back?"

Camaro shrugged one shoulder. The other one hurt too much. "No way to know."

"I'm gonna miss you."

She looked at his eyes. They were moist and earnest. She couldn't look long. "You're not so bad yourself," she said finally.

Pope arrived at her window. "My offer of relocation still stands. We did it for Faith Glazer, we can do it for you."

"No," Camaro replied.

"So you're going to rely on Carlos Lorca's goodwill to keep you safe?"

"He has to find me first."

Ignacio's tone was sober. "How hard do you think it's going to be?"

"No one ever came around here."

"How many people do you have looking for you?"

The slightest of smiles lifted the corner of Camaro's mouth. "That's my problem."

Ignacio turned to Pope. "Special Agent Pope, do you mind if I have a few minutes with Camaro alone?"

"Sure," Pope said. She glanced at Camaro. "I don't think she'll listen to me anyway."

Pope went to where the landlord stood watching, the house keys in his hand. Camaro was aware of people looking on from other yards.

"Hey," Ignacio said. "Listen, I don't want you to take this the wrong way, because I know we're not going steady or anything, but I'd like you to stay. If you'll stay. You need someone to watch your back. And you need a friend."

SAM HAWKEN

He put his hand on the edge of Camaro's window. She put her hand over it. "There's nothing left for me here. Not right now, anyway."

"You're not gonna miss me at all?"

"Would it make you feel better if I did?"

"Actually, yeah, it would."

"I'll miss you."

"That almost sounds like you mean it."

She squeezed his hand. "Think about it awhile."

"You know, I haven't finished showing you all the great places to eat."

"Some other time." She took her hand away.

"Faith asked about you. Want to know what she said?"

Camaro felt her neck stiffen. She looked out through the windshield. "Not really."

"Now *that* doesn't sound like you mean it at all."

Camaro didn't turn to him. "Okay, tell me."

"She said you were right. You can run and run, but you can't get away."

"Is that what she really said?"

Ignacio chuckled. "I guess you'll never know. But it sounds like something she'd say, right?"

She looked at him. "I really can't stay. I could...but I can't. No matter who asks."

The humor vanished from Ignacio's face. "Will you do me one favor at least, Ms. Espinoza?"

Pope and the landlord were talking. Camaro frowned. "What's the favor?"

"Will you try not to kill anybody for a little while?"

She tried to keep the smile away, but it wouldn't stay hidden. Ignacio grinned at her. "No promises," Camaro said. "It's been a busy few years."

"Hey, try six months for a start. If that works out, go for twelve. You don't need any more of that kind of thing weighing you down."

Camaro cocked her head. "You really *do* care, don't you?"

"I do."

Camaro started the truck's engine. "I'll see you around, Detective."

"One more thing," Ignacio said. "If you don't mind."

"I need to go," Camaro said.

"I asked you to call me Nacho. All my friends call me Nacho. I'd...like for you to call me Nacho instead of 'Detective.' You know what I'm saying?"

Camaro thought. "Does anybody really call you Nacho?"

"Of course. Lots of people."

"Do they really?"

Ignacio shook his head. "No, not really. One guy, I guess. I don't know why."

"It's because 'Nacho' is weird," Camaro said.

"It's not weird!"

"Yes. It is. And I'm never going to call you that. Not ever."

"Like 'Camaro' isn't a name somebody picked out of a car magazine."

Camaro put the truck into drive.

"How about Ignacio, then? Can we agree on that?"

Camaro appraised him. "Okay...Ignacio."

Ignacio thumped the edge of the window. "That wasn't so hard, was it? Ignacio. Ignacio Montellano. It's a good name, I think. Conveys strength."

"If you say so, Ignacio."

"Will you call when you get there?"

"I don't even know where I'm going yet."

"Well...whenever you make it there."

"Maybe."

Ignacio extended his right hand through the window. "It was nice knowing you, Camaro Espinoza. You and me, we've been through some shit together. Pardon my language."

Camaro shook his offered hand. "And that's another thing: I've heard the word 'shit' before. You don't need to apologize."

Ignacio swept the hat from his head. "I'm sorry, ma'am, but that's how the Montellano boys were raised."

Camaro laughed. She stifled it with her hand. "Okay, then. You be you."

"What do you know: Camaro's got something under the hood, after all," Ignacio said.

"That's always been the problem."

Camaro put up the window. Ignacio moved his car. She drove away.

ACKNOWLEDGMENTS

Make Them Sorry is a watershed moment for Camaro Espinoza, when the woman hidden behind a wall of emotional protection begins to show herself for the first time. She could not have gotten here without the support of many behind the scenes.

First and foremost is my wife, Mariann, to whom this book is dedicated. Mariann will not tolerate bad writing, and she has saved my keister more times than I care to admit. If you enjoy Camaro's stories, it's because Mariann was there to keep me from wrecking them.

My agent, Oliver Munson, has also been an indefatigable booster of Camaro from the day the first novel in the series, *The Night Charter*, crossed his desk. I have been, and continue to be, grateful for his full support over the past few years of Camaro's life.

Finally, I would be remiss if I didn't thank Emily Giglierano and Ruth Tross, my excellent editors on both sides of the Atlantic. Emily in particular has represented a real partner in my time with Mulholland, and the mere fact that you hold *Make Them Sorry* in your hands is due to her persistence in seeing this story through.

And for those I have forgotten: it has been a pleasure working with each and every one of you. Camaro and I would buy you a beer if we could.

ABOUT THE AUTHOR

Sam Hawken is the author of the Camaro Espinoza series, beginning with *The Night Charter*, as well as the Crime Writers' Association Dagger Award–nominated Borderlands trilogy. He was born in Texas and currently lives outside Baltimore with his wife and son.

Former combat medic Camaro Espinoza is trying to put her past behind her. She's done bad things – but always for good reasons.

Then her sister Annabel calls. She's trapped in an abusive relationship with petty criminal Jake Collier and needs Camaro's help.

Camaro has always protected Annabel, but the situation is more dangerous than she realises. Jake's own sibling, Lukas, is an ex-Marine, and together they are planning a much bigger crime.

As the federal marshals pick up Lukas's trail, and a bounty hunter closes in, Camaro knows that standing her ground is the last thing she should do. But if there's one thing she can't do, it's walk away.

Out now in paperback and ebook.

MULHOLLAND
BOOKS
HODDER